GOTTa HaVE It!

A novel by

Shawna A. Grundy

shagru-ENTERTAINMENT

A ShaGru Entertainment Production
Published by:
ShaGru Entertainment, LLC
PO Box 689
Darby, PA 19023

This novel is a work of fiction. Any references to real people, events, establishments, organizations, or locales are intended only to give the fiction a sense of reality and authenticity. Other names, characters, and incidents are either the product of the author's imagination or are used fictitiously, as are those fictionalized events and incidents that involve real persons. Any character that bares resemblance to a person, living or dead; an acquaintance of the author, past or present, is purely coincidental and in no way intended to be an actual account involving that person.

ISBN: 0-9724621-0-4
Printed in the United States of America

Cover illustration and editing by:
Leigh Woolston Karsch
www.leighwoolston.com

GOTTa HaVE IT!

www.shawnagrundy.com
sag@shawnagrundy.com

ACKNOWLEDGMENTS

This entire voyage has truly been an uplifting experience.
The feeling is indescribable.

To My husband,
*Barry, I thank you for your undying support, love, patience
and your backbone when mine no longer seemed strong enough.*

To My son,
*Sean, Thanks for helping me on those days when my head was
pounding and I was too tired to function.*

Thanks Mom and Dad for the constant encouragement
Theresa Ruffin and Robert Rickards.

And to the rest of my family, you know I gotcha! Robin Rickards, Ed Ruffin, Rai Nelson (Mom#2), Shanae Patterson, Brad Morgan – Brianna, Dejah, Amira, Shukiyah Patterson – Samiyah and the one on the way, Patricia Grundy, Tiesha Grundy – Isaiah, Wayne (the best brother-in-law ever!) & Yvette Benson – Brittany.
Bob & Lynn, Tiff & Tim – it's time for a night out!

I'd like to thank those who remained my friend while I transformed into **many** different people . . . **many** times!!
Rajé Shwari – I hear you doing your thing girl!!)
Debbie Stephens, Debbie Atkins, Lynda Ford, Nicole Miller, Renita Murray and Ceceley Chapman.

Daaimah S. Poole, Patricia Haley, Brenda L. Thomas and Marni M. Williams . . . you ladies can get your feet out of my rear now! I finally got this thing movin'!!

Bernadette Y. Connor . . . Bern, how can I ever repay you?

To the authors who have touched my life: Marcus Major, Karen E. Quinones Miller, Nicole Bailey-Williams, Tonya Marie Evans (& Mom Evans), Solomon Jones. Michael Baisden – thanks for the encouragement and the boost you gave me with your poetry contest.

Debbie Stephens, Kim Bell, Sheila Huggins, Lynda Ford, Angie Smith, Kim Krug and Elvei Newbern – thanks for taking time to read for me. To my co-workers who I drive crazy, Ashish Patel and Wendy Wenner . . . thanks for all your encouraging words and Belinda Patrick . . . thanks for letting me vent.
Nakea Murray of As The Page Turns Book Club . . . the support you give never goes unnoticed. I can't wait to visit your club.

Emlyn of Mejah Books in DE & the Mejah Book family . . . love ya!
Donavan & Milissa of MultiMedia M.D. &
Devon & Lisa of Star Shooters . . . I hope you still love me!
John Carr . . . I hope I still get serenaded after you blow up!
Ace, Tim & Steve of Take Down Records . . . keep it goin'. . .
Jamal Hill of Super Stars . . . collaboration??? let's do it!
Cream of Cream Entertainment . . . who would've thought!

Zaria, thanks for making me smile when I needed to the most.
Snoop, I didn't forget about you boy!

. . . and last, but definitely not least, thank you to my son, God rest his soul, Jalen Breon Grundy, for bringing me closer to my Creator and myself. Without the time I spent with you, I may never have made it where I am today. Mommy Loves You.

God has blessed my family with talent.
I'd like to thank my cousin for the inspiration I receive each time I hear his music and see his videos . . .
Wanya Morris – Boyz II Men
Thanks for keeping me determined to succeed.
Keep blowin' up that mic!

Jalen Breon Grundy
May 13, 2000 – May 14, 2000

I feel your presence . . .

P R O L O G U E

It's eleven o'clock and I'm heading back home. I'm feeling really weird. I'm questioning myself over and over as to whether I should go through with popping in on Ian. Maybe he isn't really foolin' around with this Maria woman. Could I be reading more into this than is really there? Am I being overly paranoid? I could be but something's keeping my hands on the wheel and foot on the pedal! If there's nothing going on, then I'll finally get a chance to meet this person who cleans my house and is allergic to my dog. If there is something going on, well . . ."Surprise, Ian! Guess who's home!"

***

Driving into the garage of my building, I see Ian's car right away. I knew it! Why is he home? He went out of the door right behind me this morning. What reason does he have to be home while the place is being cleaned? After all, the building supervisor lets the cleaning lady in, supposedly. I wonder how many Tuesdays he's been home while she's here... while I'm working and appreciating that he cares enough to lift some of the burden off me by hiring help. And what do I get? Son of a bitch, I get my *caring man* screwing the maid!

I see several cars as I pull into the garage, but I don't know what she drives so I can't tell if she's here. Since she wears such nice jewelry, she's probably driving that black BMW next to Ian's red one. "Well, here I go," I say to myself, walking towards the door.

As I get closer, the music coming from inside is so loud that I can't really make out what song is playing. Slowly easing the door open, I recognize it clearly, "Do Me Baby," by Meli'sa Morgan. No the hell he isn't! My heart is beating super fast and my hands are starting to shake. If this bitch is screwing my man, in my house, in my bed, I'll have to kick her ass and then start on his.

I slam the door but whoever's inside obviously doesn't hear me. Maybe Ian's home alone, listening to music, chillin' out and thinking about this morning, and maybe, just maybe, he was serious about us talking later.

I still don't see any signs of anyone being here – no pocketbook, no cleaning supplies, no nothing. Hold up. Where's Snoopy? Dammit! He must be in his cage, because normally he'd be jumping up on me by now. That bitch must be here.

Heading towards the stairs, I hear one of my favorite songs begin playing – "UHH-AHH" by Boyz II Men. That's the song that was playing when Ian and I hooked up that night after the LL Cool J concert. Damn, I'm almost at the top of stairs, and I still don't hear anyone. Could it be that I've completely over-exaggerated this whole thing? Should I turn around and leave? How would I explain coming home? What would I say? Hey honey, I just came home to spy on you. I don't think so . . .I'm leaving. I'm going back to work and when I come home tonight we can talk like Ian said we would.

What was that? I stop and listen. I hear movement but no talking. Don't tell me this man is here alone, listening to romantic music and jerking off. Why would he do that? I was home earlier, trying to be sexed, and he basically brushed me off – and that wasn't the first time he's turned me down. Why would he have to pleasure himself? Oh, I can't stand here trying to figure it out. I have to go see.

Oh shit! Standing in the bedroom door, I cannot believe what's happening in front of me. I'm stuck in this spot and what's worse is, it's like I'm witnessing this in slow motion. I gasp for air as I grab my stomach. It feels like everything I've eaten since the day before is working its way back up my throat. I don't know whether to scream, run or just cry; I don't know what to do. All of my emotions are frozen, along with my feet, and not to mention my voice. How could he do such a thing? He's definitely crossed the line! Why me? What did I do to deserve this? I've been sleeping with this man. I wonder how long this has been going on and how many times have I slept with him since then – maybe even on the same day? Oh God, I'm gonna throw up!

He's so engrossed in what he's doing that he hasn't even noticed me standing here. The damn music is so loud that he didn't even hear me walking in the room or me gasping at the sight of him.

Oh! I can't take it anymore. I have to get out of here. On second thought, why should I leave? He's the man, and a diabolical one at that! He should be the one to leave.

I turn back around with tears rolling down my face. "Get the hell out! Get the fuck up off my bed and get the hell out!"

Startled, Ian tries to speak. "Ashlei!"

"Don't bother, you nasty motherfucker! Just leave!" Everything that could be said has been. "Just get all your shit and get out!" I don't know whether he understands me, because I'm screaming at the top of my lungs. I'm crying and my entire body is shaking – I think I'm hyperventilating.

I don't feel like it's necessary to get all hyped and start fighting at this point. This is not a battle that I want to win. It's bad enough that he's cheating on me, but this is inexcusable. I just want him to be gone so I can be alone in my misery and accept my defeat. I think to myself . . .

3

running, running, running
crying, screaming
out of breath
nowhere to turn
nowhere to hide
why, why is this happening
why ask
just accept it

I run no longer
instead I search
I search within myself for the answers
I've learned to conquer sadness by using it as strength

each moment of sadness teaches a lesson
lessons sometimes shaded by the darkness
but during my quest
I find the light
the light, the lesson, the answer
accept it

1

This concert couldn't have started soon enough. I'm so pumped on the day of a show! It takes me all day to perfect the look – especially when it comes to seeing LL!

These shows get better and better every time my girls and me come to one. LL is tearing up the mic and looks, what? GOOD!!

Standing in the front row, I say to Desz and Amber, "Yo! I know he keeps looking at me."

"Ashlei, you're crazy. He can't see you for seeing me," Desz comes back at me.

"Both of you are crazy," Amber says. "He probably doesn't care who's who, as long as you bought a ticket and you're here screaming your brains out. Now both of you shut up so I can pay attention to those pecs of his!"

"I Need Love" is my favorite song.

"No, you need me!" Desz yells. "I sure would like to go home with him after the show and give him some love."

Every female in the place is screaming, but at the moment I don't hear a sound. I'm in my own world. Kneeling down before my face is LL Cool J! It's all I can do not to jump up on the stage and pounce this man's bones!

"I love you, L."

He stands, licks his lips, and grabs the crotch of his jeans, winks and walks away finishing his song. I think he must have licked his lips ten times during that song. Oh! I love him.

I can't even talk. He's stolen my heart, and I don't want it back. My eyes are filled with tears and I'm in shock, not able to say anything but, "Damn he's fine!"

"That's all you can say!" Desz yells. "You make me sick. You're such a little bitch. You always get the best-looking guys and now...eww, I hate you!"

"Shut up, Desz," Amber says, laughing. "Don't be jealous. You can't have everybody. Ashlei, what did that guard come over and say to you?"

"If Desz would shut up, I could tell the two of you. He invited me to the hotel to the after-party."

"Eww! I really hate you now... Are we going?" Desz asks faster than the speed of light.

"You better believe it!"

The show is amazing. LL is such a talented performer. In my crazed state, I may be imagining this, but every time he goes past me, I think he winks! And all I keep thinking is, I knew I was going to get me a singer one day and wearing this dress tonight, helped with my mission.

After the show is over, we go straight to the car. Usually my girls and me hang around a while, but not tonight. Since our seats were in the front row, it took us forever to get out of the building and now we have to hurry and get to the hotel before we miss something.

"I can't believe we are actually going to the Holiday Inn to LL's after-party! I pray that LL told that bodyguard to invite me and the guard remembers telling me to come. I don't want to get there and be embarrassed."

"Ashlei Marie Thompson, don't you even try to chicken out now," Desz threatens. "We're going and we're not turning back. I'll kick your ass if you try and turn around!"

"Yeah right, Ms. Desiree Carter. Let me see you try!"

We arrive at the hotel and start following a group of people. Hopefully they're heading to the floor the party's on since we're completely in the dark as to where we're going. We ask the front desk clerk what room Mr. Smith is in but you know they're not giving up that kind of information on LL!

When we get in the elevator, we're the only females with six young thugs. It's very uncomfortable, but we would never let it show.

"Who y'all here wit'?" one of them asks.

Before I could part my lips, Desz answered, "Somebody from L's security team invited us. Why? Who are you here with?"

"We're trying to get in so we can meet some nice ladies like you three."

Right in the nick of time, the elevator stops. "I don't think so," I say as I step off.

We turn and walk down the hallway. I immediately recognize the man at the door as L's bodyguard who invited me. As we walk up, he opens the door for us. "Wait for me inside," he says.

Thank God. I didn't want to argue with Cooly-Bop from the elevator, who's getting turned away at the door. I can hear him saying some obscene things about me but I don't care. I'm in here and he's where...gone! The guard took care of him. As big as that guard is and as small as Cooly-Bop is, I hope he just shuts up, takes his too – young – looking friends and heads back to the elevator. The door opens and the guard motions for me to come to him.

I say to Desz and Amber, "I'll be right back. I'm going to talk to this guard."

"Did they leave?" I ask, walking up to him.

"They better have. I don't put up with no bullshit, and I surely don't let just anyone in this door."

"But you let us in – or is it different for ladies?"

"I invited you."

"I'm surprised you remember me with all the women you see in one night."

"I remembered your face as soon as you stepped off the elevator, and I definitely remember that dress!"

Of course you know I can't hold back the blush. I think it was more like a cheez! Tonight might really be my lucky night!

"My man isn't coming down to the party."

"Why not?" I ask.

"He was sick with something like the flu while he was performing, but he was determined not to cancel the show."

"Well, why'd you tell me to come here? I thought I was going to meet him."

"You look like the type who enjoys a good party. Am I wrong?"

"No, you're quite right, but . . ."

This six-foot-five-inch, dark-chocolate man with this huge chest says as he looks down at me, "Look three can stay and party with us. I'll make sure you have a good time." He winks as he opens the door to let me back in, making sure there's just enough room for me to come through but not enough to slide by without brushing up against him.

I walk over to my girls saying, "I can't believe it; we make it to an LL after-party and he's not even coming!"

"Why?" Desz asks.

"He's sick. Oh well, what do you two want to do? We're here and the party's jammin'. No reason to waste a good party, especially since we look so hot in these dresses!" My dress has a low V in the back and in front, showing lots of cleavage. The three of us have no problem getting on the dance floor. Even though it was meant for LL, this dress is getting me some attention. I knew it would work. I'm dancing with this gorgeous guy who will not let me off the floor.

Desz and Amber aren't doing badly either. They're both tied up with two very chocolate honeys. They always go for the darker men, while I prefer the light to medium-brown complexioned with light eyes.

This guy and me are dancing and dancing, moving closer and closer together. Every now and then we make eye contact and smile at one another. Every time I turn my healthy booty around towards him, he comes rubbin' up on me. I do have to admit . . .it does feel pretty good.

It's been a while since I've been out dancing; actually it's been a while since any of us have. We were all tired of meeting the "average" men at parties, and taking that roller coaster ride of getting to know them. It's obvious they're hanging out looking for someone, just like we were. Now, I don't know about my girls, but as for me...when I find that someone who's satisfying me, I'm chilling out. The men I'd meet never seemed to be satisfied and they were always out there, on the prowl for fresh meat, so to speak. So, my girls and I decided to take a break from dating for a little while and when I start again, it'll only be with a man who can lead me to my dreams.

The DJ slows the music down. Let me get off this floor because I know if I slow drag with him it'll only start something and I don't know if it's worth my time. Dammit! He grabbed my hand. I look up at this tall, copper-tone complexioned man with full lips, sparkling' eyes, broad shoulders, nice chest and as my mom used to call them, "thunder thighs," and I'm trying not to think about that bulge I could feel when I'd turn my rump to him. I just can't say no. Actually, I don't say anything.

After we start dancing he asks, "So, what's your name?"

"Ashlei. And yours?"

"Ian," he says, and then asks, "Are you having a good time?

"Sure I am," I say, smiling seductively.

Well that was it for words between us. I look over and see that my girls and their dance partners are also engaged in slow grinds of their own, so I may as well relax and let Ian take me into his world for a few minutes.

I feel him squeezing me a little closer, so I follow his lead and hold him tighter. Before I know it, our knees are interlocked and the groove is definitely on. I don't want the song to end, but I hear it winding down. Since a good DJ

9

always plays two in a row, neither of us is letting go.

Oh no, trouble! "UHH-AHH" by Boyz II Men . . .my absolute favorite. Without even realizing what I'm doing, I begin singing softly.

"Sounds nice," he says.

Oops! I didn't realize he was listening to me. When I hear this song I imagine myself in the video with them and picture myself in a champagne bubble bath. "Glad you're enjoying it," I answer.

"That's not all I'm enjoying," he moans.

As he says this, he gets as close to me as possible and I'm telling you, it feels like he's mounting a log between my legs. I feel him pressing and rubbing his pleasure inside my thigh and on my frontal. Oh! This shit is all right! The more intense the song gets, the more I sing and moan "UHH-AHH" and the harder and larger it seems to be getting. I gotta have this man and I don't even know him! "Here I go again," I think to myself.

At the end of the song, he kisses me softly on the cheek. And it's a good thing the room is dark because I don't want anybody to see what I was feeling on that dance floor. Actually I don't want to see it either, especially since I'm already tempted to explore, but I'm playing it cool. We move to the side of the room to talk.

"So, Ashlei, who are you here with?"

"My two best friends," I say, pointing them out.

"What made y'all come here? Do you know somebody?"

"Now I know you and that's all that matters, right?" I know I'm laying it on a little thick but that's how men always do us women. I figure I'll get the next question in before he has a chance to. It's time for me to be in the driver's seat. "I'll ask you the same question, do you know somebody?"

"Besides you? I manage a rap group called The

NewComers whose CD should be releasing soon. There's one of the guys over there by the bar and the others are around here somewhere. I try my best to have them anywhere I think they may be able to meet the *right* people."

"Oh, so you're a manager?" I ask, trying to hide my excitement.

"Yeah. Does that bother you?"

I wish he was a singer but a manager is close enough, I guess. Bother me, shit! He's good looking, has a big package and a promising career. It's time for me to live out my dream! I knew one day I'd be in the right place at the right time and I'd make my connection to the entertainment world. Sounding much calmer than I'm feeling, I answer, "No, but that probably means you're always busy right?"

"I'm busy, but not too busy to have a life. I try to make sure I always have time for me, and although they have a deal on the table, they aren't signed yet so they don't have as tight of a schedule as someone on a label. Why? What's on your mind?"

"Me and my friends, Amber and Desiree, are having a little barbecue at my place. Why don't you stop by? It won't be a lot of people."

"That's what I like…a woman who's not afraid to ask for what she wants no matter how long she's known you. That sounds good."

Rubbing my hand down his chest, stopping at the top of his jeans, I hook my finger in his belt loop and say, "And after we all eat and have a few drinks, maybe you can hang around so we can get to know each other a little better." With that look in my eyes, I know he won't say no.

"Now, that really sounds good," he says with a sexy, we're-on-the-same-page smile.

We exchange phone numbers and I give him my address. Amber and Desz come over and introductions are made. We all agree that we need to be going so we can get up early to prepare for tomorrow.

We say goodnight to Ian, Reggie and Dave. Reggie gives Amber a hug and a kiss on the cheek. Dave hugs Desz and says he'll see her tomorrow. Ian pulls me to the side, puts his hand in the small of my back and kisses me. I bite a little lip – being sure to make a lasting impression.

"Call me tomorrow morning for directions. I'll see you later."

"You better believe it," he responds.

As we walk to the car we talk about how much fun we had.

"Desiree," I say sarcastically, "how's Dave going to see you tomorrow if you'll be at my place barbecuing?"

"Oh! I invited him. Hope you don't mind."

"Well…I don't know…" I pause. "Just joking girl. I invited Ian too! It's about time we all loosen up and have some fun again."

"What about you Amber?" Desz quizzes.

"Dag, Desz. Why you always asking me questions? I don't have to do what you two do . . ." She pauses and then blurts, "But you know I did! He'll be there and then I plan on having *him* for a nightcap!"

"I know what you mean! We need to take control of these relationships and have some fun on our terms and not always on theirs. I'm not holding back nothing, not waiting for nothing. I know we always say that we should date these men for a certain amount of time before we let anything happen, but I'm tired of that. We've tried the easygoing route for years and we're still alone. So what's the use? I might as well put my thing down NOW! I may get lucky this time!"

I go on, "Hey, and guess what? If I don't feel like being bothered with him anymore after tomorrow, then I won't. That's how they do us. Love us and leave us!"

12

Amber and Desz agree with me. We roar with laughter as we get into the car. After we calm down, the remainder of the ride home is quiet. I'm imagining Ian singing "Share My Love," but when I snap back to reality, I realize its LTD! We all need to relax and cool off our hot booties so we can get a few hours' sleep. 8am will be here before we know it and these two will be pounding at my door. Tomorrow should be interesting.

2

I had such a good time tonight that I'm still all keyed up. I need to mellow so I turn on some soft music and jump in the shower. For some reason, singing in the shower tonight is bringing back some childhood memories.

My love for music started at a young age, but one particular Saturday morning comes to mind. Mom was listening to her music while doing her cleaning and I tiptoed into the room. I caught her with the broom, pretending she was singing into a microphone! When she noticed me, she waved for me to join her. We had done this so many times that we had actually memorized a couple of dance routines for what I guess were her favorite songs. For instance, "Ooo Baby Baby" by Smokey Robinson. We laughed so hard every time we did our little performance.

I helped Mom finish the cleaning and we got dressed for the rest of the day. She'd brush my hair and say to me, "Mommy's little girl is so pretty and you have such beautiful hair." At that time I had long ponytails. She continued, "You know for a little gal, you sure can move on that dance floor. And that voice! Girl you better use that voice to make you some money! I wish I had listened to my mother when she told me *I* should become a singer."

"Why didn't you, Mommy? You have a beautiful voice."

"Because I didn't believe I could do it. Then when I met your daddy, he wanted to be my manager, but by then it was too late. Ashlei . . .She paused. "Whatever your dreams are, go for them. Do what you have to do to achieve what you want."

"I will Mommy," I answered with tears in my eyes. Mom seemed so sad. "I'll make you proud of me, and Daddy too. I promise."

14

Daddy, oh Daddy. My daddy was a famous musician. He always told my mom he was going to take her to the top. She believed him and he was doing as he promised. My mom told me about how she met my daddy one night at some club called the Royal Lounge. She was out with her girlfriends, having a few drinks, after coming from a concert. One of her favorite song came on and she was singing her heart out. The next thing she new, she was being tapped on the shoulder. When she turned around it was one of the band members from the group they had just seen perform. She couldn't believe he wanted to talk to her but he loved her voice. That man became my mother's husband and my daddy. Before she knew it, she was singing in local clubs and people were enjoying her singing. They were known as the performing duo, Alyce and Mark Thompson.

Then one night, Daddy was playing with his band and Mommy was home waiting for him. It was way past time for him to be home. Mommy was really worried about him because it wasn't normal for him to do this. She sat up waiting for him as long as she could, only to wake to the morning sun . . .my daddy still not there. Hours later, a knock came at the door. It was the police. They were there to tell my mother that a man they believed to be my father had been killed in a car accident, just blocks from our home. My mom passed out and had to be taken to the hospital. Before they could treat her, they had to run a series of test. That is when she found out she was pregnant with me.

From that afternoon forward, my dreams began: what would it be like to be famous or at least have a husband who was famous like my daddy?

As a teenager, that dream stuck with me. My girlfriends and I used to pretend we were in a group and I'd always be the lead singer. We'd pretend for hours about everything from having husbands to the big houses we would own. I did a lot of singing in the mirror, but eventually the same fears that my mother had, I began to experience. I did however, start writing a reflection of my feelings in poetic form in my diary. I never showed anyone, but I liked being able to express myself in that manner, privately.

I never forgot the promise I made to my mom that I'd make her and my dad proud, so I knew I needed to come up with a plan. I figured it all out. Shoot! My master plan was to graduate from high school, attend Howard University because Roberta Flack, Donnie Hathaway and my daddy attended school there. As fine as my daddy was, I knew I'd meet a man there who'd be equally as good looking and would be going into the music business. I was fascinated with the entertainment industry for some reason; maybe my love for music was hereditary or maybe it's the money, fame, parties, clothes or the fun they seem to have, and did I mention the money! I planned to complete my studies in business management while traveling and partying with my man on the weekends, holidays and vacation breaks from school. Then, after graduation we'd get married. I'd take some time off to travel with him before starting my own business, a business that he'd help get off the ground. My plan was to work with R&B artists of various ages. I wasn't quite sure in what capacity I'd be dealing with these artists but I had time to figure that out.

A few years after running my own business successfully we'd have a baby. I'd be able to continue working because I'd have a home-based office in our huge ten-room house which I'd design and he'd have an architect do the formal layout, using my sketches, and he'd have it built. I'd also have a nanny/housekeeper, who'd have an apartment-style wing attached to the house, so I'd be able to leave freely to attend meetings and various events.

Wow! Now that was some serious dreaming in the shower. That sounds real good. I guess that smooth running,

16

fairy tale stuff may be true for someone out there but it definitely wasn't the path my life took. As I step out the shower, I snap back to reality.

In my new event specialist position at Winer Pharmaceuticals I'll be planning all corporate events. It'll require me to be on the road, but that's fine – at least I'll have my own administrative assistant to keep things going smooth while I'm out of the office. One of the perks with this job is I'm able to drive a company car during work hours, if necessary. Also, it pays me just enough to afford my bills, some going out money, and five hundred dollars left over each month, for my savings account. And it allows me free time to pursue clients for my personal business which is also event coordinating that is related to the entertainment industry. I'm still determined to find a man in the industry, so attending after parties at the hottest clubs and networking while I'm there is essential.

Looking the part is important too but I never have to worry about that. My mom has always been very clothes conscious, which resulted in my extravagant wardrobe. It's always been just me and my mom, so she may have spoiled me a little but all she wanted was to make sure I look my best at all times. That theory stuck with me. I'm not a duplicate of one of the perfectly portrayed women who's tall, with a light complexion, exceptionally beautiful with hair down her back but I'm nowhere close to being dog ugly either. Believe me, I turn many heads...sometimes even make 'em spin.

However, I'm very conscience of my weight. I watch everything I eat because I'm scared if I don't, it'll stick right to the bod, so I also go to the gym regularly. I used to wish I was the exceptionally beautiful, model-type woman I'd see on TV or always read about – but not anymore. I hate the way women are sometimes portrayed; even in the books I read every woman is always "perfect." I often think to myself, "Damn, don't they ever get a blemish, diarrhea or a yeast infection?" Well, guess what? I do!!

My two very close friends, Desiree Carter and Amber Brinkford, and me used to go to all the concerts that came to town. They're both attractive too. Desz is about the same height as me – five feet-four or five inches, with a medium-tone skin and a short-tapered hair cut. Amber is tall, thin, with light skin and long black hair." We've been best friends since grade school. Our families lived in Yeadon, a small suburb, just outside of Philadelphia. I guess you could've labeled us as "groupies," but that was cool! Like Mom said, "Do what you have to do!" Desz is the wildest of us three. When it comes to hanging out, she's the one to call. Amber can be a lot of fun too, but sometimes she goes into her own little world and seems to distance herself from us. Amber grew up in a very religious home, so after hanging out with us and being a slightly on the wild side, she'd feel a little guilty and would spend a lot of time in church with her family. She keeps in touch with us on a regular basis even when she's taking a break from hanging out for a few weeks. I've always known that no matter what our futures hold, we'll always be friends.

I tell you what, when the three of us get together... watch out!! We've spent countless nights hanging out at the clubs and going to after parties! I've met lots of men while we were hanging, out but none of them have ever turned out to be that "dream person" and I've dealt with enough bullshit to realize when it's time to take a break. Wouldn't you know it? I decide to take a break and now my kind of man comes along! I hope!

With the ceiling fan on medium, I lay across my bed in my favorite nightie, staring at the ceiling between the movements of the blades, my thoughts racing as I reach for my journal and begin writing...

18

Have you ever just sat somewhere . . .
no lights, no music, no television
and just visualized what you want out of life
who you want to become
who you want to share your life with
how you want your life together to be
and where you two will live out that life-long commitment?

I feel myself finally beginning to doze off, but I can't shake the thought of that long, long slow grind with Ian. I can't wait until tomorrow.

3

Damn, I can't believe I overslept. "Here I come. Calm down!" Why didn't they call before they came over? "Damn! Quit pounding!" As I reach the door I say, "All right, all right. Stop being so damn impatient!"

I open the door, and without looking turn to go back down the hall towards the bathroom. When my feet touch the floor, my bladder automatically thinks it's time to empty! Quickening my pace I holler, "You two could at least say hello since you decided to not call first to wake me the hell up!"

"Hello, Ashlei."

I turn around so quickly that I almost lose my balance. "Oh shit," I shout, knowing the voice I'm hearing is not that of Desz or Amber! I snatch my silk scarf off my head, then cross my arms in front of my chest grabbing the opposite shoulder, trying to cover my very erect nipples.

"No need to do that. You look gorgeous!"

"What are you doing here Mr.?" I don't know his last name.

"Klarke, with a K and an E!"

"Well, what are you doing here Mr. Klarke?" I can't believe Ian is standing in my apartment!

"I couldn't wait until this afternoon to get another one of those hugs from you and I was curious to see what you look like in the morning when you wake up."

"I'll be right back." I'm really about to pee myself right in front of him, especially since he's succeeded in scaring the shit out of me. I can't imagine what I must look like, having just rolled out of bed. I need to get my ass to a mirror fast. With the way he turned me on last night, I don't hardly want to turn him off before I have my chance to finish what we started. I can't believe he came over here like this. That's a little

20

strange – but hey, some men do strange things and confuse them with romance. He could be strange or maybe he really did "lust" me last night like I did him, and he really couldn't wait until the barbecue to see me. Let's hope it's the latter, because I don't have time for a weirdo right now!

"What are you doing in there," he asks standing outside the bathroom door, his voice making my hair stand up on my arms, "after giving up all that mouth when you opened the door?"

"I'll be right out. Remember you did wake me the hell up." I make sure not to sound too happy, but at the same time I don't want him to think I'm pissed off either. What I'd really like to do is take him in my room, undress him and sit him on my round, high-backed, red velvet chair over by the window, take this nightie off and, facing him and the window, lower myself onto his lap. With the morning sun peeking through the blinds, making my skin glisten, I'll make sure my nipples that already feel like they're ready to burst stop at his beautiful lips. I can only imagine sitting on that mass I felt last night while we were dancing, those big hands gripping my cheeks and pulling me closer. I bet that would be the best seesaw ride I've ever had! Whew! Just thinking about it makes my pointers ache and my inner thigh muscles tighten. I grab my robe off the back of the door to cover myself, while trying to regain my composure.

I open the door to find him still standing there, waiting patiently. I look up, smile at him and head towards the living room. Knowing he's gazing at me, I make sure to "shake what my momma gave me," erasing the devious little smile from my face by the time I sit down on the couch. I look at Ian, who appears to have been absorbing my body into his memory bank. I wonder what he was thinking while he watched me switching across the floor? "Why are you standing there Ian?" I inquire, knowing he wasn't expecting me to go towards the bedroom. As much as I want to, I don't want him to know that's what I want . . .not yet anyway. Maybe on our next date!

Ian seems to snap out his trance and responds, "I was admiring that walk of yours. For someone whose only about 5'5" and 140 pounds, you sure got a lot goin' on back there! No, seriously, you walk with so much confidence. I like that, but as much as I hate to admit it, your smooth caramel-colored skin and the way your hair bounces when you walk has been on my mind since you left the suite last night."

"Why do you hate to admit that?" I ask as I sashay over to put on my Silk CD. When I turn around he's standing in front of me.

"For one, because you probably don't believe me and you'll assume it's a line; and two, that I'm soft or something for saying that."

"Well, which is it? I think corny."

"You're crazy as shit! I'm far from corny." He grabs me around the waist and pulls me up against him. "It's just that usually most women think a man can't have a sensitive side. But we do and when we let it show, y'all act like we're just frontin' so we can get some."

"Well I don't think that way and I'm glad you've been thinking about me. I've been thinking about you too."

"Oh yeah? What about?"

"Last night before I fell asleep, I was thinking how I couldn't wait for today so I could see you again. I really enjoyed dancing with you last night and I figure there has to be a lot more to you than a good dance."

"That sounds about right."

I ease away from him and return to my seat on the couch. He joins me. After about thirty minutes of talking about our jobs, my dad and the things that we have in common like our love for music, it occurs to me that Desz and Amber still haven't shown up. "Look at the time! I need to call my girls and get dressed so I can get things together."

"Are you having a lot of people over?"

"It started as just the three of us, but with you and the two guys they met last night, it'll be the six of us."

"Well, I'm gonna get out of here and I'll be back later." He moves closer and whispers, "Before I go, can I taste that sweetness you let me sample last night?"

Now how can I turn this offer down? We engage in a long, stimulating kiss. Timing couldn't have been better. "Freak Me Baby" starts playing and sets the mood. His embrace is strong, making me want more. His tongue feels so good massaging mine. Loosening my robe, Ian gently rubs my back. "Umm," I moan, still kissing him. His hands feel too good moving slowly up and down my silk nightie. Damn! This dude got my girl jumpin'!

"What are you doing? Standing at the window waiting for us to drive up? You got the door all unlocked and what not, listening to your love music!" Desz says as she opens the door.

Ian and I jump. "Oops," Amber whispers, snickering under her breath.

"Sorry, Charlie. Don't stop on our account! We'll just go in the kitchen and you two can continue where you left off – or is it where you were all night? I could have sworn you came home alone last night. Sike, what's up, Ian?" Desz says with her smart-ass mouth. The two of them go in the kitchen snickering.

"Hey, you two," Ian calls after them.

Ian and I look at each other and smile. "I'll see you later. I'm sure lots of girl talk is getting ready to happen up in here." He raises his eyebrows and tries to conceal the hard-on he has to leave with.

I smack him lightly on the arm, glance down at what I want later and walk him to the door. "I'll see you later, Mr. Full of Surprises!"

He looks down at himself, then slips me his tongue and

says, "That's not all I'm full of."

***

The cookout has turned out to be fun. Desiree and Amber have been dogging me all day because of what they saw when they walked in this morning. I haven't told them how he ended up here, so naturally they think he came over last night after I got home. I love keeping them in suspense; it keeps a fun feud going on between us.

"Anybody for frozen strawberry daiquiris?" I offer. Although Dave brought a case of Corona, I'd rather have something smooth and fruity. Ian showed up with champagne, but I think I'll stash that for us! Reggie, who must be a romantic, came with flowers for Amber and marshmallows for us to grill later. I almost forgot about the small stuffed animal that Ian had hidden in his pocket. He must have seen my animal collection when he was here earlier.

After a few drinks, everyone's flirtatious nature begins to surface. I lighten the air by asking, "Hey, anybody for a game of Monopoly?"

Desz screams, "I can't believe you pulled that out!"

Ian shouts, "Aw. . . that's my game! It's what...ON!!"

I caution, "We have to promise to each other that we'll end the game at a decent hour because you know a Monopoly game can go on all night and I'm not trying to spend all night with all of you!"

The game is fun and loud. I'm kicking Ian's butt. Every time I play I have to be the dog, and somehow my little doggie always manages to land me a home on Boardwalk and Park Place. Every time Ian comes on that side of the board, he lands on one of them. I love taking his money.

"Damn, it's 1:00am." I say, thinking that by now we've all had too much to drink or maybe just enough so that we're feeling quite heated beneath our clothes.

24

Ian whispers in my ear, as he grabs my hand under the table, "Babe, the next time you land on one of my properties, you have to take off a piece of clothing." As he's saying this, he slides my hand over what feels like a huge cucumber on the inner side of his thigh. I can barely contain my smile or the juices that are moistening my readily waiting putty cat.

I know it's time to end the game now and move on to other things. I clear my throat and say, "Well I don't know about you all but I'm getting tired. I'm calling it quits."

"Yeah, I bet you are. I saw that whispering going on over there," says I-spy Desz.

I should've known she'd seen him. She's on everything. "If you must know, Ian was merely suggesting that this game convert to Strip Monopoly! I thought it would be better to just stop now!"

The room explodes with laughter, with the guys slapping and shaking hands. Ignoring their little celebration, I start putting the game away while Desz and Amber grab some leftovers. Then the three of us say our byes and everyone, except Ian, hits the road.

He and I can barely wait for the door to close. We both know what's up and there's no need to pretend. Before I can turn completely around from closing the door, Ian has me pinned against it. He manages to lock the door before gripping me by my outer thighs and lifting me so I can feel what he's been teasing me with. There's no hesitation when it comes to me opening wide tonight.

He kisses me with more passion than I felt earlier today, if that's possible, and I know with his bone all up in my twat, there has to be a huge wet spot on the crotch of my pants. Now I'm ready to take charge.

"Put me down."

"What? Why? What's wrong?"

"Come on."

25

As soon as we get in the room he starts taking his shirt off. "No, let me do it."

I light the candles, turn off the lights and I undress this gorgeous, and I do mean gorgeous, man from head to toe! I gently kiss each part of his body as I uncover it.

Now that I have him completely nude, I back him up towards my chair. I want it just like I'd imagined earlier, minus the sun. As soon as he sits down, I lean over and start kissing him like it's our last kiss in life. His hands are everywhere and his firmness is all over my leg. I start taking off my top while standing between his legs. His kisses are stimulating my entire body. He's biting my nipples through my bra.

"Damn, this shit feels good," I whisper between moans. My lady is screaming and his man is thumping all up on her while he's devouring my tits.

Backing away, I turn and walk towards the bed to take my pants off. With my back towards him, I lower my pants. Thinking he's still sitting down, I jump slightly when I feel him touch me.

"Sorry, I couldn't resist." Not letting me return to a standing position, he's rubbin' his shit all on me from behind. I hope he doesn't think I'm going that route cause ain't nothing happening and if that's what he's after, he should consider the night ruined.

Fortunately, my thoughts are totally off about his intentions. Ian couldn't be gentler. He kisses me on my neck, across my shoulders, down my back and then starts nibbling on my ass. He slowly moves me forward until my torso is touching the bed, puts his hands on my inner thighs and starts eating me like I'm his last supper. Not yet at my height of arousal, he lifts me up by my thighs and gives it to me like I've never had it before. Now reaching my peak, I can't even plant my feet. I have no choice but to scream!

He lets me down gently, turns me over and kisses my

stomach. I sit up on the edge of the bed in the position that I'm sure leads him to believe that I'm getting ready to return the favor – but I'm not. Again I kiss him, edging him over to the chair to bring to life the picture I envisioned this morning. I sit him on my red chair and pause while he puts on protection, then I mount on his saddle and start riding this horse. I have to stop, turn around and remount. As he starts reaching his hurdle, he's pumping fast and furiously. Before he was smacking my ass, but now all he can do is stretch those long legs out, hold onto my hips and give me all he's got.

Whew! I can barely breathe! Rising up, I look down to make sure the condom held up, because that was a rough ride.

Several hours later I wake up, trying to recover from our night of endless sex. I can't ever remember being with a man who could sex me that many times in one night. Realizing we've slept the entire morning away, I ease out the bed, careful not to wake Ian. After coming out of the bathroom, I go into the kitchen to call my girls and tell them about this prize I found!

"Yes."

"Damn, Desz! You tired or something? Hold on, let me three-way Amber."

"Hello."

"Amber, it's me and tired ass Desz!"

"What's up, y'all?"

"I had to call and tell y'all that I'm in love! Yo, Ian was all that and ten bags of Homegirl chips! There was no stopping him and I can't lie, I've never had anything better. That man is mine and I'm never letting him go."

"Damn, slow down girl! You can't be in love already," Amber yells.

"Let her go ahead. Did you look at that man yesterday? I know you noticed how fine he looked when he was all up on her yesterday morning. Then during the Monopoly game, the vibe was undeniable and he couldn't keep his hands to himself under the table. I'd be hyped too!"

"See, Amber, *she* understands. Anyway, I know already that he's the one. And get this . . .he manages a rap group. Finally I hit the jackpot! Girls, you have met my husband."

"I hope you didn't tell him all that," Amber warns.

"Of course not, Amber. What do you think I am, a fool?"

"I don't know, girl – he's got you zoomin'. Lighten up honey-child, I'm just looking out for you. I can't talk this time, though. I didn't think Reggie was ever going to leave. I thought he was trying to hang in here for dinner! Remember those marshmallows that we never got around to cooking over the fire last night? Well, let me tell you how great they must taste when they're sautéed in a li'l Amber flavor!!!!"

"Amber!" says a surprised Desz.

"Amber, you didn't! I can't believe what I'm hearing. Not innocent Amber, who always pretends like she's the goodie-two-shoes of the bunch. I just know you didn't let that man go downtown?"

Laughing, Desz manages to say, "And I know you didn't return the favor?"

"Both of you shut up – and your answer is no, Desz. What? Can't I have a little fun? I deserve a little action too every once in a while. Unfortunately, he seems like the clinging type and I can't commit to that right now, so I hope he can deal with it. If he can't, then oh well. He'll just have to find another meal somewhere else! Remember what we said about being in control?"

Clearing my throat I ask, "And you, Ms. Desiree? I know your hot butt got some."

"Maybe so, but I don't kiss and tell like you two."

"What? I know you didn't go there," Amber squeals.

"Well I don't have much to say, only that I can't talk

long because Dave went to the store to get us something to eat and he should be back in a few."

"What? Dave? He's still there? You are *so* slimy! You let me go on and on about Ian and you never said a word!"

"Problem? Jealous?"

"Girl, you are crazy. And Amber thought I was bad. Well I'm hanging up. I don't want you calling me a blocker!"

"I'll talk to you two later," Amber says.

"Okay," I reply.

"See ya," Desz says, still laughing.

4

For the past several months Ian and I have had some good times. We've gone to concerts, Sixers games, more movies and nights out to dinner than I can count. We're together almost every night and on Friday nights after he's done working. When we're not sharing an intimate date we're at an industry party or an after-party, both in town and out. Sometimes when I'm alone, I smile while thinking about how good things have been between us.

The phone rings. "Hello."

"I'm on my way over," Ian says dryly.

"Okay. See you when you get here."

He sounded bothered. He didn't say much, but I can sense that something's up. I unlock the door, and then grab this month's Essence to keep my mind from wandering and jumping to conclusions.

A short time later, he's standing in my living room. "What's up with you today?" I question. He's unusually quiet, like he's extremely preoccupied with something.

"I'm just thinking about a few things, that's all."

"A few things like what? Anything to do with me?" My tone is now snappy and my mood is impatient.

"Yeah. Actually it is about you."

"What's on your mind?"

"I'm not sure how to say this because I don't know what your reaction will be. I enjoy spending time with you and don't want to mess anything up by saying the wrong thing."

"Just say it Ian. What's going on?"

"You know the past few months things have really picked up for me and the deal for The NewComers is, you might as well say, 'signed' and they'll be releasing almost immediately, so money is getting ready to be a lot better for

30

me."

"Yeah, so?" I snap. "That's a good thing. So what's the problem? Are you dumping me because you're blowing up?" Immediately, I regret asking that. I just opened the door for him to walk out with ease.

Without response, Ian walks away, goes over to the stereo and exchanges one of the CDs in the disc changer for Luther's, "Never Too Much." Now my sixth sense is taking over. Is he really planning to leave me? Why didn't he answer my question? "Ian?"

"No Ashlei, I'm not dumping you."

Just at that moment, "House Is Not a Home" begins playing. He walks over to me, sliding his fingers between my legs and causing my sweat pants to go between my now parted lips. When he touches me like this it quickly elevates my sexual nature – mostly because he once told me that the way my cooch feels when he does this makes him want it in his mouth.

Knowing what he's started, he smiles, removes his hand and continues talking. "Listen, I've never wanted to be with anyone more. I've been doing some thinking, some searching, and I think I'm ready for us to live together." Now with his hands on my shoulders, he looks directly in my eyes. "There are these really nice townhouses in the city that I checked out today, called Pier 16 Quarters. They have one available. We never talked about taking our relationship a step further so I wasn't sure how you'd feel. I don't want to ruin what we've got going, so if you're not comfortable with this, I'll understand."

"Whoa, guess I was completely off base with this one, wasn't I? Here I am thinking you were going to dump me, and you're asking me to move in with you. Well, I haven't really thought about it, but I don't see what would be wrong with it. We're together all of the time anyway."

"Are you sure? I don't wanna rush you into anything. If

you're not ready for this, I can just take the spot now and you can move in when you're ready."

"No, Ian. I'm fine with it." I feel like I'm gonna burst but I'm trying to play it cool. I'm thinking this will be good for me. I won't have to pay all these bills, so I'll be able to sink a sizeable amount of money into advertising my business. "When can I see it?"

"We can meet there tomorrow."

"Okay, write the address down for me. We'll have to do it in the morning because I have a dental appointment in the afternoon."

While Ian's writing the address down, I start drifting off into my own little world . . .It's hard to believe that six months ago I was searching everywhere for a man and now I'm about to move in with the best thing that has ever happened to me. We're growing together as a couple, a real couple. I can't wait to tell Desz and Amber my news, but right now I'm gonna sneak up behind my man and have me a little fun.

As Ian stands up from writing the address, I step up behind him with my shirt and bra off. The CD changer moves to a new selection and Babyface starts singing "Sunshine" in the background. Ian turns, takes my breasts in his hands and begins pinching my nipples, oh so slightly. The music is flowing, our bodies are moving and I feel him beginning to stiffen. I open his jeans and slide my hand in to do a little exploring. Damn he feels good! His jeans drop to the floor and it's like he's hearing SWV singing "Downtown!" He lowers himself to his knees and begins french kissing my navel. He slides my sweats down, moves my thong to the side and begins...

"Hold up, baby. Come here," I whisper, moving to the couch because my legs are feeling a little weak. I sit down on the edge of the couch, lean back and use my eyes to call my man back downtown.

"Shit! Ooh, Ian, that feels so good," I moan.

32

I look down at Ian and he's looking up at me. His eyes have this sexy glare that leads me to believe he's enjoying this as much as I am. I feel myself getting ready to climax and I want him inside me. I use my toes to pull his boxers down but he's not stopping.

"Uh-uh," he grunts.

I grip the cushion above my head, tilt my pelvis towards the ceiling and scream, "Ohh!"

Ian rises up with his sex in his hand, but before he can enter me, he lays it on my girl. We're holding each other tight, he's breathing hard and moaning, "Umm." I feel the wetness between the two of us.

Damn! I'm convinced he's the shit and the one.

We top off the night by ordering a couple of juicy cheese steaks and some fries. Normally I'm not one for eating greasy foods, especially late at night, but sex with this man makes me work up a serious appetite.

5

Luckily, I had several appointments out of the office today so I was able to use a vehicle from the company fleet. I call Kara to let her know that I'd finished my meetings and will be back in the office after running an errand. I head over to meet Ian. Approaching the front of the building, the first things that impress me are that it sits on the waterfront and has an underground garage. I turn to enter and I'm stopped at the security booth. "Can I help you?" the gentleman in the booth asks.

"I'm here to see one of your units."

"Sorry, miss, parking is only permitted in the garage if you're a resident or on a list provided by a tenant. There are private entrances to each unit. You'll have to park on the street and enter through the front door."

"No problem," I reply, "I can appreciate this type of security." He permits me to turn around, then I find a parking space on the street and, as instructed, I enter an automatic revolving door trimmed with brass at the front. When I walk in, the elegance of the lobby has me in awe. The floors and walls are covered in marble and there are beautiful chandeliers hanging along a long corridor. On one side of the lobby there's a regular door, also trimmed with brass and on the other side there's an older gentleman positioned behind a high glass desk. On the wall behind him written in brass is Pier 16 Quarters. If this lobby is any indication of what the apartment looks like, I'm sold.

"Can I help you, miss?"

I don't see Ian yet so I think I'll ask the guard a few questions about the building. "I'm meeting a friend so we can look at one of your units." I extend my hand. "I'm Ashlei Thompson."

34

"Well hello, Ms. Ashlei. Garvin James, but you can call me Mr. Garvin. You said you're meeting a friend?"

I smile. "Yes." He seems very nice, kind of grandfatherly.

"Mr. Garvin, can you tell me what it's like living here and in this area? I've never lived in the city before, only in the suburbs."

"The building is very secure. There's always a guard here at this desk and at the booth outside. The owners focus on security since we know it's a concern for our tenants, who are insistent on the utmost in safety and security."

He goes on talking about the building. He walks me over to the chandelier-lined corridor, points and says, "This leads to each unit's entrance from the lobby and there's also a private entrance from the garage. It's a real nice place to live. Everyone here has very busy lives so you won't have to worry about the 'nosy neighbor syndrome'."

I feel a tap on my shoulder and jump slightly.

"Sorry, I didn't mean to scare you."

"I'm so busy talking that I didn't even see you coming. Mr. Garvin, this is my friend Ian, that I've been waiting for."

"Nice to meet you, young fella. I hope you two will decide to take the unit. I think you'll be satisfied."

"Thank you," I say to him, thinking to myself how comfortable I felt talking to him. He has such a warm smile and a soothing aura.

"Ian, Mr. Garvin was telling me all about the security here. It's very impressive. I can't wait to see the unit."

"Well, let's go talk to Ms. Karigan. She's the woman I spoke to yesterday."

"Mr. Garvin, could you please let Ms. Karigan know that Ashlei and I are here? Thank you."

Within minutes a woman wearing a sharp black pantsuit who looks to be in her forties walks through the doors to the right of the guard station.

"Nice to see you again, Ian. And this beautiful young lady must be Ashlei?"

"Yes. Nice to meet you, and thank you." Looking around the lobby I add, "What I can see of your building is quite impressive."

"Thank you. I'm glad it meets your approval! Well, let's go see the unit that's available."

Ian answers, "That sounds good."

She leads us to the far end of the corridor, telling us about the unit. "The units are constructed exactly like townhouses but they call them bi-level apartments. They have two bedrooms, two and a half baths, living room, den, an extra large kitchen, a laundry room and another small room that some tenants use as an office. Also, each unit has a patio off the living room." We reach the last unit on the right and she unlocks the door for us. In only a short amount of time, I'm already imagining my décor. After seeing both floors, I exclaim, "This apartment is absolutely beautiful. I love it!"

Ian puts his arm around me and smiles. "I knew you'd like it. Are you sure this is what you want to do?"

"You better believe it!" Now my excitement is showing, but I don't care. I'm not about to let this get away from me. This is only a stepping-stone towards the house in my "master plan," but it's a lot closer than where I live now. My apartment's nice but nowhere near this level of luxury.

"It meets her approval, so I guess we'll take it. Ms. Karigan, how long will it be before we can move in?" Ian asks.

"The unit is ready. We can go to my office now so I can get some information from you. If you have a little time, you can wait to see if you're approved."

"No problem," he responds.

We sit in the waiting room of the management office waiting for Ms. Karigan. When she comes out, she shows us

36

into her office, only to give us bad news. "Unfortunately, Ian has some things on his credit report that prevent us from approving your application."

I didn't know about any credit problems but how would I? We've never had a reason to discuss our credit. "I can't imagine his credit being all that bad. He has a beautiful BMW!"

Ms. Karigan assures us, "It's nothing major, but the owners are very critical when there's anything derogatory on the report. However, there's a solution. The apartment can be in your name, Ashlei. Since I know Ian will be here with you, I'll fudge your income a little. Your credit is A1, so with a slight salary increase, there won't be a problem getting you approved."

"That's fine. Do whatever you have to do."

"Are you sure you don't mind putting it in only your name?" Ian asks.

Is he crazy? I gotta have this place. No minor blemish on his credit is going to interfere with that. "Are you sure you don't mind it being in my name?"

Without either of us answering, Ian turns to Ms. Karigan. "Sounds like we're in agreement. Where does she sign?"

For the first time in my life, I'm getting ready to live with a man and I'm liking the feeling. Ian has a way of making me feel so good about myself. Who cares about the little credit issue? He's truly a dream come true!

Before leaving, Ian writes Ms. Karigan a check to cover the deposit and she hands us our keys. "You two can move in immediately."

"Thank you so much for all your help." We shake hands and she shows us out.

In the hallway I tell Ian, "I'll go to my landlord tomorrow to give notice. I know I'll have to pay next months rent, but I don't care. I turn and leap into his arms with child-like excitement. I'm going home to start packing!"

Ian smiles. "Dag, Ash! I knew you'd like it but I didn't think you'd like it this much! I don't know…is all this excitement about living with me or because the place is so plush?"

"Both." I can't let him think the apartment is beating him out.

"Well good, but unfortunately you're going to have to calm yourself down."

"Why?"

"Did you forget that you have to go back to work and that you have an appointment?"

"Oh shit! I did forget. I have to hurry. I have to get back to work to wrap up, turn in my car and then catch the train. But more importantly, I can't wait to call my girls!"

"I hate you catching that stupid train. I have to look into getting you a car. You can't be living in a place like this and not have a car."

"It really doesn't bother me, Ian. I've always lived near the train or when I'm in the city, I catch cabs and that has always worked well for me. I know I'll need a car eventually because with the number of personal clients I now have to see, I'll need to be more mobile. When I'm ready, I'll get something, but right now I want new furniture."

"There you go, being Miss Independent. It would be a gift. Damn, can't a man buy his girl a gift?"

Sure he can and I love it when he calls me his girl. "Yeah, whatever. I guess it's okay, but let's get our new place furnished first. I've been on the train this long; it won't kill me to ride a little longer. But you know what you can do since you hate it so much? You can pick me up after my appointment!"

"That'll work…for now," he says with a sly grin.

"Wait a minute, babe." I walk towards Mr. Garvin.

Seeing me approaching his desk, he stands. "How'd you like it?"

"It's beautiful. We start moving in tomorrow. Thanks so much for taking time to talk to me."

"No problem, little lady. I'll be seeing you two." He smiles, waving at Ian.

"I think you like that old head. You gonna trade me in for him after we move in?"

"You better believe it! In all honesty Ian, there's something about him that I really like. He has this parental quality, I'm thinking . . .similar to the father I never knew."

"Maybe so but he better not be trying to take my girl!" He taps me on my butt, gives me a quick kiss and we head for our cars.

Driving back to work I realize this took longer than I expected. I have a few phone calls I need to make before I leave for the dentist.

***

Returning to the office, I greet my administrative assistant. "Hey, Kara!"

"Whoa! As fired up as you are, you must've had a good meeting with someone."

"Yes I did. I just signed the lease for a new apartment located on the waterfront. It is truly fantastic. I can't wait to move in."

"So you're moving into the city? Congratulations! I hate to ruin your mood but did you remember your two o'clock dentist appointment?"

"I did and I didn't. I'm leaving right after I make a few calls." Looking at my watch I see I don't have enough time. "On second thought, I better get to my train before I miss it."

"I'll see you tomorrow."

"Okay, Kara. Have a good night and thanks for

everything."

***

I rush to the train station because they're usually punctual at this time of the day. I'm glad there aren't many people waiting. Ridership is a lot lower now than during rush hour and the class of people seems to be different. After work I'm used to seeing the working class, business-suit-wearing types, but during the middle of the day, it's a different bunch altogether.

I grab a seat in the car that has the least amount of people. There are two small kids sitting a few seats in front of me with their mother and grandmother. Grandma is speaking to the girls in this annoying, whiny tone that makes me want to smack her and tell her to talk right. Kids are human too...they don't need that baby-talk gibberish, and these girls are at least two and four. Thank goodness their mother is quiet. At 30th Street Station, the last stop before the train becomes an express, they along with several others, get off.

The few people remaining on the train look like they might be students or people who no longer work full-time in corporate America and just work part-time jobs. Yet, how do I know that these people didn't have the day off or that it wasn't dress-down day at their jobs? I don't, but I always like to create my own scenario for strangers. Now that the kids are gone and the conductor has checked tickets, I can relax and read for the next thirty minutes.

In my peripheral view, I see a young woman sitting on the opposite side of the train and one seat in front of me. She looks to be maybe twenty-two or so, with auburn colored, permed hair that's scrunched and hanging down just below her shoulders. She has on a cute little sundress with tropical flowers that caught my eye when I passed her. There's something strange about the way she's playing in her hair.

40

Maybe she has a fixation with her hair, a nervous condition or could she be hyperactive and always needs something to do with her hands? Is she trying to entice someone – but who? No one's sitting with her or even seems to be taking notice of her except me.

There is a young man sitting behind her, dressed in shorts and a polo-style shirt. He appears to be around twenty-eight or thirty years old, very refined and very straight-laced. I guess he's a student since he has a Jansen backpack sitting on the seat beside him. But he's too busy looking out of the window to notice she's sitting in front of him.

She's now separating small sections of hair, running her fingertips through it and then twirling it around her index finger. She keeps doing it, one section after another.

The backpack man is no longer looking out of the window. He's now watching her play with her hair. Maybe he's trying to figure out what her problem is too. He keeps moving around in his seat, like he's trying to get comfortable or something. I wonder if she's annoying him as much as she is me. Yet, I don't even know why. It's not like it's my hair she's messing up. Uh oh! Maybe I pegged him wrong – he looks like he's getting aroused!

I'm trying to read my book, "Milk in My Coffee," in an attempt to ignore the hair-crazed lady. Even though I truly don't want to watch her playing with her hair, there's something peculiar about the man behind her who now appears to be ever so interested in her actions.

I'm willing to assume that this man must not care that I can see him or maybe he thinks I'm not paying attention to him since I'm reading my book. He must have never heard of peripheral vision. I can see him out of the corner of my eye and it looks like he's rubbing his manhood. Eww! He is – he has that thing positioned on the inside of his right leg and is rubbing away. The more she twirls, the more he rubs. I can't believe what's happening!

Finally she stops and, believe it or not, so does he. I'm so uncomfortable and I want to say something but I don't know if that's wise. I don't want to just get up and move, both because that'll be too obvious and a person has to be careful of what she does and says to people. He may go off on me for bustin' his groove. I wish this wasn't an express train because I still have at least another twenty minutes before I'll reach my stop. I wonder why she couldn't hear him back there getting his jollies off? Or, does she know what she's doing to him?

Oh, it's getting better, for him anyway. She tilted her head, fluffed all of her hair forward and flipped it back, showing more of its length and fullness. Can't she feel his attention on her? Her hair is hanging slightly over the back of the seat and this outlandish man has leaned forward and is sniffing her hair!

There she goes again, and immediately his hand is working its way back to the stiffness that has made a defined imprint in his shorts. He still hasn't looked my way. I turned my head away from them, trying to continue with my reading. I check the time, seeing that it'll be approximately ten minutes before we reach my stop. Inconspicuously, I continue to watch because this act is amazing me.

Eww! I should've kept reading my book or should've kept my head turned towards the window. Slyly I watch this fool, who is no longer rubbing his thing through his shorts but has succeeded in working the leg of his shorts up and has his beef stick in his hand, rubbing up and down on it. The entire time he appears to be concentrating on the chick reveling in her hair.

That's it! I can't sit here any longer. I don't care if he does snap out. All I know is I'm out of this car. I stand and head for the door, but he doesn't stop; he never takes his eyes off her. It's like I'm invisible. I look back at the few people who were sitting behind me. They're seated so far towards the back of the car that they can't have a clue what's going on up here.

I pass between the cars, knowing this is dangerous, but right now I don't care. Shit! I almost lost my balance. I grab onto one of the handles and regain my footing, attempting to do the same for my composure. The next car is a little crowded and right away I feel more at ease. I take a seat next to a professional-looking woman. Luckily it's a three-seater so she and I don't have to sit too close. After witnessing an episode of Sex on the Train, I don't want to be too close to anyone. For all I know, when the train shakes and shifts, she may get turned on.

"Hello," the woman says in a soft and pleasant tone.

I return the gesture. "How are you?"

"Excuse me for prying, but was there something weird going on in the other car?"

"Weird is not the word. These two people . . . I don't want to talk about it."

"I knew it," the woman relies. "You look distraught, so I figured there must have been a reason for your passing between cars while we're still moving."

I stare at her wondering how she knows. "How'd you know?"

"I see them on the train often. The first time I saw them was about a month ago when I was in the same car with them. When I saw what was going on, I was so shocked and unsure of what to do that I wouldn't get up and move. The fact that he looked clean cut and like a student and was doing something like that with me right there worried me more because I figured he must be unstable and might do something to me if I stood up."

I exclaim, "I didn't want to stand up either!"

She goes on, "So I just sat there and tried to pretend that I didn't see them, but I kept watching to make sure he didn't get up and come near me."

"So you sat there until he stopped?"

"More like until he finished!"

"YOU HAVE TO BE JOKING!"

"Afraid not. If you weren't sitting across from him, you would have never known this was going on. He kept going until he finished...on the floor."

"Ugh! That's disgusting! But wait, I notice you said 'them.' Does she know he's doing this?"

"Oh, most definitely. That's the most disgusting part of it. When we finally reached the stop, the two of them stood up, and when they stepped out into the aisle they giggled, kissed and got off together."

"Now, that's crazy. How can the conductors allow this to go on?" I inquire.

"If you didn't notice, they have their little thing timed so that they don't start until after the conductor comes through to take everyone's tickets. Once the conductor does that, he doesn't need to come back in the car until we reach our stop since this is an express train. That's why since then, every time I get on this train, I check to make sure I don't see them and if I do, I don't sit in a car that they're in. I don't know if they do that all the time, but I have noticed that not many people sit in the same car with them."

"Well, thanks for letting me know. I don't normally ride the R3, but if I ever have to catch this one again, I'll be sure to watch out for them."

Just then the conductor announces that we're approaching my stop. Sure enough, as I step off the train, they're holding hands, getting off too. He glances over at me and has the nerve to smile. I want to throw up.

I'm right in time to catch my connecting bus, trying to get what just happened out of my mind. The recent memory of signing my new lease replaces the horrid memories of the train and my spirit begins to lighten. As I walk into the dentist

44

office, the receptionist Diane greets me and asks me what's new. The first thing that surfaces in my mind is mine and Ian's new home. I paint a vivid picture of the apartment and upon finishing, Anita, the hygienist, calls me back for my cleaning.

I'm a wuss in the dentist chair. Dr. Nabs calls me "Xtra-Xtra"! But I don't care; give me my nitrous and let me relax!

When I come out, Ian is waiting for me. After he finishes turning on the charm for all the ladies in the office and I said my good-byes to everyone, we go to his car and I fill him in on what happened on the train.

"Isn't that enough for you to not want to ride the train?"

"It has never happened before, Ian."

"So what! You don't have to ride the train. You could be driving . . .your own car."

"Okay, okay. I'll start looking."

"You do that and until you decide on something, I want you to rent a car if you have somewhere you need to go outside of work."

"I'll do that for you."

Ian drops me off and goes back to the studio. I go in my apartment feeling all tingly inside. Aside from the adventurous train ride, my day was better than any day I can recall.

***

I can't even get my key in the door and the phone is ringing. "Hello?"

"Hey girl!"

"Hey, Desz! Girl, you must have been reading my mind."

"Why? What's up?"

"You will never believe what happened today!"

"You met the man of your dreams?"

"Funny! I met him six months ago! We signed the papers for our new apartment!"

"Girl, he's moving you to another apartment? Is he buying you a car yet?"

"You're a trip! No he's not moving me…we're moving together and as a matter of fact, I'm getting ready to start looking for a car!"

"Go, Ash. Do that thing girl! You must've put it on him right!"

"Shut up, Desz. I'm really into Ian."

"What? Oh, I see…he's must've put it on you!"

"You make me sick. He's so good to me and for me and he's really helping my business get off the ground. We're good together; we really click. We spend quality time together and he includes me in his professional life, which you know I like. His job is the shit! I love being around the people he associates with, watching them interact and enjoying the luxuries that they have. I know one day we'll have the same things. Ian's becoming very connected in the industry and one of his groups has been offered a deal. When that happens, he's set and I'm sure his other groups will get deals soon too. He's even talking about financing my business so I can do it full time. He says he sees me being a major PR person in this area."

"A PR person? Where'd that come from?"

"I coordinated a book release party for Daaimah S. Poole, a local author of the book "YoYo Love," and Ian went with me. He was shocked at the support she received and he was quite impressed with the publicity she got because of my planning and contacts. He watched me all night and commented on how I seem to be a natural and how happy I look while I work."

"So when's this going to happen?"

"Soon, girl. I have to expand my client base, but that's where he comes in. I'll coordinate events for him and he'll introduce me to influential people."

"Go on, girl! You have your master plan working along

with his. Just make sure you don't forget that you have a best friend."

"Stop that. Well look Desz; I have to run. I want to start packing because I plan to be out of here by the weekend. I'll call you tomorrow to give you the new address and phone number. You and Amber have got to come over to my place this weekend, even though we'll all have to sit on the floor."

"That's cool with me. You pack and I'll call Amber to share your good news with her. We'll see you this weekend. Don't forget to call me tomorrow with the information."

"Gotcha."

6

The phone rings. "Ms. Thompson, Ms. Carter is on her way back."

"Thank you," I say to the guard at the booth.

I wait at the door for Desz to finish parking.

"And to what do I owe this surprise?"

"Hey! I can only stay a minute. I'm out doing my running around and I had to stop by to check out the place, now that it's all furnished."

"Well come on in, miss. Let me take you on a tour!"

"Ash, it looks so nice. I can't believe you did all this in just two months."

"That's the same thing Ian says, but you know me, no matter how much I have to do or how tired I am I can still shop. You know, Desz, I don't think I ever thanked you for going out with me all those times that Ian was too busy. I think he appreciated it even more than I did."

"Girl, you don't have to thank me and Ian thanked me enough by treating us to dinner every time we went out. I think he did that because he knew we weren't coming in 'til the stores closed. What more can a woman ask for? Speaking of Ian, how are things going with you two lovebirds?"

"Real good. I love my place and now, my man more than I thought I ever could."

"That's so good, Ash. I'm so happy for you. When I grow up, I wanna be just like you."

"You're such a smart ass!" I say as I smack her on the arm.

"Well, I gotta run! If I keep talking to you, I'll end up here the rest of the day."

"Call me soon."

I close the door and lean back on the wall. Desz is right,

48

what more can a woman ask for? Even though I don't see him as much as I used to, I'm so happy that I found Ian. Now, with two groups signed to labels, he's crazy busy. He's even hired an assistant to do the administrative work, but he won't take on a partner. I don't know what he's waiting for – he's constantly being approached. Some dude named Davon calls here at least once a week trying to get in with him. I think he likes being the only one, at his level, working with the groups and I tell you what, the money is damn good! Unfortunately, the busier he gets, the less I see of him.

But my business has also picked up, so I'm out after I get off work or I'm up early and in the office working. It's becoming a challenge juggling my demanding full-time job and maintaining my personal client relationships. I've made it work up 'til now because of the time I get to spend away from the office, but it's becoming a bit overwhelming. Luckily I have Kara. We have such a good working relationship at Winer's that I brought her on to help me at ShaGru, which is what I've decided to name my event-coordinating business.

When I finally make my move and begin running my company full-time, Kara will be coming with me. We actually end up doing some ShaGru work during the day because there are times when calls have to be made during "normal business hours" but we're able to schedule most meetings in the evening. I turned that extra room into an office just like Ms. Karigan said. I really wanted to use the extra bedroom, but Ian and I decided against that because we were almost positive we'd need it at times for guests. Kara comes here after we get off work to concentrate on paperwork, and if we have an event she's right there with me.

My home office is large enough for my desk, a smaller one that's made to fit in the corner and a stereo/TV unit mounted in the other corner. Luckily, most of the events have been during the week, which works out great. That gives us time to breathe on the weekend and get ready for the next week. It also gives me time to spend with my man so I can make sure everything stays fresh.

Meanwhile, Ian uses the den. He had it soundproofed and made it a studio. It wasn't closed in, so he had sliding glass doors installed. It looks so nice.

Needless to say, things have gotten extremely busy for the two of us, but we both knew that eventually it would be this way because our careers and our financial freedom are things we both want. I don't usually mind as long as when he has free time, he spends it with me. I'm usually more flexible than he is, but it works out. So going away with him on his weekend trips keeps me satisfied because we get to hang out and party with the entertainers and then return to our room for a private escapade. He knows how to keep me happy!

7

It's Friday and I'm beat. I don't know if I can hang with Ian tonight. I've worked all week at the office and I had three consecutive events – Tuesday, Wednesday and Thursday. I just want to go home and chill out for the rest of the night.

A nice quiet evening at home is definitely what I need. After showering, I put on my favorite T-shirt, my big, blue fluffy slippers, pop some old-fashioned popcorn, smother it with butter and salt and plant myself in the corner of the couch with my feet up. I'm going to watch TV until I fall asleep. Ian should be coming soon. He'll be surprised to see me all prepared to stay in tonight. I seem to recall that tonight may be a big night at the club, but I can't make it. Ian's group, The NewComers, are in town this weekend and if I'm right and tonight is the night, he'll have to understand and go without me.

I wake to Ian's voice, talking to someone on his way in our apartment door. Who the heck is with him? I'm not even dressed.

"Oh, babe, I'm sorry. I should have called you first to let you know that my man is with me. Are you okay? You're not sick are you?" He was surprised to see me, lying around.

"No Ian. I'm just tired. It's been a long week and I need to relax tonight. I'm fine."

"What about tonight? You know tonight is the first formal appearance for The NewComers here in Philly. I know you're planning to come."

"I'm sorry, I didn't get your name," I say to Ian's friend.

"Mike. I recently started working with Ian."

"Nice to meet you, Mike." I guess he doesn't have a last name. "I'm Ashlei, but I'm sure you know that already. You can have a seat. Please excuse my appearance. I don't normally look so casual when I know company is coming."

"It's okay. I've heard a lot about you... and you look fine by the way," he says showing those beautiful pearly whites. This man I know is making some woman very happy. "I was hoping you'd be joining us tonight. I heard you have a lot of connections too."

"Back to tonight, Ashlei," Ian says throwing a you're-getting-too-friendly look at Mike. "I know you're still coming, right?"

"Ian, I have to pass on this one, please babe? I'm really beat and I just want to chill tonight. I'm sorry honey; I'll make it up to you."

Mike interrupts, "Ian, we're going to be late. Let your lady rest."

Ian shoots Mike a look, telling him without words to chill. Before Ian can say anything, I break in, "Besides Ian, their release party is in a couple of weeks and I wrapped up all the plans for that today. It's gonna be all that! There are celebrities coming from everywhere for this one. R Kelly, TLC...just to name a couple."

Mike blurts out, "I know I'm coming to that one! Oh, that is if you'll add me to the guest list Ashlei."

"You got it Mike," I say smiling.

"Okay. With that news, I guess we can survive without you. I need to introduce Mike to some people at the club. Mike has an R&B group that he's looking for some help with. I heard their stuff and I'm really likin' their style so I'm bringing them into the studio one day next week. They have someone who's going to manage them but they're looking for someone who can help them get on a label – and you know I'm that man." Ian checks his watch. "Mike, I'll be right back. I have to run upstairs for a minute."

With Ian gone, I try to keep on with the small talk. "Sounds like things are going to work out for you and your group. Good luck with everything, Mike. I know Ian will introduce you to some good people. I just hope whoever this person is that's going to manage you is ready to be as busy as Ian is."

"Thanks. I hope after I get started I can find somebody sexy like you to chill with when I'm not busy."

Feeling a little uneasy with his last comment, I respond, "I'm sure you will."

Hearing Ian coming down the stairs, he blows me a kiss, turns and says, "You ready yet man?"

"Yeah." Ian walks over to me, kisses me, and they leave.

That dude seems a little shady. As a matter of fact, Ian better be on his P's and Q's because Mike acts like he's one who needs watching.

8

While riding in to work this morning, I'm thinking back to only three months ago when I was bragging to myself that Ian's the best thing that could ever have happened to me. Now I rarely see him and when I do it's so late that it doesn't matter. I can't even remember the last time we had fun together. Yeah, we still live together, but what difference does that make if he's never home? My schedule is busy too, but I'm still able to make time for him. I feel like I need to schedule an appointment to see my own man. Some of the most important people in the world manage to still maintain a family. You would think Ian has the weight of the world on his shoulders and taking one minute out for me would cause it to crumble.

A couple of weeks ago when we went car shopping was more time than we've spent together in a while, even though it was far from being romantic. I didn't mind that night because for both business and personal reasons, it was time for me to get some type of vehicle. Plus, I'm out a lot more at night and my only option if I had a full calendar was to rent a car.

It took us a few nights of looking around for me to decide what I wanted. I knew I wanted an SUV, but I wasn't sure what kind. I decided on a Pathfinder for its versatility between sporty for me, and luxury for the clients. Of course Ian got me exactly what I wanted, fully loaded with extras, and I drove it home that night.

The next night, he was right back doing whatever it is he has to do all the time that keeps him away from home. I've tried to talk to him about it, but he just says he's working and to stop giving him a hard time. What can I say to that?

I'm getting real tired of this shit. We don't go anywhere anymore, and every time he has a show or something, he goes without me. He always manages to come up with some crazy excuse why I shouldn't go. Again I go to sleep alone, with my relationship in limbo.

***

Now I'm here at my office early, trying to clear my head and get ready for my workday before anyone else comes in, but it's hard. Tomorrow we're leaving for a show in New York. I'm shocked he included me, but it probably is because of my bitchin'! I can't help but wonder if the plans will be changed.

The ringing of the phone startles me. "Ashlei Thompson," I answer, wondering who would be calling before office hours.

"Hey, Babe. I thought I'd get the voicemail. Bad news...there's been a mix-up so we're only going to have three rooms...one for the band, and me and the group will have to stay in the other two rooms together."

"So what are you saying?"

"Look, this group doesn't have money like that yet. They're still trying to get up there. The reservations weren't done at our end. I'm sorry, but you won't be able to go this weekend."

"I don't mind paying for my room. I . . .we can afford it."

"I'll think about it," he says. "I'll see you when you get home."

I knew something would come up. Well, I'm glad I thought quickly. I'm not changing any of my plans. I have a five o'clock appointment to get my hair done, so I'm leaving work a little early so I can get in and out, and plus I have the day off tomorrow.

***

I leave the salon, pick up some Chinese food and when I

55

get home it's around seven o'clock. I change into my t-shirt, sweats and fluffy slippers, grab my chicken and broccoli and plop down on the couch with the remote.

When I get up to throw my trash away it's eight-thirty and he's still not home; nine o'clock still nothing.

It's a little after ten o'clock and I hear his key turning in the lock. I keep watching ER like I don't even hear him. I know he had things to do to get ready to leave tomorrow but for some reason I have a serious attitude. He could have at least called. Something's going on. He never used to do that; he'd always call. Now, since we got a place together and he started talking long-term stuff, he's doing lots of dumb shit…the same dumb shit that the boyfriends who never amounted to anything used to do. I always promised myself that I'd never compare one man to another, but I can't help it this time. I also promised myself that I'd never live with a man unless we were married, and I broke that promise too.

I hear him talking as he's coming up the steps. Who the heck is he talking to? I hope he didn't bring any of those guys home with him because we have to finish packing.

"Hey, babe," he says all cheerful.

I don't answer; don't even flinch.

I feel him coming up behind me. I'm thinking he'll bend over and kiss me on my neck, the way he always does when he knows I'm pissed – but boy did he fool me. What the hell? What's cold and wet on my ear?

As I reach up I feel something furry. I jump up, turn around and he's holding a beautiful little black, white and brown puppy with long ears and the saddest looking eyes I've ever seen.

"Ooh! Where'd he come from?" I scream as I take the dog from Ian, forgetting for a moment that I'm pissed.

He licks me all in my face, my ears and all up in my hair. I just love dogs and Ian knows it.

56

"He followed me home. Sike! I drove to Lansdale to get him. I saw an ad in the paper earlier this week and I called to find out when the puppies would be ready to wean. The lady said they'd be ready by the end of the week. So, I arranged to pick one up next Monday."

"So why'd you get him today? We're going away tomorrow and now I'll have to find him a vet and leave him in the kennel all weekend. He'll be scared. You should've waited 'til Monday like you originally planned," I say with a snappy tone.

I'm arguing with Ian and thinking to myself, Snoopy. That's a good name for him.

"Ash, I told you the deal with this weekend. I wanted to give you the dog before I leave because I feel bad."

"Yeah right you feel bad. I told you I could just pay for my room. What's the big deal?"

"You don't need to do that and you know I wouldn't let you pay for the room anyway. I'm only going to New York and I'll be back early on Sunday. Besides, the hotel is booked and I really don't want to stay somewhere different than everybody else. You can just go next time."

Here he goes again. Damn! I feel my temperature rising. Something's up with this man.

"You're so full of shit! If you didn't want me to go, you should've just said so. What's up with you anyway? For the past two months you've been acting real shady. I realize you've been extremely busy because you've picked up some new talent, but you don't even work from your home studio as much. We don't do shit! We don't even get champagne, some take-out, rent movies and end the night with some good sex anymore. You act like you don't even want THAT anymore! I need to have Dru Hill come sing for us because that must be what's going on . . .their song 'Somebody's Sleepin' in My Bed'!"

"Ashlei, please don't start! Can we not argue before I leave? I'll be back on Sunday. It's not like I'm going away for weeks."

"It doesn't matter. All that matters is that again, I'm not going. You must have some bitch traveling with you! We used to have fun when we'd go away, and now you act like it'll kill you to take me along. If there's someone else, Ian, please tell me so I can move on."

Grabbing me by the shoulders, he yells, "I've told you before, there's no one else! I wish you'd stop saying that. I'm tired of hearing that shit from you just because I'm out doing my job. Girl, don't you know that my career is my life? I don't need no bitch because I'm away from home."

Pushing his hands off me I shout, "Oh, now I'm a bitch, huh? Fuck you, Ian! If you don't want me, somebody will. Keep fucking with me. Just like I grinded on you at that after-party, I can do it again. You think you're the only one out there with a dick?"

"I wish you would. I'd . . ."

"You'd what? You'd what? It'll be your fault. You're the one not taking care of home."

"Not taking care of home? I make sure you have a nice place to live..."

"Oh, and I didn't have anything to do with that? How soon we forget."

"Whatever...I bought you a truck so your ass wouldn't have to catch the stinkin' ass train, I even got you somebody so you don't have to clean – and I'm not taking care of home?"

"What about me? Not all the material shit? What about sex? What about taking care of this?" I yell, pointing at my womanhood.

"Girl you need to stop fuckin' trippin'. Look, I'm not arguing with you anymore. Everything you need for the dog is in the kitchen. I gotta get some rest."

58

What type of shit is this? What kind of man let's you talk to him like that and just goes to sleep? What's up with this dude? Who does he think he is, Mr. Golden Dick? He *can* work it, but damn. I'm not gonna to let him treat me like shit.

"How can you just go to sleep in the middle of us arguing?" My voice changes to an erratic tone as I say, "You know what? Go the fuck to sleep, Ian. I'm not gonna sweat your dumb ass. If this is how you want it then fine."

I go in the living room and lay on the couch but can't relax enough to fall asleep. I scoop Snoopy up, lay him beside me and watch TV until I finally fall asleep.

***

I can't believe this, it's midnight on Sunday and I've spent yet another weekend alone. This is the first time he's ever stayed longer than what he originally planned and I know it's not because of our argument. There have been so many shows that I haven't gone to lately that I'm starting to lose interest in his career. New people I'm beginning to meet are starting to look very appetizing to me.

The phone startles me. "Now who could be calling here?" I ask myself. "I know it's not him.

"Hello?"

"Hello, is Ian in?"

"No. Who's this?" I'm not normally so snappy but I don't feel like being bothered.

"Davon Matthews. Can you let him know I called?"

"Sure."

"Sorry if I disturbed you."

"Excuse me?"

"You sound disturbed. Sorry to bother you."

"Oh, don't worry about it. I'll tell him you called."

"Thanks."

See what I mean? Even he sounded good and I can't see

him. I never thought this would happen. For some reason, this weekend felt different. "Yeah, right. You know the reason," I try telling myself. Things between Ian and me have been less than pleasant lately.

Sex? What's that? I can't even remember the last time we had some good sex. I mean GOOD sex, not a quickie or a meaningless moment. I'm usually asleep when he gets in and he never wakes me. When I ask him why he didn't wake me, he tells me it's because I was sound asleep and he didn't want to bother me for something that we can do later. Later? When is later? He's hardly ever here.

I know what his automatic response will be to any challenge from me. *"Ash, don't even try it. You know I have lots of things going on. Hopefully, one day soon I'll be able to build a management team to help me with some things, but right now I don't want to put out that kind of money on something I can do myself, with my administrative help. Please be patient with me. We have the rest of our lives to make love. We're not going anywhere. I'm trying to give you everything you want so you won't have to work anymore. I know right now you enjoy what you're doing, but one day I'd like us to start a family."*

A family? Picture that. I may have believed that before, but we are at such a distance that I can't think like that anymore. Sitting here, I think back to the first night Ian and I met at the LL after-party, our first sexual encounter, and the next night of the cookout…

"Excuse me. Didn't you hear me come in?"

"Actually, I didn't."

He came over, gave me a peck on the neck. "I see you have your toy in bed with you."

I guess I drifted off after the thoughts of our first night together led me to inviting my battery-operated man to bed with me. I didn't even hear Ian come in. "Well, what else am I

60

supposed to do? You leave me here by myself and it's not like you've been giving me any. I'm sure somebody's getting it, though."

He just shook his head and started getting ready for bed like everything was okay. "It's cool. Better that than another man. You know you better not go there."

I didn't bother to justify that comment with a response because if I wanted to fool around I could and he'd never know. I have enough free time on my hands and I meet enough eligible men who are making good money during my travels to take on a few, but for some reason I'm not interested in doing that right now.

"Night, babe," he grunts as he lies down and turns away from me.

"So how'd it go this weekend?" I question.

"Everything went good."

"Ian, you can't even tell me what went on and how the show went?"

"I told you, it was good. Ash, it was a long weekend and I'm tired. We'll talk in the morning."

I guess that's why he gave me Snoopy. It would give me someone to talk to so I could leave him alone and that's why he doesn't mind me using the imitation dick . . .that lets him off the hook. "All right, Ian," I say, again feeling hurt.

I reach for my journal and begin writing…

Someone's always saying…
"You two look so good together
You seem like the perfect couple
I hope one day I'll have a relationship like yours…
And so on, and so on…"

These words make me feel so good
When I hear someone say them
But who can see deep inside those words
Inside there's an emptiness
An emptiness I've never felt before
Where did all the fulfillment go?
Where did it all go?

So many days wishing for happiness
So many nights filled with lovemaking
So many dreams
So many so many
Where did it all go?

Please tell me…
Where?

***

Monday morning and I'm off to another hectic day at work. It's so hard to feel powerful at the office when home is so unsettled. I figure I can talk to Ian some more when I get home tonight. I'm surprised after a few morning meetings to hear from Kara that Ian is on the phone on hold for me.

"Thanks, Kara. I'll take it in my office."

At my desk, I pick up the receiver and say, "Hello."

"Hey! What you up to?" Ian asks.

"Nothing much. I was actually sitting here thinking about you."

"Oh, shit. What about now? What did I do this time?"

"Ian, why do you have to say it like that? You know damn well that I'm upset about the weekend and the fact that you just came home and went to bed like nothing was wrong."

I heard the bell ring. "Okay, Ash, I just called to say hello. I gotta go."

"Who's at the door?"

"It's Mike. You remember you met him a few weeks ago? I'm riding with him to meet this guy Davon at the studio. He's interested in managing Mike's group and wants to talk business."

"Oh yeah. He called last night."

"Thanks, he told me. I talked to him this morning. I'll talk to you later, babe."

"All right, Ian. Bye." I hang up on him. So many things are racing through my mind. I just can't believe that something's happening to us. I'm not liking this. I can't let this fall apart.

When I get home later he's nowhere to be found. Then I see a note on the kitchen table saying he had to go to a meeting that was scheduled at the last minute and that he'd see me later. And he took his car this time because it wasn't in his spot.

Again I go to bed alone, fighting back the tears. If it weren't for him my business wouldn't be prospering the way it has been and I wouldn't be where I am. What will I do if we're not together?

9

I've basically spent the past couple of days alone. Ian has managed to be away most of the time so I haven't had a chance to talk to him. He knows I'm still pissed, but I'm not about to sit up in the middle of the night arguing with him only to then walk around exhausted the next day. If he wants to keep ducking me, that's fine. Eventually, he'll think I've gotten over finding that earring in our bedroom and then I'll throw that shit in his face again.

Maybe what I need is to start getting out more – the way I used to when I first started dating Ian. With the exception of work, I've been keeping myself too secluded from the things I used to do socially with my girls. My world now revolves around him and I only have myself to blame for letting it get like this. Well, there's no need to sit around beating myself up about it. I just have to make a change. Desz, Amber and me are always talking about females who see shit ain't right but yet they just keep on hanging on. To what? False hopes? Been there, done that. And I'm not doing that again or should I say, any longer. I shouldn't have let myself get in this far but I did and here I am. I have to handle this without losing my mind. Even though I've gained several clients through Ian, they're not even worth me dealing with a man who cheats on me in our own bedroom. I need to get out and have some fun. As a matter of fact, let me call my squad and see what we can get into this weekend.

"Hello! I'm sorry I'm not in right now . . ."

I knew I'd get her machine; her hours always fluctuate. "Hey, Desz. Call me when you get home. I need a night out in the worst way. I'll tell you about it later. See ya."

I try my other partner.

"Hey, Amber."

64

"Hey, girl. I know the voice but I can't say I remember the face," Amber says sarcastically.

"I know and it's been too long. That's why I'm calling. What are you doing tomorrow night?"

"As of right now, nothing. Why? What's on your mind?"

"I thought the three of us could go out and hit a couple of dance floors like old times."

"Now Ash, you know I don't hang out like we used to."

"Come on, Amber. I'm not sayin' go out and leave with plans to lay somebody down. I just want to go out to dinner, go have a couple of drinks and get my dance on."

"Why this sudden urge to go out?" asks Amber.

"I knew you'd ask sooner or later. I guess I might as well tell."

"Tell what? Are you pregnant?"

"No girl! Hell no!"

"Whew! Thank God. Well what then?"

"Wait a minute. Let me try Desz again so I only have to say this once. Hold on."

I click over and call Desz. After three rings I hear the phone pick up. "Yes?"

"Desz. What's wrong honey?"

"Hey, Ash. What you been up to? Nothing's wrong. I thought you were this guy who's been calling me non-stop ever since I met him at the Bark's Deli near my job. What a mistake it was to give him my number! Anyway, what's up with you?"

"Same ole'. But hold on; Amber's holding on the other line. Let me click her in."

"Amber?"

"Yeah?"

"Desz?"

"Yeah?"

"Aw-shucks now!!! Here we go!!! Just like old times!"

"All right, Ashlei, Desz is here now. What's going on? What's with this sudden urge to do one of our 'hang out 'til we drop nights'?"

"What? Something's going on?" Desz says.

"Hold on to your thongs. I'm getting ready to tell you." I pause, trying to think of how to say this with dignity. Well, you know that things haven't been great for Ian and me, right?"

"Right," Desz says.

"Okay," Amber joins in.

"And you know that I've been sinking money into a savings account. Well, I'm getting an office, leaving my job soon and operating my event-coordinating business full time."

"What brought on this sudden change?" Desz asks.

I explained, "That was my intention anyway but I'm doing it a little sooner than I'd planned."

"Okay, Ashlei, what does this have to do with things not being good with Ian?" Amber quizzes.

"Are you ready for this one?" I say jokingly, trying to keep my spirits up. "Night before last, I found a medium-size, platinum diamond hoop earring in my bedroom, on the floor by the nightstand, on *MY* side of the bed. When I asked him, he said it was probably Maria, the cleaning lady's and he took it from me to give back to her."

"Now wait a minute, Ash," Desz starts. "Aren't you jumping to conclusions? She *is* the cleaning lady. She could've dropped it while she was cleaning your room. Have you ever seen her wearing earrings like that?"

"I've never seen her, at all! She always comes on Tuesdays when I'm working."

"Then you really can't be sure," Desz replies. "I know Ian's been spending a lot of time away, but if he was gonna cheat don't you think he'd do it with someone wherever he is, not at home with his maid?"

"That's the truth, Ash," Amber adds. "Why would he

choose someone he hired to clean your home when he can pick one of those little groupies running around ready to give it up, you know . . .like we used to?"

"Wait, I'm not finished. Two weeks ago, I found a platinum, a beautiful platinum bracelet in the bathroom . . .in the tub."

"Wow, what did he say to that one?" Amber asks.

"He said that it was a gift to himself that he thought he lost. He acted pissed and said that he was going to take it and get his money back. I never saw him with the bracelet on, but it all seemed believable so I gave it to him and didn't think anymore of it until I found the earring. Amber, you've always told us that things happen for a reason, so why do you think these things have turned up?"

"Yo," Desz blurts out, "if Maria is making enough to buy jewelry like that then I need to call Ian and see if Ian can give me some part-time work waxing your floor!"

We all laugh at that one. "Desz, you are stupid," Amber says cracking up.

"No, Ian's stupid if the thinks I'm gonna sit here while he screws the cleaning lady, in my room, on my bed, while I'm at work. No wonder he's always so tired at night. He wears himself out on her during the day."

Amber's protective nature kicks in. "Ash, you need to calm down. I understand why you're upset, but don't blow up at him until you have more to go on. There ain't nothing worse than telling a man about himself and being wrong."

"Oh I know, girl. That's why I've decided to put my business plan in action a little sooner. I know the shit's gonna hit the fan soon and I need to be ahead of the game. I'm going to look at a couple of nice offices tomorrow; then to the gym and I'm hoping after I'm done, we can hook up and have one of our famous girls' nights out. Then I can start checking out some other options, if you know what I mean."

"That'll work," Amber responds. "But Ash, what you said about other options . . .you know that either way, you don't have to have a man for your career to be successful. You're already rolling. You can do this on your own."

"I hear you, Amber, but right now, I gotta do what I gotta do. Ian has introduced me to some influential people and I have to be sure doors keep opening for me, if not through him then with someone else.

"Desz, I hear you flipping pages. Are you free tomorrow or what?" I say to her.

"Can I find the page? And you call me impatient. It's cool; I'm there. I thought I had something on my calendar, but I don't. So, let's do this!"

"Oh wait!" I say kind of loud. "I forgot to tell you last week I came home and all of Snoopy's stuff was in the closet, including his feeding bowls. You know I flipped. How's he gonna put my baby's bowls away? I asked his dumb ass about it and he got this peculiar look on his face."

"What did he say?"

"Again, he blamed it on Maria. He said that one time she mentioned that she is allergic to dogs and she doesn't like to touch Snoopy's things when she does the floors because it makes her hands itch."

"I have to admit," says Amber, "Maria's name does come up a little too often."

"Right! And do you think I care about her allergies? She best take a Benadryl before she comes here and leave my dog's stuff alone . . .See, now I know I'm not losing my mind. Well, guess what? Next Tuesday Maria and I will meet because I'm taking the day off. I want to see what this chick is all about."

"Go Ashlei, go Ashlei. Kick your shoes off, kick your shoes off. It's your birthday, it's your birthday!" Desz chants.

I cut in on the performance, "Enough about Maria for

now. What time tomorrow?"

"How about if we meet at your house around seven o'clock? That way I can get to see my Godson, Snoopy. I haven't seen the little guy in a while," Desz laughs.

"That's cool with me," Amber says.

"Alright. I'll see you two tomorrow night at seven o'clock. Make sure you eat your Wheaties because we're not stoppin' 'til we drop."

"All right, Ash. See ya Desz."

Desz follows, "Talk to you two tomorrow."

"Hey, thanks you two. I really need this."

I'm feeling a burst of energy. I feed Snoop and take him out for a long walk. At one point, we even pick up a slow jog. It feels good to know that I have a plan, a plan to get my life back on track. I've wasted so much time sitting around because of this man. I do love him and it hurts knowing there's something going on, but I can't let him walk over me like I'm a doormat. I have to do what I know is best for me. Meanwhile, I have to uncover whatever or whomever he's keeping warm with.

***

"Coming out tonight was a good idea, Ash," Amber says.

"I know, y'all. It feels good to be out just chillin'. I mean, I'm in the clubs every week, but that's work. I had a function here at Club Escape last week, but the atmosphere is completely different when you step on this side of the table."

"Well, you know me. I'm getting ready to go get my groove on. I'll be back in a few," Desz says as she prances her hot ass towards the dance floor. I don't know when she'll finally settle down. She's still seeing Dave, but that doesn't stop her from having her fun on a regular basis. She still calls him a friend.

"Amber, look at the guy over there . . .the one with all black on and those hazel eyes. Do you see him?"

"Yeah, I see him – and I think he sees you."

"Yeah, right," I say, doubting Amber's observation. "He is fine, though, and he definitely has the look."

"Yes he does. It's a shame you're taken!"

"Yeah, and it's a shame I actually feel guilty about sitting here checking out another man. Amber, I really love Ian. I don't want things to come to an end for us. I've always thought of myself as being a strong woman and thought I could deal with an industry man, but I don't know anymore. He always blames it on work, but I just can't believe that everyone in this business, who has a significant other never has any time to spend with that person. Ian used to be all over me. I guess I could deal with everything else if he just showed me some affection when he comes home."

"I understand what you're saying Ash. You're going to have to really rethink everything. Look, things are going good for you and it sounds like the music scenario has worked but the man is slipping out of it. Like I said before, I don't know why you always think you need a man to get where you want to be. You're almost there now and I bet you could have made it to this point on your own if you would just believe in yourself and your talents. Will it really ruin your career if you don't have the man – or just your ego?"

"I don't know Amber. You're probably right. I'm sure it's more my ego. I know my career is strong. I've gained a lot of respect at Winer for the work I've done and my plan is in action to take ShaGru to a full-time level soon. Oh, I forgot tell you that Kara has agreed to come with me. I just need to hang in there a little while longer."

"Well, if that's the case, you don't need him. If he's not treating you like you want to be treated then leave."

"I can't just leave. The place is in my name."

70

At that moment I feel someone touch my elbow. "Would you like to dance?"

I look into the face of a tall, thin, dark-skin man with locks and tinted glasses on. "No, thank you," I say with a smile. I hate not being able to look someone in the eyes. His locks look nice, but why does he have on tinted glasses like the sun is shining in here?

"Well, can I at least buy you a drink?"

Now he sounds like he's begging. "No thanks. I'm okay. I'm just chilling with my girlfriend. Thanks anyway."

He seems disgusted as he twists his mouth and walks away.

"Ashlei, why'd you do that?"

"What? Tell him no?"

"That too, but why'd you put that place in your name?"

"Cause he's not my type, dag. You can't even see him behind those glasses. Ian had some credit issues. I really don't mind so much – anyway, he pays the rent."

"Suppose he had just up and left you. You would have never been able to afford that place alone."

"Maybe not in the beginning, but after a while I was making enough for me to carry the load by myself. That's when it seemed like everything started changing. I'll be okay for now but when I'm ready I'll find a replacement for him. Right now I have to try to play it cool until I have some proof that something's going on with Ian. I bet I'll have it next Tuesday!"

"We'll see. Right now what you definitely have is an admirer."

Amber thinks she's slick. Just as she says that, she turns and walks away. Before I can say anything to her I hear this deep, sexy voice behind me.

"Excuse me."

I turn slowly, "Yes."

"I don't mean to seem presumptuous, but it seems like

we've been catching each other's eye since you came in."

"Oh, does it?"

"Am I wrong? Before you answer, would you like a drink…" he pauses as if to imply my name should now be inserted.

"It's Ashlei, and yes I'll have an Amaretto Sour, thank you. As for your other question, I'd say you must be overly confident or paranoid to think that I've been looking at you since I got here. Which is it?"

"Neither – I'm just honest."

I can't help but laugh because we were definitely staring at each other and no matter how hard I tried not to look his way, I couldn't help it. It's not often that you see someone with dark complexion skin with light eyes. He is *so* fine!

"Why are you laughing?"

I answer, "Because, I have to admit, I did look your way a few times. I'm sorry if I offended you."

"Believe me, no offense taken. I'm quite pleased with what I'm seeing. I wonder if someone is looking at the same sight on a daily basis."

Ooh, good one. I never heard that one. "It just so happens that I do have someone, but I don't mind having a drink with you . . . "

"Thanks for being honest, and my name is Dee."

"Dee. That's it?"

"That's what everybody calls me. You need more?"

"Yeah," I say in the midst of another giggle. I don't know what it is about this guy but since I don't know what's going on between me and Ian right now, I'm going to keep my options open and make sure I get this man's phone number. That's one thing I've learned over the years about dealing with men…always have a plan B or in this case, plan D.

The DJ spins "Summertime" by Philly's own DJ Jazzy Jeff and the Fresh Prince. I start moving my head to the beat. I know it's old but it's still one of my favorites."

"Do you want to dance?"

As I follow Dee to the dance floor, I notice the guy that asked me to dance earlier. I feel him staring at me. I can't see him but his head is turned this way. While we're dancing, I position Dee in front of him to avoid his awkward glances.

"So, Ashlei, you and your girlfriends just out for a little fun tonight?"

"Yeah. We used to do this on a regular basis but we've gotten away from it."

"I'm here by myself tonight checking out some new talent I recently moved here from North Carolina."

"Really? I'm surprised you didn't go to Atlanta."

"I thought about it, but I visited Philly and New York several times and I prefer the pace in the north better. Besides, I think I had a dream that I'd meet a beautiful woman by the name of Ashlei if I moved here."

Smiling, I say, "Oh really. Cute!"

I can't imagine where Amber has disappeared to but I haven't seen her for over forty-five minutes. I decide to head back to the bar where we were before Dee came over. "Thanks Dee. I'm going to look for my friend." I turn to leave the dance floor, wondering if he will follow.

"Wait," he says reaching for my hand. "Can I buy you another drink?"

I hesitate, "Um . . .sure."

As I'm walking back to the bar area I'm thinking, isn't this the way it usually goes? It's like when you're job hunting and not having any luck and as soon as someone hires you, everyone wants to call and offer you a job. This man not only knows people here but down south too. I need to be his friend. He may be able to help me expand what I'm doing to another state. Damn, why didn't I meet him first? He probably has way more connections than Ian – and better ones.

He orders drinks for both of us. "I hope I run into you again."

"Let me give you my business card. I'm an event specialist. If you or someone you know is having an event, I'd be more than happy to handle the planning."

"Is that the only time I can use this number?" Dee asks.

"Is that the only time you want to use it?" I come back at him.

"Not hardly."

Damn, this man looks good and his eyes are sparkling. The timing is so wrong – or is it? I'm not closing this door. Right now I can't promote anything more than a business relationship, but I may be available soon, so I'm leaving the ball in his court. "Well, you're a grown man. Use your own judgment."

"I'll do that. Well, I'm getting ready to get out of here, Ashlei. I'll talk to you soon." He pays the bartender for another drink for me, looks at me with those sexy eyes, reaches over, takes my hand and very lightly, kisses me on the cheek. "It was nice to meet you, Ashlei."

I smile as his lips touch me because he gave me a chill that made my nipples stand up and say hello. "Nice to meet you too, Dee."

He leaves me sitting there mesmerized. I can't believe he has me feeling flustered like I'm a teenage girl. This man has sex appeal that I can't even explain. Whew, I can't even imagine . . .no, won't do it to myself!

Amber manages to find her way back over to me. "So, your new friend is gone?"

"What were you doing, hiding somewhere watching us?"

"Basically," Amber admits cockily. "He's fine, girl! I saw that kiss he gave you on your cheek. I know your shit started leaking."

74

"Amber! I can't believe you're talking like that! You never cease to amaze me. I knew it. You come off so innocent but the freak is still in there and . . .you're right!"

"Hey, after dealing with crazy-ass Reggie for three months and it taking three more months for me to make him realize that I didn't want him, I've decided I don't want to deal with anybody right now. I'm focusing on my career, which by the way is going very well. But just because I choose not to deal with anyone, that doesn't mean my little man in the boat is dead. I keep it alive myself and when the time comes, I'm sure the right man will help me out."

Confused I ask, "Amber, you've been seeing him all this time and never said anything to us? I know we talked about him but you said you were through with him."

"I *was* through, but he didn't want me to be. I didn't talk about him because as far as I was concerned, there was nothing to talk about. Done deal."

"I hear you girl. I know you had it under control. Let's go find Desz so we can get out of here. I thought I was going to dance all night but the *brown-eyed man* has stimulated my circulation enough for one night!"

"Oh, he has a nickname?"

"Well, ya know!" I say slyly. "Now, back home to reality."

10

It's Tuesday at six o'clock. The alarm goes off and I start getting ready for work as usual. I throw on some sweats so I can take Snoop out before getting in the shower. When we come back inside, I notice that Ian has already showered and is in the bedroom. There's no conversation between the two of us but that's not unusual for us in the morning. I've never been much of an early morning person anyway and he doesn't usually have much to say either.

I remember when I was younger, my mom would wake me up for school and it would take her four or five tries before she could even get me to wake up. "Ashlei Marie Thompson, you better get out of that bed," she'd say when she'd burst into my room. Then it would take me another ten to fifteen minutes to even raise myself to a sitting position. But mom, oh she had plenty of energy. I wouldn't even have a chance to get that hard, rock-like stuff that older people call "sleep" out of the corners of my eyes before Mom would be talking away. And about what, I don't even know. I'd be so mad that I'd purposely forget. If it were anything important she'd leave a note anyway. After our forced conversation everything would hurt . . .my head, my stomach. I'd have done just about anything so I could get a few more minutes in bed and if I was lucky I might get to stay home that day. Mom wasn't having that too often. If I complained of a stomachache, she would always say, "Go to the bathroom. It'll make you feel better." Why do older people always think that a bowel movement is the cure for everything? I think going through that with Mom is why I enjoy quiet time in the morning.

So now, as an adult, my defense to any unwanted conversation is the radio. Perhaps the humor from The Dream Team on Power99 FM will keep me preoccupied. Sometimes they say some real off-the-wall shit.

I'm not sure why, but I just feel like aggravating Ian this morning, so after showering, I waltz in the room with a fluffy, shrimp-color towel wrapped around me with my hair pulled up. As I enter the bedroom, I look at the clock, drop my towel, lie on the bed and exclaim, "Whew! I'm still kind of tired. I think I'll lay down for a few minutes before I get dressed."

"What, you're not going to work again?" He asked with a parental, I'm disappointed in you, tone. "You stayed home last Tuesday."

I'm screaming inside, yeah I stayed home but little Miss Maid didn't come! Wasn't that a coincidence that she called and couldn't come on the day I stayed home to see her? "Nobody said anything about not going to work. What I said was that I'm laying down for a couple of minutes and what difference does it make? If I stay home, I'll be here alone. You wouldn't dare stay home with me. I'll just be here with the stupid, allergic cleaning lady who loses things in my bedroom. That is, if she shows up this week!"

"Here you go. Why does she have to be all that?"

"Oh, now you're defending her, Ian?" I'm so frustrated I could throw something at him.

"No, I'm not defending her…here we go again! Why does everything have to be an argument with you? I hired Maria to take the load off of you. But you don't appreciate that. If I couldn't afford to do that, you'd be mad that you have to work and then come home and clean. I get someone to come in and clean and now you have to talk about her like a shit."

Unable to control my anger any longer, I jump up off the bed, grab my clothes and start getting dressed. "Whatever, Ian. I still don't understand why you're defending her. Do you want my opinion? And too bad if you don't – I'm giving it to you anyway. I think you got her for *you*."

"For me? What sense does that make?"

"For you to screw."

"That's crazy. Now you are really losing it."

"You say you hired her for me, but you seem to be the only one who even knows who she is or what she looks like. I've never even met the woman."

He's so infuriating to me and it becomes more and more clear through all the things he's not saying, what is actually going on. I can't hold back any longer so I fire at him with a final blow. "I can't even lay here nude and get a little attention from my 'suppose to be' man because all you're worried about is what I called your sorry-ass little housekeeper."

"Look, Ashlei!"

I ignore him, storm out the room and busy myself with making sure Snoop has water and food. He always looks so sad when I'm getting ready to leave. I lean over to pet him and whisper, "I'll see you soon, Snoop, much sooner than you think. Love ya."

I go back in the room to get my pocketbook and Ian's standing there with this stupid look on his face. "Look, Ash, I didn't know that's why you laid back down."

"Forget about it, Ian. I understand perfectly. You don't want me like you used to. It's quite obvious that there's someone else that you're sleeping with because you sure ain't sleeping with me. I just wish you'd tell me so I can or better yet *you* can, start making other arrangements."

"Girl, you're crazy. This is us here," he says pointing to the floor and meaning the apartment. "We are not going nowhere. We'll talk later. I promise."

"Promises promises," I say to myself as I turn and leave for work.

***

When I get to work I ask Kara to come into my office.

"Kara, I'll be leaving around eleven o'clock and I'm not

78

sure if I'll be back today."

"Are you okay, Ashlei?"

"I'm fine; just need some time. Nothing major is going on today. There's a lot of paperwork that needs to be caught up. Here's my cell phone number in case something comes up that can't wait until tomorrow."

"I'll be fine, Ashlei. Please let me know if there's anything you need."

"Thanks, Kara. I will."

***

Even though I've imagined myself doing this, I can't believe I'm actually going through with it. When I was younger I always used to play detective to find out what naughty things my boyfriends were doing behind my back. It's unfortunate that as a grown woman, I'm back at it again. I'm heading down the street towards my home, the home I share with a man I thought would one day be my husband and I'm anticipating catching him with some woman. The thought that he may be bringing someone into our home and into our bed disgusts me. I don't care if I'm being childish and immature. I owe it to myself to check this out no matter what may be running through my mind. If something's going on, I need to know about it today. If there's not, no harm will be done. And if I'm wrong, I'll go to the store, buy groceries and fix Ian a nice dinner tonight. I don't have to tell him what is currently racing through my mind, nor do I have to tell him that I took the rest of the day off to cold bloodily bust him.

***

As I get out of my car, I can hear the music blaring from inside the apartment. Approaching the door, with butterflies in my stomach, my quest begins. I don't know why I'm so nervous, but I'll soon find out. From the door to my bedroom seems longer than ever. Son of a bitch! My first suspicion was correct. I knew it! Instead of that bitch cleaning under the bed and making sure her earrings weren't left behind, she's doing maintenance on my man and making sure he doesn't have any energy left behind for me. I knew I wasn't wrong. I knew it!

The butterflies have quickly dissipated and now the rage rushes in. My body is shaking and I feel like I can't breathe, almost like my lungs are being squeezed. I can't stay here right now. I need to get out of here before something happens. I think I'm okay; no, I'm not sure. I'm not sure of anything right now. I need to grab my dog and get away from here before something happens that I'll regret for the rest of my life.

"Ashlei!" He has the nerve to run behind me screaming my name.

"Get the hell away from me, Ian. Don't call my name, don't say a word to me and you damn sure better not touch me. Just get your shit and be gone by the time I get back. Make sure you take all your shit too or you won't get it back – ever!"

I jump in my truck with Snoop and pull off with him still pleading behind me. There's nothing left to say.

"Ashlei, wait! Let me explain!" He's still screaming as I pull out of the garage.

I think to myself, explanation? What's that? For what? Who needs it? I just need to get away from here and hopefully when I come back . . .no, not hopefully; when I come back he better be gone.

He gives up trying to catch up with my truck. I can still see him through my rear-view mirror, standing in the middle of the garage in his jeans, no shirt and no shoes. Someone so fine now looks so disgusting to me. I should put this truck in reverse and run him over. But it's not even worth getting myself into that kind of trouble, especially for his sorry ass.

Thoughts of all the time we spent together, all the things he said, all the things he promised keep running through my mind. Everything was a lie. What was the purpose? Why me? What part did I play in his little fairy tale? I need to know. I never want to speak to him again, but I really need to know. I can't go through this not knowing why. I can't put myself through this without him suffering. I won't let him continue his little whatever-he-wants-to-call-it without being bothered with me. I bet that shit turned him on, probably made him feel powerful. He probably patted himself on the back everyday, thinking, "Yeah, I'm the man."

"Oh, I hate him!" I scream. I can't let this make me crazy. I have too many positives going on in my life. I have two great friends who will be right there if I need them. I've got a great job. I've started my own business and through the contacts I've made I've built a strong foundation for myself. I've been saving a lot of money to build a cushion for my future and most of all...I'm young. I have plenty of time to find a new man, a good man, and until then, I'll have a little fun. Right now, I just need to get away from everything. I need to give myself some time to cool off and get my thoughts straight because I don't like the anger I'm feeling. I can't deny the pain he caused, but I'll be okay.

All this drama . . . Is it really worth it?

7

Snoopy and I ride around for hours, listening to music. He's sitting in the passenger seat, periodically putting his head out the window. I think it's so funny how dogs like to hang their head out the car window. I used to play like that as a kid and have done it as an adult as well. On nights when my girls and me are out and we're acting crazy, I'll imitate Jim Carey in one of our favorite comedies, "Pet Detective." We always get a good laugh when I do that.

Every now and then, when I bring the truck to a stop, Snoop looks over at me. He looks like he wants to ask me, "Why are you crying, Mommy?" I reach over and pet him. Although he's a product of this horrible relationship, I really love my Snoop and I'm glad I have him. Over the past several months I've found out that a dog can be a great companion. All those nights when Ian wasn't there, Snoopy would curl up beside me and we would sleep for hours. I knew that no matter what, he would be there with me – unlike that disgrace of a man. Without saying a word, Snoopy comforts me. He's like a child, and at the rate I'm going, he may be my only one.

I'm not going back home and take the chance of him being there, waiting for me. After stopping at about five hotels, I stop at the Holiday Inn in Bensalem and finally I've found one that will allow pets. Not a minute too soon either…I'm getting tired. Snoop and I check into our room and I immediately give him some water. I can tell he's real thirsty because his tongue is hanging out and he's breathing hard.

I lie down across the bed and cry myself to sleep. I wake feeling hungry – and no wonder. It's seven o'clock and I haven't eaten today. I order a pizza and some wine from room service, and then hop in the shower.

I keep thinking about what I just saw. I've been hurt

before by men I've dated but I truly thought I was doing things differently this time; paying more attention to things going on around me; asking more questions about what he was doing and where he was going. Everything was fine until he started taking those trips without me. "It's okay. It's business," he'd say. I didn't think it would be right to put conditions and rules on a person's livelihood. I didn't want that done to me so I didn't do it to him. "Is this my fault?" I ask myself as I cry.

Turning the water off, I get out of the shower thinking how my perception of a good relationship includes one with a strong presence of trust. Obviously, my recipe is incorrect. I trusted him, but in this case I shouldn't have. I got sucked into the idea of that dream of mine. It was fun at times but it wasn't worth all this.

I take the gym bag that I'd put it in my trunk when I left home earlier today and change into my sweats. I can't bear to put back on the clothes I wore earlier. Everything about those minutes in that room, watching him, just being near that man, makes me feel so dirty.

The feeling comes back over me and makes me weak. "Oh God, I can't believe this. Please help me get through this," I pray. Amber always tells me that when she can't handle something that's going on in her life, she prays on it. She says she turns it over to God and he will lead her in the right direction. "God, I know I haven't talked to you much in my life and I'm sorry, but Amber says that you'll forgive me. Please forgive me and please help me get through this. This has to be the worst thing I've ever had to deal with. Thank you, God. Amen."

A knock comes at the door. "It has to be my pizza, Snoop, because no one knows we're here." I know Snoopy understands what I'm saying to him. At least he always looks at me like he does!

I open the door, turn and walk away, flopping back on

the bed. "Bill my room please."

"How are you tonight?"

I don't look up to acknowledge the delivery person, because I don't feel like exerting any more energy on anyone. Irritated, I finally look up at him and ask, "Why are you still here?" I've never seen a delivery person in a shirt and tie.

"I'm sorry. Actually, I was checking out your dog. He's cute."

"Thanks."

"Can I ask you a question?"

"What is it?" Why can't he just deliver my food and leave?

"Why does someone as nice looking as you come off so mean?"

Oh, now he's giving me a reason to tell him off. I continue giving him the evil eye and prepare myself to tell this well dressed, delivery boy what to do with his question. But this time when I look at him, I notice that he's very handsome. He appears a little younger than me but I may be wrong. He's very clean cut and has nice hands. Nevertheless, he still overstepped a stranger's boundaries by asking me something personal. The last thing I want is for someone to be personal with me.

"Look, whatever your name is..."

"Kevin."

"Whatever..."

"Wait. Before you snap on me, like I can tell you're about to do, answer this question, what foolish man would let someone who looks like you, with the cutest dog, be away from him for the night?"

Okay, that's it! He has definitely gone too far. "How do you know I have a man? What, are you some kind of psychic or something?"

"I could tell when I saw you come in that this wasn't a

84

planned stay."

"What? How'd you see me come in? Were you watching me?" I can't believe this dude was watching me and I didn't even notice him. I didn't see anyone outside when we were coming in.

"No! I was on break and went outside for some fresh. Tonight's been slightly hectic. I'm the night supervisor and several people called out, so we're all trying to pick up the slack for others. That's the only reason I'm bringing your pizza. Plus, I was standing there when the call came in and since it was coming to you, I saw that as an opportunity to meet you personally."

That explains the shirt and tie. "Oh, I see. Humph. A little young, but obviously independent, responsible, nice looking, big hands, nice voice, strong chest showing through his with arms that look like the ones that give you those "don't let me go" hugs. His pants fit nice – loose but not falling off. Whew!! This young man looks GOOD! I can't believe I'm thinking like this after…

No. I refuse to dwell on that every second. A little diversion might be just what I the good doctor ordered. "What did you say your name is?"

"Kevin, Kevin Sanders."

"Kevin. What are you doing?" Yeah I'm being bold, and so what.

"No, really. Why do you ask?"

"I thought maybe you could come back when you get off. I could use some company, and since you have the gift of gab, you might as well come and keep me company."

"No problem. I get done around midnight. Will you still be up?"

"Probably."

"Are you sure?"

"I invited you, didn't I?"

"All right. I'm sorry; I don't remember your name."

"That's because I never told you!" I snicker, knowing he checked that out before he came here. "I'm Ashlei."

"Ashlei, nice name. Sure, I'll come back to keep you company, on one condition . . ."

Here he goes. He ruined it already. Who does he think he is asking something of me? He doesn't even know me. "What?"

"Dag! Don't bite my head off. I only want to suggest that you lie down, cuddle up with that nice puppy and take a nap. Try to rid your mind of whatever's in there causing you to be so defensive."

Boy did he fool me. I'm ready to take his head off and he's actually looking out for me. That's a welcome change.

"Oh. Okay. I'll do that, just for you." This time I speak with a sexy smile. This man is FINE!

Not long after Kevin leaves, I finish devouring my pizza and Snoopy helps with the crust. I feel myself drifting off, and instead of thinking about the awful thing I just witnessed, I find myself thinking about Kevin. Maybe I shouldn't have invited him here, but why not? I've been hurt bad and I think I'm entitled to a little spontaneity. He really may be just what the doctor ordered. He's already somewhat taken my mind off the situation. Imagine what will happen when we spend some time together. We may turn out to be good friends...or maybe just lovers.

1
2

Back at home; I try to get my place in order. The ringing of the phone interrupts me. "Hello?" I answer on the first ring even though I'm thinking that I should have let the machine pick up because I really don't want to talk to that loser. After two nights at the hotel, I figure enough time has passed for Ian to pack and get out of town with his damn group. Hopefully he won't bother me when he gets back. Even though I want to know why he did this to me, I don't want to see his face. He knows he was wrong and there's nothing for us to talk about.

"Ashlei! Where have you been?"

"Oh, hey Desz."

"Oh, hey Desz? That's all you have to say? Where have you been? We've been calling you non-stop since Tuesday and Ian has been calling here. He came by here talkin' about he didn't believe me when I said I haven't seen or heard from you. He thought you were hiding out over here. What's going on with you two?"

"Girl, I was with this great guy."

"What do you mean you were with some guy? Who is he? Where'd you meet him? I never heard you say anything about seeing someone else. When did you start cheating on Ian?"

"Desz, calm down. I don't have to tell you everything."

"But you do, whether you have to or not, and I'm really not believing you right now. He told me you had Snoopy with you and I don't think you'd take Snoop on a hot date with someone you're seeing on the side. What's going on Ash, for real?"

"Damn, Desz, calm down. I broke up with Ian. I told him to get out. I was too embarrassed to even tell you and

Amber after the way I'd bragged about him. I needed to handle things on my own first, and I swear I was going to call you today."

"So what happened? I know you've been feeling a little less than happy about him lately, but what brought this on so suddenly? When we talked the other night, you didn't say anything about putting him out. Oh shit, Ash! You said you were going to sneak home to see if you could catch him with your cleaning lady. Did you? Was he with, what's her name, Maria?"

"Desz, this is a nightmare. I don't want to talk about it over the phone. Let's meet up for dinner. Can you call Amber to see if she can come too?"

"All right. How about the Olive Garden on City Line Avenue? Do you feel like that tonight?"

"I don't care what kind of food we have, as long as we have drinks!"

"I'll see you around seven o'clock. I'll call Amber now and make sure she can be there."

"And Desz . . ."

"Yeah, Ash, what's up?"

"I really was with a great guy. I'll fill you in on all the details over dinner."

***

It took me a few to go into the bedroom but I wanted to make sure Ian took everything. Unfortunately, his packing only included his duffle bag and what he could fit in it. He hardly took anything, probably thinking that it would give him an excuse to come back here and see me again. I have a few hours before meeting Desz and Amber, so I'm packing his shit and taking it to the security booth on my way out. I'll leave it with them and remove his name from my list. I see that his things are still in the studio, so he'll have to make arrangements to get them. I'm so glad that we put everything in my name when we moved here.

I hate to admit it, but it's painful packing his things, well, actually, bagging his things. I'm putting all his clothes in big, green trash bags along with the sheets that were on the bed the other day, the towels that were in the bathroom and the used condoms I found on the floor. It's disgusting to put them in the bag, but I have to. It's the only way I think I can get closure from what happened that day. Besides, I want to give him a memento!

This is harder than I thought. I plop on the bed and break down. The sound of me sobbing makes Snoop cuddle up beside me. I hug him tight and tell him that we'll be all right. I don't know how I let it come to this. Why didn't I see it? How could I have been so wrapped up that I couldn't pick up on the signs? Were there any? I'm still am not sure, but what I do know is that I want him to feel bad, really bad, about what he did. In anger, I throw the bag on the floor and finish kicking the other three condoms in there with his clothes. What the hell are these beads? I've heard something about people using beads. I'll ask Desz; she'll know.

The phone rings. After four rings I listen to my voice, and after the beep, I hear a male voice. "Ashlei. I just want to check on you before I go to work . . ."

It's Kevin. I forgot I gave him this number. I hurry and grab the phone before he hangs up. "Kevin?"

"Hey, I wasn't sure if you'd be there. I thought I'd check on you, to see how you're feeling."

"I'm fine. Thanks for being concerned."

"Ashlei?"

"Yeah."

"You're such a nice person. I don't know why someone would do something so horrible to you. I just needed to tell you that."

"Thanks Kevin, that means a lot to me. I'll talk to you soon."

"You promise?"

"You got it."

"By the way Ashlei, if your ex comes back and gives you a hard time, remember I'm only a phone call away."

"Thanks, Kevin, I'll keep that in mind."

"Bye," he says in a low, sexy voice.

"Bye-bye."

I stand here for a moment, thinking about how Kevin's so nice to me. He stayed with me for two nights and we were complete strangers and now he's calling to check on me. At first I thought he was being nice to me and staying with me just so he could get some poonani, but I was wrong. Well, he did end up getting some, but only because he made it easy for me to force the issue, but not before he let me pour all my problems on him.

I load the bags in the truck and take them to the gate. The security guard has no problem keeping them there and removing Ian's name from the list. I request, "Can you see that my locks are changed immediately?"

"No problem, Ms. Ashlei. It'll be done tomorrow and we'll hold the key here for you."

"Thank you." That makes me feel a little better. I don't know how I'd handle seeing him again, especially if I were to come home and find him in the living room or bedroom like nothing ever happened. I know eventually I'll have to talk to him, but I can't do it yet.

***

I pull up to the restaurant knowing Desz is going crazy waiting for me. She hates being left hanging.

"Hi, can I help you?" The hostess has one of those bubbly, 'you're so phony' kind of voices.

"Hi. I'm meeting friends here. They've probably already arrived."

"Oh yes, they're here and they seem very anxious for you to join them."

"It's only been a week since we last saw each other. You know how it is when you're in love!" I say laughing. She looks at me like I'm crazy and she doesn't know whether or not to take me seriously so she giggles, turns and with frowning eyebrows, shows me to our table. I cover my mouth and laugh. I have to do something to humor myself.

"All right, girl," Desz practically screams. "Sit down and let's have it!"

"Don't start, Desz. Can't we order our food first before we get into this?"

"Let's get that waitress over here then. I had a hard enough time waiting for you to get here. I literally wanted to stand in the street and clear a path for you through the traffic!"

"Shut up, Desz. You just don't know what to say," Amber finally manages to get a word in.

"Hey, Amber. I was hoping you'd be able to make it."

"Now, Ashlei, you know if you need me, I'm here. I'm just mad that you didn't call me, but I'll handle that at another time."

The waitress is taking her time, so of course impatient Desz goes to find her. She returns with some girl who must be our waitress. We end up ordering the same thing we always order when we come here: Desz gets chicken marsala, Amber gets vegetable lasagna and I have chicken parmesan. My appetite has been off and on and they're so nosy that they'd rather drink and talk than eat anyway.

Desz starts, "Okay, now down to business. So Ash, what happened? I can't believe you didn't call us. Something was so bad that you left home and you didn't even call your girls? It must've been real deep."

"Girl, deep is not the word. I was lost for words. I needed to be by myself for a while to clear my head. I know I was wrong, and seeing now how it upset the two of you, I'm truly sorry."

"It's cool, Ash. We understand. Next time at least leave us a message or something so we know you're okay. Tell us what happened," Amber says readjusting the tone of the conversation.

"Remember the situation with Maria the maid and how I was planning to leave work early to go home to see if he was there with her? Well, I did."

"Oh shit! You caught 'em didn't you?" Desz interrupts.

"No . . .yes . . .well, I don't know."

"What do you mean you don't know?"

"Desz, if you'd hush I could get my story out."

"Hurry up then. I'm about to make one up and tell it for you!"

I explain how I felt when I was going home; how I had second thoughts about the whole thing until I pulled in the garage saw his car. I broke it down step by step about the loud music, Snoop being in his cage, not hearing anyone, until I decided my hunch was wrong and I'd go back to the office . . .but I didn't.

"Why not? Did he see you?" Amber asks, now beginning to sound impatient too.

"As I was going back down the hall to leave, I heard some type of movement. I still didn't hear any voices, so I thought he was in there jerkin' off. I was pissed because he would always act like he was too damn tired to do anything with me and that would've meant he'd been taking care of himself."

"What? You weren't getting any and you didn't cheat on that fool?"

"Desz!" Amber scolds.

I continue, "I turned around and headed towards the room with the intent to cuss him out. When I reached the door I couldn't believe what I saw."

I pause to get myself together because I'm determined not to cry. I think they must be able to see how shook up I am because neither of them press me to go on this time. After a minute or so Desz asks, "Was he with Maria? In your bed? Did you kick her ass?"

Amber, the voice of reason interjects, "Calm down, Desz. Let Ashlei finish telling us."

"I stood at the door and watched for what seemed like forever. They didn't even know I was there. I couldn't move or speak. I was frozen and I couldn't believe what I was seeing." I pause again, and look at them hoping I can hold back the tears. "He was with another woman. I don't know if it was Maria or not. I didn't take the time to ask for ID."

"Damn, Ash!" Amber blurts out.

"I was still standing there, staring and that's when I noticed she was wearing the earring – like the one I'd found on the floor, the one he claimed was the cleaning lady's. This woman lying on my bed was wearing . . .the earring. She looked to be medium height with dark brown skin and twists in her hair. Besides the earrings, she didn't have on any jewelry that I could see – and I could see everything, and I mean everything, except the left side of her nude body. No, I'm wrong. She did have one small ring on the pinky of her right hand. I only noticed this because of the way she was holding her hand, guiding my man's very erect sex into her mouth."

"Oh Ash, I'm so sorry. I know you were losing it."

"You're right, Amber, but that's not all."

"What else?" Desz asks with anger in her voice.

"She was laying on her back under Ian. He was raised above her on his hands and knees with his masculine parts well engaged with her lips and tongue. She had her other hand

93

between her legs giving herself enjoyment while he was getting his. While I watched, I gasped for air and could feel the tears filling my eyes. I couldn't help it. I couldn't stop this feeling. I never imagined anything like this. How do you deal with walking in on your man and another woman? Your man, another woman and another man."

Desiree and Amber's eyes almost pop out of their heads. Just then the waitress comes with our food. As soon as she steps away they exclaim, practically in unison, "You're lying!"

Amber asks, "Wait a minute, Ash, did you just say another man?"

"Yeah, another man. Standing behind Ian was this, I'm sad to say, gorgeous dark chocolate, bald-headed man with a huge hairless chest. He looked kind of familiar, but my head wasn't clear enough to figure out where I'd seen him before. He had his eyes closed, head tilted slightly back, holding my man's hips and giving it to him. Ian was loving it. I could see it on his face. He was in the best of both worlds. His eyes were closed but he kept biting on his lip in an aw-shit-this-feels-good kind of way. And you're not going to believe this one. The dude was wearing the bracelet that I found in the bathtub, so it was quite obvious that this wasn't their first rendezvous. I couldn't take it anymore; I couldn't continue watching until they got their shit off. I finally felt like I could move and I just wanted to run out of there. I wanted to get as far away from there as I could but then something said to me, 'Yo! Why should I leave? This is my place! He's the nasty-ass cheater! He can leave.' So I turned back around and screamed at the top of my lungs for them to get the hell out. I told them to get the fuck up off of my bed and get the hell out! The three of them jumped. I guess whoever she was forgot to open her mouth when they jumped because Ian grimaced, grabbed himself and let out a painful screech. I almost laughed, thinking . . . good for your ass, or should I say your dick! He had the audacity to

94

try to talk to me like he wanted to explain something. Explain what? That picture needed no explanation."

"Meanwhile, the bitch was trying to grab her clothes and get them on. She acted like she was scared to death. But I had no intentions of trippin' on her. I walked in on my man in our own bedroom, in the middle of a ménage à trois. Dude was taking his time getting dressed. He got left hanging, and hanging large I might add. I bet he was making some woman very happy at night while he was keeping Ian busy during the day! Can you believe it? My ex is bisexual and I didn't even know it. But don't get me wrong; I don't have anything against gay or bisexual people. I'm just not down with it. I feel that an individual should be given a choice whether or not they want to be with a partner who has bisexual tendencies. I wasn't given that choice."

"Then what did you do, Ash?" Amber asks, with tears in her eyes.

"I grabbed Snoopy, his food and I got out of there. Ian came running after me, but I wasn't hearing anything he had to say."

"Damn, Ash, I'm sorry that happened to you like that. The ménage à trois isn't the bad thing – the bad thing is that he didn't let you know about his sexuality."

My eyes are bulging in shock. "What are you saying, Desz? Are you saying that you've been in a bisexual situation before?"

"Well, Desz?" Amber asks.

"Look. All I'm saying is don't completely put something down because you've never tried it. What's good for some may not be good for others, but that's a part of life. Ian should've let you know that bisexuality is a part of his life, but a threesome isn't as horrible as what you're thinking."

"Damn, Desz! Is there anything you haven't done? You know what, don't answer that."

Amber changes the subject. "Where is he now? I mean he wasn't there when you got home was he? Have you talked to him yet?"

"He had to go away on a planned business trip. I stayed away until I knew he was gone. I haven't talked to him, but he left me a few messages. When I got to the house I noticed that he only took a few things with him. Before I came here I packed the rest of his things, left them at the security booth and took his name off my visitors list."

"Will the guards let him in anyway, since they're used to seeing him?"

"They're not supposed to. They'll get in trouble if they let somebody through the gate who isn't on the list, and I don't think any of them are willing to lose their jobs for Ian. Anyway, I put in a request to have the locks changed, just in case."

Amber reaches over and puts her hand on top of mine. "How are you feeling?"

"I'm trying to handle it, you know? I met a nice guy at the hotel where Snoop and I stayed. That's another reason I didn't rush to come home. I was only going to stay for the one night, but I was really enjoying Kevin's company and the attention. If you remember, I hadn't been getting the proper attention from Ian for quite some time. You two will meet him soon, I'm sure."

"Dag, girl, you sure don't waste any time!" Amber seems completely confused. All this is moving way too fast for her.

"Please, as deprived as I've been, I need a distraction. Don't get me wrong, it's tearing me up inside, but when you have a shoulder to lean on it helps to ease the pain."

"Now Ash, you know it's not right to use that man. He'll get all hooked up on you, when all you're doing is trying to get past what you're going through." Amber is forever trying to be like a mother and tries to shine the proper light on every situation.

"It's not like that. Well, maybe! But either way, I enjoyed his company and I'll just have to make sure he understands that we're just friends because he's definitely not the type I'd settle down with."

"Yeah, well, I hope that works for you because you know how it is when you don't want them . . .they always want you," Desz adds. "But you know what I say girl . . .go for what you know!"

Desz makes a valuable point. That does seem to be the way it goes for us. Neither of us have had much success in holding on to anybody for any length of time. I think my relationship with Ian was the longest out of any of the relationships any of us have had. We always seem to get wrapped up into some man and the next thing we know, he's gone. I don't want a relationship with Kevin, only a friendship.

The waitress comes over to take our plates. We order another round of drinks and keep talking. Even though we don't always have a chance to get together, when one of us is down, we're always here for each other.

"Well, Ash, you know if you need someone to talk to, I'm here for you. I know it'll take a while to get over this, but I think you're on the right track. You sound better than I would be; I would've been trying to fight all three of them." Desz's tone is that of someone who's ready to fight this very second.

"Thanks, girl. I'll remember that when I can't sleep at three in the morning."

"Yeah, okay. You know what? Just think about it this way . . .you got your truck out of this rotten deal and my cute little buddy, Snoopy."

We sit there chatting for no less than three hours, through several rounds of drinks. When we finally decide it's time to go, Desz and Amber say almost simultaneously that they're there for me if I need them. Just then I remember the beads that I kicked into the bag.

I lean over to Desz and whisper, "When we get outside I need to ask you something."

"What?"

"Just wait until she brings our change back and we get outside."

We talk for a couple more minutes and promise that we'll get together and do this again soon.

We pay our check and walk outside. "Ash, what do you need to ask me?"

"Oh! When I was packing his crap, along with the rubbers I also found some beads. I remember in one of our descriptive conversations some time ago, you told me about beads that people use when having sex. What are they all about?"

"Well? Since they were doing some erotic shit anyway, it truly doesn't surprise me. When I tell you the name of them, you'll completely understand. They're anal beads!"

"Say no more. How disgusting! Oh yeah, hell yeah, he needed to have the two of them to have sex with because I'm not about to use anything like that!"

"I told you before…don't knock it."

"Desz! Damn! Is there anything you haven't done? We gotta love you, girl!" We hug and head for our cars.

"Ashlei, don't forget, if you need to talk, call me no matter what time it is," Amber reminds me.

"Thanks, Amber. Love you guys!"

"Love you back," they say.

I start my truck and begin pulling out of the lot. My cell phone rings. "Hello?"

"Ash?" Amber says in a strange tone.

"Girl, didn't I just hug you? What? You need more?" I laugh.

"No, seriously Ash. What will you do when Ian shows up and the guards don't let him in?"

"Honestly, Amber, I don't know, but I can't worry about that. That's the price he has to pay for doing what he did. I can't just forgive him and let him back in. I'm sure he can stay with someone or rent a hotel room until he can get an apartment. I'll say it again – I cannot worry about that. I have to do what I have to do to get this nightmare over with."

"Do you think he'll get hostile?"

"I doubt it. His career is starting to jump, so I doubt if he wants to end up in all the newspapers for domestic violence and let his little secret lifestyle get out. He knows he did me wrong and I truly don't think he's going to make a big fuss."

"All right, but if he does, you call me and maybe you should call your new friend. What's his name again, Kevin?"

"Yeah. I'll tell him what you said. It'll be fine Amber, trust me. I'll keep you posted."

"Make sure you do."

"Oh, Amber! Before you hang up…"

"What's up?"

"I forgot to tell you and Desz about the office I found. I love it and I can move in as soon as I want. I left a deposit today."

"Ash, I'm so happy for you. You're finally doin' it, girl! I knew you would."

"All right, I'll talk to you later."

"See ya, and congrats!"

1
3

As I expected, things have been quiet. It's been weeks and Ian hasn't bothered me, hasn't even bothered coming over here for the rest of his things. I did hear from some mutual acquaintances of ours that he had asked how I was doing, but that's the only communication that's occurred. That is, until Tuesday, when Ian tried to get in the apartment while I was at work. He was pissed when he discovered he couldn't get past the guards, so he left me a note. Now I'm listening to a message on my answering machine, from him, cussing me out because of some equipment that's still here in the apartment and he needs it. I was surprised when he left and didn't clean out the studio, but that's his problem. He should've thought about that before he decided to try to have the best of both worlds in our bedroom.

After receiving his nasty remarks on the machine, I call Jodi, his assistant. Reaching only a machine I leave this message:

"Hello, this is Ashlei. Ian's equipment can be picked up but only when security is available to accompany him. I've already spoken to Mr. Garvin to arrange this, so Ian should call him to set up a time. Mr. Garvin understands that I will not be there and nothing else is to be removed except the things in the studio. If there's any problem, you can call me, but I'd prefer Mr. Klarke not ring my phone. I appreciate you helping me with this."

I hang up and take Snoop for a stroll. The fresh air does both of us some good. When we get back, I hear the phone ringing, but I can't get there in time. I wait a few minutes and check the messages.

"Hi, Ashlei. It's Jodi. Just want to let you know that I'll take care of everything and there won't be any problem. Take

care."

Good! That'll be taken care of and without the hassle of dealing with Ian.

I'm getting used to being here without him, and actually Snoop and I are getting along just fine. At first I was worried because the rent on this place is a little high, but my income has become very consistent. Money is coming in steadily and it's enough to cover my expenses, plus I still have a little stash from when Ian was pushing money at me all the time to make up for his ass not being around. My momma didn't raise no fool! I always make sure I have something for a rainy day. I have to get back out there so I can hook up with somebody else who can help keep me connected to the industry people. The most important thing now is to keep my foot in the door and not let things drop off.

The phone rings. Who could be calling here? "Hello?"

"Miss Ashlei?"

"Yes?"

"It's the front desk. There's a Davon Matthews here to see Ian."

"Davon?"

"Yes. He says he and Ian have an appointment."

"Who? Oh, Davon. Okay. I guess Ian didn't contact him to tell him that he isn't living here anymore. You can send him back. Thank you."

Now why didn't he tell this man that he wasn't going to be here for this appointment? His admin really slipped up on this one. I'll let him know and give him the number to reach Jodi. I hope this dude doesn't try to get nasty because he came here for no reason at all. And I thought I was going to have a peaceful Friday night.

A knock comes at the inside door before I can throw my sweat pants back on. Hopefully it won't offend him when I answer wearing this spaghetti strap tank top and "booty" shorts.

Oh well, its not like he's here to meet with me.

As I open the door I begin talking, "Davon, I am so…"

Damn! Now who's shocked? I can't believe who's standing in front of me, in *my* apartment door. I can't even finish my sentence, nor can I close my mouth.

"Ashlei?"

"Dee?" It sure the hell is, looking better than he did at the club. He's more casual tonight, wearing Guess jeans and a polo-style shirt.

"Whoa! Did I knock on the wrong door? Or," he says with a sly smile, "did I knock on the right door but at the wrong time?"

"Neither. Damn! Excuse me but you've really caught me off guard. Come on in."

"So you're the Davon that's been calling Ian?"

"In the flesh."

"He told me about you, and I met Mike from the group you're helping."

"Mike? There's no Mike in any of the groups I'm working with."

"Wait a minute. First off, why did you tell me your name is Dee? Second, I met this guy named Mike and Ian said that the person who was supposed to be managing his group was named Davon. He even told me about a meeting that he was supposed to have had with you."

"I'm sorry, Ashlei but you must've been mistaken. I've been trying for weeks to hook up with this Ian cat. I ran into him a few times at the Black Lily and once in New York, but it's hard to corner someone for a business conversation in a club. Besides, he always seemed to have the same dude around him who I figured was his bodyguard or one of his moneymakers that he was promoting real hard. So, he told me it would be better to give him a call to set something up. I've heard he's a good contact, and like I told you, I recently moved

102

here. I was hoping Ian could help me out with a few R&B singers that need some rap tracks on their songs. Unfortunately, every time I've scheduled something with him, he's called and canceled. Except for this time. So you must be thinking of someone different because it wasn't me."

"It was you. I even answered the phone one time when you called and I took the message. He must have given you our home number," I insist, telling him the number.

"Yeah, that's the one I've been calling. I do remember that call. Damn, so Ian is the lucky man?"

"Lucky? I don't know if I'd call him that. And he's not my man. Things have changed since that night I met you at the club. Ian doesn't live here anymore, but I can give you his office number. Maybe you'll have more luck reaching him there."

"Thanks. So, now that I'm here and you're no longer involved do you want to grab something to eat? I haven't eaten and I'm starved," he says with a hypnotizing smile.

What's with these men and these smiles? Someone must have told all the men with beautiful smiles to find me because that's what works! Since I haven't eaten either, I can't say no. "I just got home from the gym so I'll need to jump in the shower. I'll make it quick."

"No problem. Oh, and Ashlei, my name is Davon but most people, once they get to know me, call me Dee."

"Then I prefer Davon if you don't mind," I say smiling.

He looks around like he's trying to find something to keep himself occupied with while I get dressed. "Do you mind if I put some music on?"

Please . . .I don't mind what he does. This man looks like he needs me to give him some *Ashlei work*! He looks like he could be my next man. He already has stature in the music world, so all I need to do is get up on him and become his woman.

"Of course I don't mind." Walking over to show him where all the CDs are, in case he wants some older ones, I see the intense stare he's throwing my way. He's licking his lips, the same way LL does. Damn.

I hit the power button and start the CD that's already in the changer. "There are more CDs down here in this case," I tell him as I bend over to open the cabinet. "These are the older ones and the newer ones are up top." When I stand back up and turn to look at him, I almost knock him down because he's standing practically on top of me. "I'm sorry. Didn't realize you were that close."

"No. I'm sorry. I shouldn't have come up on you like that but...woman you are beautiful. How could that man have let you go? For someone who's supposed to be so business savvy, he must not have used his smarts at home or he would have never left you."

"He didn't leave me. I put him out." My eyes lower and my voice sounds a little funny.

"I'm sorry. Did I hit a bad spot?"

Just as he asks that, the CD begins to play the "Waiting to Exhale" movie soundtrack. I reach up and advance it to track two, "Why Does It Hurt So Bad" by Whitney Houston, and start walking away. "It's cool. I'm going to shower."

As I pass him my boobs brush up against his arm. "Excuse me." He stretches his arm out and grips my side furthest away from him. Of course I stop and look up at him.

He begins to speak, "I'm really sorry. I just thought..."

"I know. That's what most people think, isn't it? Everybody always thinks the man left the woman. I don't know why people don't seem to think that the woman, who probably had enough of the man's shit, may have put his ass out. It's cool, though. It's a horrible double standard but that's society."

He turns me towards him and says, "Forgive me. I didn't mean to assume and I'm sorry if he hurt you. Go shower

104

and put something on so I can take you out for dinner and a few drinks. If you need to talk, I'm here. You know I wanted to get to know you better when I met you at the club and I didn't hide that, but I respected the fact that you were involved. Well now you're not, and although this situation is now in my favor, I won't take advantage of you, I promise."

Looking up into his eyes, those beautiful brown eyes, is a mistake. He winks at me. He's so sexy! We stare at each other and before I know it his lips are touching mine. At first I try to pull away but I give in. It feels too right. I don't know if this is fate and the two of us were supposed to meet again like this or if I just really don't like being alone. But here's this sexy man, making me feel like he really wants to get closer to me. Does he just want some? I should be asking myself that question! All I know right this minute is, he feels so good and I'm enjoying him. I'm gonna relax and go with the flow. Whatever happens, happens.

I finally relax and enjoy his kiss, his touch. I reach up and hold his neck as he slides his hands down my sides, to my hips, around my back, easing them downward. He stops at the bottom of my coccyx bone and I feel him pulling me closer to him. It's feeling too good for me to resist. This is so different, so natural. This man has some serious sex appeal. Our kisses are passionate but very gentle. He stops, kisses me lightly, slowly…then he leans back and looks at me with those pretty eyes and starts again but with his tongue. I can hear TLC singing "Take It Slow" in the background, but I'm trying not to comprehend.

I ease away. "Uh…I thought you said you're starving."

"I am, but…"

"Let me shower and get dressed so we can go eat."

"Okay."

I'm halfway up the stairs when I notice Davon is right behind me.

"What are you doing? Why are you following me? I thought you were listening to some music."

"I am."

When I reach the top of the stairs, I start laughing and running towards the bathroom. He catches me just as I reach the door. Facing each other, he backs me up against the wall and starts kissing me with incredible fervor. It's feeling too good for me to stop him, so again I give in. I slide my hands inside his T-shirt and start rubbing his back. His grinding on me has me horny as shit. I want him and obviously the feeling is mutual. Our sensual biting while he's lifting my tank top and I'm unfastening his belt leads me to believe that we've decided to have each other for dinner. Within seconds we're completely nude. Damn, I need to take my shower.

"Davon, wait. Let me get in the shower first."

"What?" he asks, soft but deep.

"I just got home from the gym. Let me shower."

He sighs. "Okay, but be quick."

I start the water and leave him standing in the door.

"Can I watch?"

Now that's some sexy shit! No one's ever asked me that before, but why not? I'm feeling daring tonight. "Sure, if that's what you want to do."

Before I step in the shower I walk over to him and give him a little peck and take another look into those eyes. I wash using my bath sponge and try not to look at him, but I can't resist taking a peek every now and then. His aroused nature is looking better by the second. He's leaning on the wall, just inside the door, looking at me with his head tilted back. He's taking his tongue, running it along the bottom of his top teeth and then biting his lip. No, don't do it. I knew it! He takes his hand and lightly rubs himself. He's staring right at me now, smiling. He takes his monster in his hand and strokes it, real slow, pointing it at me, rubbing out and in. Then when he knows he has my full attention, he gets faster. Damn, he looks good! Leaning back on the wall of the shower I start washing my breasts with the sudsy bath sponge. With my other hand, I follow the suds, down my stomach to my valley. Instead of using the sponge on my girl, I use my hand. We're staring at each other and the temperature is definitely rising. Both of us are breathing hard and staring at each other. This is the most intense foreplay I've ever experienced without touching. It's so erotic. My heart's thumping and all of a sudden, words come to mind and start flowing...

when i met you, you seemed to possess a mysterious side
squinting those eyes ever so slightly
light reflecting off them
casting a peculiar shine
is it that you wanted to know me
or was that all in my mind

as you spoke, i watched your lips and imagined the taste
the aggression while they caress my body
        I know will be pleasing
just waiting to steal a heart that wasn't meant to be stolen
but in life
        do we actually choose when these feelings come about
do we choose who they'll be directed towards
or do those feelings choose us
i didn't know before I walked in the room
that your presence would totally consume my thoughts
your persona houses much sex appeal
your words supported by extreme force
your eyes, yes those eyes
i wonder what you're receiving from me

my stare i know is intense

as i watch you do your thing
can you hear my heart thumping
tell me, what's on your mind
do your thoughts match mine
can you stand a little bump
then hopefully more than a grind
will your body ever touch mine
making us wish we could halt time
our lips, ooh when they meet
will they cause glaze to secrete
naked – umph, umph, umph
yeah us, in the tub
you make me scream when *you* rub
and now *my* sensuous spot
oh shit I'm too hot
I can't believe how you've made me feel

the words have ceased and the moment has ended
the passion – was it merely a façade?
eroticism never to be real?
damn, all I can say is . . .

what's on that mind, you brown-eyed man?

His motions stopped when he moved closer to hear my words. At the end of my thoughts, I refocus on him, now sitting on the side of the tub, staring at me in disbelief. "They were your words?"

"Yeah. You like it?"

"I'm gonna make you my star!"

I smile thinking how special he made me feel when he said that. No one has ever said anything like that to me. A star? Just what Mom always said I could be. I can't explain the connection between the two of us, but it's strong. I switch the shower to pulse and reach out for him with tears in my eyes. He steps in the tub and once again takes me in his arms. The intensity increases as the shower beats down on us, tears rolling down my face, him kissing me like he's never gonna stop, my body aching for him and his man waiting for me to get on him. I remember I started keeping condoms in the cabinet inside the shower. You never know when a condom will be needed as a bathing essential. I turn to grab one, but Davon doesn't stop. With him feeling my breast, rubbing his nature on my ass and kissing me on my shoulders and back, I find it very hard to get the cabinet open and get one out. I'm tingly all over and I feel weak. I turn back around and face him, trying to gain some control. I readjust the showerhead and partially raise the tub stopper. Gently, I back him up towards the rear of the tub. Now kissing him the way he was kissing me, I feel his chest going in and out, harder and faster; I hear his breathing picking up. I lower myself, kissing his chest and stomach on my way down. I take his man in my hands and put the condom on. Never breaking eye contact, I stand and motion for him to sit down. Before lowering myself on him, I stand very close to his face. Still looking at me, he begins to french my girl. I don't let that stop me from lowering myself on what I see standing beneath me.

"Ahh. This feels good," I moan.

"Yeah it does. Damn girl, you are beautiful."

I think he must have said this to me ten times tonight and he hasn't even been here for an hour. I knew I wanted this man from the moment I saw him at the club. As much as I didn't want to admit it that night, I knew then that something would happen if we were ever given the opportunity.

"Ahh," I breathe as he enters my territory. The water's splashing between us, his hands clinching and separating my cheeks, allowing me to feel every inch of his manhood inside of me. He has taken control of my body and the rhythm of our

109

bodies has surfaced sexual emotions that have been buried away because of neglect and lack of attention. My body is shivering and my thoughts are racing. "Don't stop," I scream. With every thrust, I feel him swelling . . .Oh no he's not! I didn't even get going good and he's done! It did feel damn good, but I'm only saying, if I'd known that was all I was getting I would have let him work the jaw longer.

Don't get an attitude, I think to myself. He was impressed with my poem and no one besides my mother has ever complimented me like he did. His time is short but his parts aren't and his foreplay is damn good. I'm holding on to him, no matter what. I'll just introduce him to my toys.

We shower together, get dressed and leave for dinner. Because of the time, we decide to go to South Street. We end up at Copabanana's.

After enjoying margaritas, while we waited for a table, our conversation becomes a little more intimate. "Davon, I have to admit, this is a little – no a lot different for me," I confess, breaking the ice.

"Is that a good or a bad thing?"

"Well, it feels good if that's what you want to know." I'm not lying; it is good and the chemistry is definitely there. Who knows, maybe the lack of stamina was from the intense foreplay. We'll lighten up next time.

"It's ironic…I came there for a business meeting, only to find out that the person I was supposed to be meeting just happened to be your man, who is now your ex and is no longer in the mix. I come in, we talk and then we end up in the bathtub having the most passionate sex I think I've ever had with a stranger. But it's all good. If I had the choice, I'd do it again."

"Oh really?" He grabs me and we hug. "Davon? What happens when you finally meet with Ian and you two start doing business together?"

"What do you mean?"

110

"I don't want to sound like I'm jumping the gun here, but I'd like to keep seeing you and how will you feel if you're working with him?"

"That'll have nothing to do with us. I plan to keep seeing you too. I didn't meet you through him and he's no longer in your picture, is he?"

"Except for business, no."

"Business? What do you mean?"

"I told you, I'm an Event Specialist. I also try to touch on a little PR upon request. I have several things pending on my books for him and we'll probably be doing more in the future. But business is business, so I have to deal with that. So far I've only talked to his assistant, and in all honesty, I don't ever want to talk to him again."

"That breakup must have been really bad for you to feel that strong about not seeing him."

"Yeah it was, but I don't want to talk about it. I'll just say that I was in love with someone I didn't know. For over a year I was with someone who wasn't even true to himself. If I had had some warning, I may not have taken it so hard, but out of nowhere, it smacked me."

"Damn. I'm sorry you had to go through that. You seem like too nice of a person to be put through a lot of bullshit."

"Thanks. So, if you and I do continue seeing each other, I'm sure at some point, the three of our paths will cross."

"Don't worry about it. If you two broke clean then it won't be a problem, honestly. Things like this happen all the time in this business. People break up and then you see someone else with your ex. You kind of get used to it. I've been so involved in my business that for the past couple of years, there hasn't been any room for a serious relationship."

"Oh. Is that a message to me?"

"No. If you noticed, I said for the past few years. I've

111

now gotten my career, my financial situation and myself to a point where I am very comfortable. Most of the groups I've handled have gotten very lucrative deals, so I've been able to expand my company and relax a little more. I think we've met at a good time. I'd like to spend some quality time with someone who is about something and gives me good sex! What more can I ask for?"

"Well that's good. I'm glad that working with Ian won't interfere with us because you really seem like a nice person and I do intend on getting to know you a lot better. Not to mention the sex."

After eating, Davon takes me back home. We enter through the garage so we don't have to walk as far. He's impressed with the security.

"Do you want to come in for a few?" I ask, not sure what will happen if he says yes.

"For a few, but I can't stay long."

"Do you have a busy day tomorrow?"

"Believe it or not, I don't have anything scheduled for this entire weekend. One of the groups went home because two of them are brothers and their mom's birthday is this weekend. So I gave the girls I'm working with a couple of days to rest. We've been really pushing it to the limit lately and I think we all deserve a weekend off."

"Well good. It's settled. I'll make some of my famous strawberry daiquiris!"

"That sounds good. I'm down."

"Oh, one condition."

"What's that?"

"You have to come with me to walk Snoopy!"

"No problem. I can use the walk after all the food I ate."

"Let me whip up the first batch so it can sit in the freezer while we're walking."

After walking Snoop, we have a few daiquiris. The combination of sex, the food, the walk and the alcohol lands us cuddling on the living room floor, while watching "Love Jones." I'm not sure what time we moved to my bedroom, but the next thing that's clear to me is the ringing of the phone and the morning sun. I grab for the phone reluctantly. "Hello."

"Hey, Ash."

"Kevin?"

"Yeah. What's up? You're still asleep, as late as it is?"

"What time is it?"

"Eleven o'clock. I thought you'd be up and ready for the gym by now."

"I'm sleeping in this morning."

"Do you want to grab some breakfast or something?"

"No, not this morning. I think I'm going to chill this week. I'll give you a call later, after I'm up and moving around."

"Who's that?" Davon asks barely awake.

Instead of answering, I lay my hand on his chest.

"Are you sure you're okay?" Kevin asks.

"Yeah Kevin, I'm fine. I'm just tired, that's all."

"Okay, call me later."

"I will."

I hang up and say as casually as I can, "That was Kevin, a good friend of mine. We try to do breakfast on Saturdays."

"Do you want me to leave so you can go? I don't want to mess up your plans."

"Davon, they're not plans. It's just something we do sometimes; it's not carved in stone. He's a good friend...he'll understand." Climbing up on him I say, "And anyway, I wish you would try to get up out of this bed!"

Rolling me over he says, "What you gonna do? You can't beat nobody!"

"Man, I'll sic my dog on you!"

113

Just then Snoopy comes over to the side of the bed whimpering because it's past time for him to go out. He knows that by now he's usually been outside and he's ready to go. "I have to take him for a quick walk."

"You want me to come with you?" Davon offers.

"Sure if you want to. But on one condition."

"What's that?"

I demand, "You resume the position when we get back."

"No problem." Davon gets up, throws on his jeans while I throw on some sweats.

Today's walk takes a little longer than normal. Davon tells me he really likes animals and wishes he could have a pet. He asks for his leash and they pick up a little jog. When I start jogging to catch up, Davon starts running. Snoopy looks so cute with his ears flying back. I'm laughing so hard I can't even run. When I finally manage to catch them we're all out of breath. Davon grabs me and lays a nice, long kiss on me.

"Now how you gonna jog back with that?" I point to the big bulge in his jeans.

Laughing he says, "Hold up. Let me run in here for a minute." Davon runs into The Coffee Room Café II, a little coffee shop on the corner of Spring Garden and Delaware Avenue; it's the sister shop to the one on South Street. He gets two hot chocolates for us and bottled water with a cup for Snoopy.

Walking, talking and drinking hot chocolate with him seems so normal. I can't believe how fast things have happened between us. I guess it's meant to be.

When we get home, we run in the door and collapse in the middle of the living room floor. After a brief rest, Snoopy falls asleep while Davon and I resume the position!

14

"I'm sorry, Ashlei. I didn't know you were on the phone," Kara says as she barges into my office.

"It's okay. I was just hanging up with Mr. Garvin. Ian picked up the rest of his things today. I knew everything would go smooth as long as he and I weren't there together."

"That's good. I'm glad that part is over for you. Here, you had a delivery while you were on the phone," she says with a sneaky grin as she hands me a bouquet of flowers with a stuffed dog.

"Who in the world could these be from?" The person who comes to mind first is Davon, but I don't remember telling him where I work during the day.

"Things should've been different," the card reads.

"I know that stupid-ass Ian is not sending me flowers and a stuffed animal. Throw these things away. I don't want anything from him."

Not even two minutes later the phone buzzes and catches me off guard. "Yes, Kara?"

"Kevin's on the phone for you."

"Thank you."

"Hey Kevin, what's up?"

"Just calling to say hello since you never called me back the other day."

"I'm sorry, I was a little preoccupied." I hear him making some kind of noise. "How are things with you?"

"Good. Do you want to grab something to eat after work?"

"I'll have to let you know. I'm not sure what time I'll be done working. I may have to meet with a client when I leave here."

"Well, let me know."

"I'll do that. Wait, Kevin. Did you send me something?"

"No. Why?"

"I just received flowers and a stuffed animal but there is no signature on the card and I just thought...never mind. I'll talk to you later."

Okay, it wasn't Kevin and I know it wasn't Davon, so it must be Ian who sent them. Well, I'm not responding anyway, so he shouldn't have wasted his time.

My day is very busy – but Mondays usually are. I have a corporate dinner scheduled for tomorrow night and last minute preparations for that have taken up most of my day. Some of the contacts I made while working for Winer's ask me to plan things for them. I also have an after-work meeting with the Tyson Sisters about coordinating a launch party at Club UnderGround.

I think I'll give Davon a call when I get home. Hearing his voice would be therapeutic.

When I finally arrive home I find my little partner anxiously waiting. We go for a quick walk and head back home. On our way back in the door, I realize that I never checked my messages.

"Ashlei, it's Davon. I wanted to call your cell phone but I knew you had a meeting. I'll try to call you back later but tonight's gonna be hectic. I know you have that big party tomorrow, so if I don't talk to you, good luck . . . like you really need it. Later, beautiful."

Oh, that man sounds so good! I hope I'm not wasting my time with him. I wish I could've talked to him.

Oh well, I guess I'll call Kevin and see if he wants to meet somewhere for a quick bite to eat. I get his machine. *"Hey Kevin, it's me Ashlei. Call me when you get a chance. I thought we could meet somewhere to grab something to eat. Talk to you later."*

116

Not even ten minutes later my phone rings. "Hello."

"Ashlei, its Kev. Where'd you want to meet or do you want me to swing by and pick you up?"

Ever since I met him, Kevin's been a good friend. We go to the movies, dinner, breakfast or just sit and talk when our schedules permit. He calls me almost every day to say hello and see how I'm doing. "Okay, I'll be ready whenever you get here. I'll let the guard know you're coming."

Lately, he's been calling more frequently. I hope he's not starting to like me too much. Even though our two nights at the hotel included some casual sex and we hooked up a couple times since then, it was just that . . .sex. Since neither of us is romantically involved, I thought our relationship could be an occasional shot between friends. When I was upset, he made me feel better, and just knowing that he's here has helped tremendously. I hope he doesn't view things as more than they are.

When Kevin arrives, I meet him in the garage and we leave. We take a short ride to What's the Scoop, a quaint little ice cream parlor that also serves food. We finish off our meal with ice cream sundaes. I order what I consider to be the best sundae in the world: french vanilla ice cream, chocolate syrup, pineapples and extra whipped cream on a belgian waffle. It doesn't come any better than that. You would think that a man took me out and spent a million dollars on me when we go for ice cream sundaes. Kevin always orders a banana split because he thinks that his being bigger than mine makes it better. Wrong answer.

Arriving at Kevin's apartment, I sense something's going to happen. Why did I say yes when Kevin suggested we come here? First of all, it's a work night, but we're having so much fun laughing and talking that I let things get a little carried away. I should've said no to his invitation to have a glass of wine before going home, but I feel guilty since I backed

117

out of breakfast over the weekend.

I enjoy Kevin's company; he helps keep my mind off of things. Last week, Ian called and had the nerve to try to make up with me. With Sade's "Love is Stronger than Pride" playing in the background, he asked that I find it in me to forgive him and try to have an open-mind about his sexuality. I got really upset. I felt like I'd been dealing with things through my anger, but I hadn't actually talked to him until last week, and when I did, the hurt came back. Of course he wanted to see me but I refused. What do we need to see each other for? What's he gonna do, tell me how to do what he did? Oh, no! Maybe he'll tell me how to get a maid or a butler like those two. I don't think it's necessary for us to see each other.

But Kevin always seems to pop up when I'm having a moment. He called me right after Ian and I hung up. He could tell there was something wrong. I wish it hadn't irritated me so much when Ian called but it did. So Kevin insisted that I meet him for a few drinks. We met at Who's Lounge, a small bar near his job and we ended up having a great time until this guy came in, with what appeared to be a white pupil and it gave that one eye a glowing appearance. Thinking back, I can clearly remember our conversation . . .

"Kevin, that guy over there is freaking me out," I said.

"Where?"

"Over there; the one with that spot in his eye."

"Oh. Why? He's over there and you're over here. He's not doing anything to you for you to be freaked out." That was a different type of response from Kevin. He's usually very attentive to me but that night he seemed slightly agitated by my mention of this guy.

Mine and the man's eyes seemed to meet every time I scanned the room and no matter how far away he was, I could still see that spot. I understood what Kevin meant, but I was picking up some strange vibes every time that guy looked at me.

118

It seemed like I remembered seeing him before. There was something familiar about him, but I couldn't pinpoint it. I would've thought that I'd remember that eye. I decided to just try to put it out my mind and Kevin didn't hesitate in doing that. We had fun, and as usual, that night Kevin was a welcome distraction.

However, tonight there's no need for a distraction. Even though we were never "officially" romantically involved, our sitting here laughing and talking feels different for me tonight. Maybe it's the alcohol. We haven't been intimate for a while and I was hoping we were on the same wavelength, but I guess not. I can't let this happen now. I'm seeing Davon, and Kevin is going to have to understand that we're just friends.

He's being very persistent tonight and slightly on the rough side. He must have more than two hands because it feels like there all over me. "Stop, Kevin. Don't!" I can tell he isn't happy when I push him away after he attempts to kiss me.

"I wish you could stay here. It would be like the nights we spent together at the hotel."

"You know I can't. I have to go home."

"I can take you first thing in the morning."

"No. I have to go," I repeat, feeling very uncomfortable.

He gives up. We get ourselves together and he takes me home.

"I know you're going to walk Snoop, so I'll stay and walk with you since it's so late."

"You don't have to."

"I know I don't, but I want to."

This is what I'm talking about. I think he's letting our friendship get to him. I don't think he can handle this. What's he going to do when he finds out I'm seeing Davon?

"That's fine, Kevin, but please know I'm cool with taking him out. I do it every day."

This is odd. Snoop is always so excited to see me when

I get home, but tonight he's not; something else has his attention. Why does he keep runnin' to the front door? We always leave through the garage.

"What's that?" I ask Kevin.

"What?"

"It looks like something is under the door. That must be what he's after."

"Come here, boy. Let me get that," Kevin says, approaching the door.

He's really good with Snoop. He has even come over to feed and walk Snoop for me a couple times when I had events and couldn't come home first.

I can't believe my eyes. A dozen white roses!

"Who the hell?"

"Looks like you've got a fan; flowers and a stuffed animal earlier today, more flowers tonight. You must be the woman," he says as he hands them to me.

There's no name on the card. "Kevin, you didn't send these?"

"No, Ashlei, I didn't."

"Whoa, why the attitude?"

"No reason. I'll talk to you later."

"Cool. See ya. Thanks for tonight."

"Yeah."

His mood sure changed. I really need to talk to him because I don't want to lose his friendship. He's been like a best friend to me, but I think I should've listened to Amber. I should've made it clear that we weren't going to be a couple.

I pick up the phone and call the security desk.

"Hello. Security."

"Hi, this is Ashlei Thompson. When I came home tonight I found something at my door. Do you know how it got there?"

"Yes, Ms. Ashlei. I put it there."

120

"Who left it with you?"

"That's the funny thing. I don't know. I was holding the inside door for one of the tenants and when I turned to go back to my desk, I saw someone leaving the building and the flowers were on my desk with your name on them."

"What time was that?" I ask.

"About two hours ago."

"Okay, thanks."

"Is everything okay, Ms. Ashlei?"

"Yes, everything's fine. There's no name on the card that's all. Thanks again."

This is really strange. I put the receiver down and pick it back up. I call Ian. Damn, it's his voicemail. *"Ian, I received your gifts and you can stop. Like I told you last week, I'm not interested in being involved with all the things you're involved in. Our business relationship is fine with me but as for you on a personal level, I can't stand you. Goodbye."*

He wasn't completely committed to our relationship, so I don't know why he keeps trying. It must be his male ego that won't let him let go, but hopefully he'll give up now.

Sometimes when I'm in the shower, I think I see someone's shadow through my shower curtain, but when I pull the curtain back, there's no one there. No one could get in here without Snoopy barking, and how would they get in, in the first place?

There have actually been a couple of times when I've come out the bathroom and things seem to have been moved around. I'm not sure what exactly, but I know something's changed. This time, I notice that Snoop even moved from the door and is now laying in the living room.

I think something weird is happening; something real weird . . .

I've been feeling uneasy since the other night when I saw that guy with that white spot in his eye and then came home to find the roses at my door. Maybe I'm just over exaggerating. That's it – I'm just a little paranoid. That man didn't do or say anything to me.

Spending time with Davon for the past couple of weeks has kept me so preoccupied that I don't miss hearing from Kevin. Since the two of us have so many things going on, we wind up accompanying each other to events so we can get some time together, and its been fun. We finally got me settled in my office. Kara and I both gave our two weeks' notice to Winer's and my business is officially operating on a full-time level. Tonight's affair is at New World, one of the most popular nightclubs in Philly, and since I didn't coordinate this one, Davon and I should be able to relax somewhat and enjoy ourselves.

"I'll be back, beautiful. I'm going to the men's room."

"Okay," I say, thinking this will give me a few minutes to get a drink and further survey the room.

122

Uh oh. I knew it would happen sooner or later. That nasty-ass Ian just walked in with his little entourage. I don't recognize any of them. Li'l Maria must not be good enough to bring out in public. I wish there was a way for me to hide somewhere so I won't have to talk to him, but I know it's inevitable. Davon won't let me do that anyway. I think he'll want to flaunt me in front of him.

I knew it wouldn't take long for him to spot me. "Hello, Ashlei."

"Hello."

"I'm surprised to see you here alone."

"She's not alone – and you must be Ian." Davon has perfect or imperfect timing – I'm not sure which.

"And you are?"

"Davon, Davon Matthews. I should thank you for not letting me know that you wouldn't be there for our meeting. It gave me the opportunity to meet this beautiful woman."

Ian looked fierce. "What meeting?"

"Last month we scheduled a meeting, but when I got there I was informed that you no longer lived there. But that's not important now because what matters is that this beautiful woman answered the door. Now, we'd like to finish enjoying ourselves if you don't mind." Davon turns towards the bar and orders drinks for us.

Ian looks like he's about to start something. He looks at me.

"I don't know why you're looking at me like that, Ian. You made your choice."

"So this is your new man? I heard you were with some new cat in the city."

I feel Davon turn back around, but I grab his hand and look at him as if to say, I got this one. "That's none of your business. I don't ask you about your m . . . Look, just walk away like you walked over here and leave us alone. A bad scene in a club isn't something either of us needs right now. And stop sending me things."

"I don't give a shit about you or a scene and I didn't send shit to you. Fuck you!"

"Oh! Fuck me? Fuck you, Ian! You weren't saying that when you were just getting started with your badass credit. You couldn't even get a place without me. And now when you're making a little money it's fuck me? No, fuck you, Ian cause I still got mine. You need to worry about what I may tell everybody about why I put your nasty-ass out!"

I'm angry with myself for engaging in a confrontation with him in public. I promised myself I wouldn't let him get to me.

"Fuck you. Ain't neither one of y'all gonna have shit in this city anyway," threatens Ian, defending his turf.

"Watch that, my brotha!" Davon says in a don't-fuck-with-me voice. "You need to learn how to talk around a lady... or maybe you don't!" Davon laughs deviously and Ian obviously gets the message and retreats.

I wonder what Davon meant by that statement. It sounds like he knows more than what I've told him. I didn't tell him exactly what happened, only that I had caught Ian messing around.

"What was that last statement all about?"

"Why is that important? I was just making a comment. Did it upset you?"

"No. Why would it? I just didn't understand what you meant, that's all."

"Well, I've heard a few things about your ex. One being, that he likes his right-hand man just as much as he does women."

"What! People are actually saying that about him?"

"Are you surprised? You haven't heard it? And what did you mean about him giving you things?"

124

I ignore his last question. "No I haven't heard those things. Nothing surprises me but...I don't know. Let's just forget about him."

"Yeah, let's."

I'm not ready to discuss my breakup with Ian. I don't think it's necessary for him to know all the details – not yet anyway. But if Ian keeps sending me those gifts I'm gonna have to let Davon get involved.

"Ashlei, do you see those cats that just walked in?"

"Isn't that..." Yes...something to divert his attention from his question about the gifts.

"Yeah, they're Dru Hill. Come on, you need to meet them. We did some work together when I was in Baltimore. They are some down-to-earth, talented brothas."

The introductions are brief. I ease away as the ladies start to swarm around them. They're lovin' them up in here, and I can see why.

The rest of the night goes really well. Ian keeps his distance – not that he had any choice – and the place is packed. Every time I turn around, I'm either huggin', handshaking or being kissed on the cheek. This party is hype and I'm feelin' this!

***

A week or so has gone by and I still haven't heard from Kevin. I guess I've been so busy lately that I haven't had time to dwell on it, even though I know he left upset the last time we hung out and hasn't called since. I should call him.

As I reach for the phone it rings. "Ashlei Thompson," I answer.

"Ashlei, it's Kevin." He sounds so dry.

"Hey, Kev! This is so ironic. I was reaching for the phone to call you and it rang."

"I was wondering why you answered so quick. Look,

125

I'm sorry I haven't called."

"Don't worry about it."

"I've really missed talking to you. What..."

Kara walks in with a bouquet of flowers.

"Kevin, sorry to cut you off. Hold on for a second . . .no let me call you right back."

"Yeah, okay." He sounds funny, but I can't worry about that. I need to know who's sending me something, again.

The card reads: *Meet me for dinner tomorrow. Seven o'clock, Rizzi's Jazz Restaurant and Club.*

I sit staring at the note in disbelief. "What's going on?" I say to Kara. "This is too weird for me."

"You must have an admirer." Kara asks, "Do you still think its Ian?"

"I don't know anymore. I told him not to call or send anything but he said he didn't send anything in the first place. We're clear tonight, right?"

"Yeah."

I pick up the phone and start dialing.

"Who are you calling?"

"Desiree. I need to get out for a few."

I dial in search of some perspective.

"Hello?" Desz answers.

"Desz, I'm glad I caught you. Do you want to grab something to eat? Some weird shit has been happening and I need to get my mind off of it."

"Sure, girl. I'm not doing anything."

"Let's meet at Outback."

"I'll see you there in about an hour."

"Thanks, Desz."

"You're not calling Amber?" Kara asks.

I had to laugh because she knows the routine. "No. Amber works in New York and doesn't get in 'til late. You usually have to give her advance notice. What are you doing

126

tonight? You want to hang out with us?"

"Are you sure Desz won't mind?"

"No, she won't care. Let's go."

Almost at the door I remember Kevin. "Oops, I forgot to make a phone call." I tell Kara to meet me at the car.

A strange voice answers. "Hello, may I please speak to Kevin?"

No response. The person sits the phone down.

"Hello?" Kevin answers.

"Kev, it's me."

"I didn't think you were calling back."

"Why would you think that? Who was that who answered?"

"A buddy of mine. Something wrong?"

"No. I was just asking. His voice sounds very familiar. Anyway . . ."

"You hung up with me in a hurry before and you sounded kind of strange."

"That's a good way to explain it. Actually, what are you doing tomorrow?" I'm going to call this number and meet this man once and for all. I'm hoping Kevin can meet me there, just in case.

"Nothing. I was about to ask you the same thing about tonight when you stopped me."

"Oh, I'm sorry. Look, how about meeting me tomorrow for dinner." I tell him where and what time.

"That's cool, but what about tonight?"

"Sorry, I just called Desz and asked her to meet me at the steakhouse."

"Don't sweat it. I'll see you tomorrow." He sounds disappointed.

"Okay. Hey, Kevin! I miss talking to you too."

I join Kara at the car and we leave to drop her car off at my house and then I drive to meet Desz.

127

This is the first time I've been out with Kara except for business. She has a very nice personality both at and away from work. We're all enjoying our meals and the conversation.

I tell Desz about the gifts I've been getting and she agrees I should go tomorrow. Kara offers to come with me, and although I appreciate the gesture, I refuse. "Kevin is meeting me there," I assure them. "I'll be fine."

"Why aren't you taking the mystery man, who I haven't met?" Desz asks sarcastically.

"Shut up, girl; you'll meet him. We've been busy."

"I bet." She throws me one of her I-wanna-hear-the-story looks.

"Davon doesn't know the whole story about Ian and I don't want him to. Kev's my buddy; he can handle things if necessary."

"Well, you better call me when you get home."

"I will."

We talk for a little while longer, before heading for the parking lot. We get in our cars and as we're pulling out of the parking lot a black Maxima with tinted windows comes up on the right side of us, swerves in front of my car and cuts me off. I slam on my brakes and barely avoid hitting him. Stopped, side-by-side, we both sit there. Then as the passenger-side window goes halfway down and I see the driver...that man with the white pupil!

I don't mention to Kara about seeing this guy before, but it unnerves me. "Are you okay?" I ask Kara.

"Yeah, I'm fine. That person's a nut! Are you okay? You look a little funny."

"I'm cool. I hate when I almost have a fender bender."

My cell phone rings; its Desz.

"Yeah?"

"Are you two all right? I saw that fool cut you off."

128

"Yeah, we're cool. Just a little shaken up, but he didn't hit me, thank God."

"All right girl. I'll talk to you later."

The ride home is kind of quiet. I can't get that man's face out of my head. Why did he try to cut me off? How'd he know I'd be there? What? Is he following me?

When we get back to my place, Kara walks Snoop with me. I convince her to stay with me instead of driving home this late. More than it being late, I don't want to be alone, but I don't want to say it.

16

I'm not sure why I'm going to this restaurant to meet this fool. I know I'm fed up with all the shit he's been sending – flowers, cards, etc. I need to close this door, once and for all. He knows I'm dating Davon and he's still trippin', even after he stood in my face and claimed he didn't send me anything.

As I walk down the stairs of Rizzi's Jazz Restaurant and Club I don't see him. I just knew Ian would already be here, gloating over a misconception that he's won me over.

The hostess greets me. I give her my name, explaining to her that I'm meeting someone. She leads me towards the back room, and in all the times I've been here I've never noticed them use it during the week. Before we reach the room, I explain that a gentleman will be coming here to meet me within the next forty-five minutes and he should be shown to my table. I asked Kevin to meet me here, but I didn't give him any details.

When I get to the room, there's no one there. I figure that maybe he's in the bathroom so I take a seat at the only table that's set.

A couple minutes later the door opens and I'm so shocked that I can't even speak.

"Oh, hell no! I will not sit here with you."

"Please wait! Hear me out."

"Why should I do that? And where is Ian?"

"I have no idea."

"Then why did you arrange this for him if you don't know where he is?"

"For him? I arranged this for me. He has nothing to do with this. I sent you the invitation."

"I can't believe all this time it was you who was sending me all that stuff! What the hell was on your mind? Why would

130

you do that? What makes you think I'd want to talk to you after what you did? What sense does this make? What are you doing...trying to help him? I told him that I hate him and never want anything to do with him again."

I feel myself becoming enraged and my voice is starting to tremble. Hold it together girl, I tell myself. I really thought this meeting would be easy. I'd tell him off, tell Ian where to go, Kevin would meet me, we'd have drinks and enjoy the rest of our night.

"No. I'm not trying to help him. *I* haven't even seen him. Please stay and let me explain."

I'm about to push my chair back so I can get out of this room but I decide, for some dumb reason, to stay and listen.

"Thanks, Ashlei."

"Don't thank me. I don't know why I'm going to listen to you. I have one question: How do you know so much about me?"

"I'm going to explain everything. That day at your townhouse wasn't my first time seeing you. We had been at a few of the same parties, but I was hanging with different groups of people. I'm basically a groupie...doin' what I gotta do, to get what I want. I started meeting celebs when I was working at the Suites Hotel and the groups would stay there. When I'd clean their rooms, they'd give me big tips and would invite me to their afterparties. Sometimes I'd even get tickets. I got used to the money and partying, and basically I fell in love with that type of life. So using a different name, I started a cleaning service, so I could get up in the homes of these men. I figured one day, I'd get to the right one and get me a husband. When I met Ian, I gave him my card, but it took him a minute to use it. Then one night I ran into him on South Street, we talked for a few and he asked me to do some housecleaning for him. He told me he had a studio at home, so I figured that since he works from home, he probably would have lots of meetings or sessions there and I mostly only get to meet people after shows and in clubs…so I agreed to do it. Ian took good care of me."

"Oh my God. I feel like I'm going to be sick."

"I wanna come clean with you because I ain't got nothing to lose. I thought you's had an open relationship. That was the other reason I agreed to take the job. He told me that when he met you, you was a groupie like me. I thought you was down wit' the fun, so I thought it was cool. He said he needed to get you some help with the cleaning because you was so busy doing parties. I figured I could have him while you wasn't there – I could do a little work, have a little fun and get paid."

I can't believe this bitch thought it was okay to be up in my house, working my man. She must be out of her mind.

The first time I cleaned your place he kept on comin' in the rooms watchin' me. I liked it, but I played it off at first. I told him I was in a hurry because I had allergies and had to hurry and get away from the dog. After cleaning for a few weeks, I showed up and all the dog's stuff was stored in the closet and he was in the cage. I started cleaning and he started that comin' in the room, watchin' shit again. So I started teasin' him by bendin' over and flashin' my shit at him. I figured I might as well since he said you were hardly ever home and that was my objective anyway, right? I was cleaning your bathroom and leaned over the tub, basically on all fours, with my short-shorts on. He came up behind me and I could feel his dick literally wedge its way between my legs and up against my shit. I couldn't deny that shit felt good, so I stayed there. The next thing I knew, he had yanked my shorts off and had me in the tub . . .taking it. That was the beginning and it was also the end of me cleaning. He had someone else do the cleaning before I'd get there."

"You're fuckin' disgusting. So, that was your bracelet I found in my tub?" I shouldn't sit here listening to this because she's pissing me the fuck off, but I wanted to know and now I'm finding out. This shit's like self-inflicted torture.

"No. That wasn't mine. I saw that bracelet myself and I can tell you about that too. A few weeks after that first time we had sex, I came over on my usual Tuesday. When I got there, it took Ian a while to let me in, which was odd.

"Oh, he used to let you in? Lying bastard."

"Yeah, usually he'd have the door cracked and be sittin' on the couch naked when I walked in. This time I had to wait, knockin' for about five minutes. I was about to bounce when the door opened and this dude came out. They shook hands and he apologized to me for making me wait. He said they were finishin' up a meeting. Even though I thought about it, I didn't question him because who was I? But I thought it was odd that he was in his robe and they both had that just-bathed smell. I just shrugged it off as if dude showed up unexpected while Ian was waiting for me.

"When I went in things weren't normal. He took me to the bedroom, which never happened before. Things were different and very quick. He wasn't the same. He kept wastin' time, playin' with my hair and shit like that. I finally got up and said I had to go.

"The next day at a get-together someone had, Ian slipped me my earring and explained that it must have fallen out the day before and you had found it. He made it seem like everything was cool."

I interrupt, "That's enough. I'm outta here. This shit is absurd! What's the purpose of telling me all this now? I thought I wanted to know, but . . ."

"Wait! I'm almost done," she begs.

"Do you think I want to sit here and listen to how you fucked my man while I was out working? You have five more seconds and I'm leaving."

She continues, "About a week or two later on a Monday,

133

I thought I'd surprise Ian. I called his business line and asked if I could stop over. He said it was cool, but I don't think he expected me to get there so fast. When I got there, that same dude was getting in his car, a black BMW. I didn't say anything when I got inside, but I felt like somethin' strange was going on. Again, Ian smelled like he had just showered. He said he had just finished an important meeting, somethin' to do with an upcoming performance date for one of the groups. After a little coaxing, I forgot and things were as normal. Afterwards I went in the bathroom and I noticed a bracelet in the tub, but I figured it was yours so I left it there and never mentioned it. When I was leavin', Ian asked me if I was still coming the next day, which was Tuesday. I told him I'd see him tomorrow and left."

"So," I reply impatiently.

"I did come back on Tuesday and everything was normal between us until the phone rang. I was in the room dressin' and I heard Ian tell security to let someone back. I heard him answer the door and I could hear someone with a deep voice talking. The person said somethin' about a bracelet. Then Ian came in the room and got a bracelet out of his drawer. I peeked to see who he was talking to and that's when I realized that the voice I was hearing was the voice of the man I saw here the day before! My instincts made me rush to the front door. For what, I didn't know.

"I figured I was at a disadvantage, so I had to watch what I said and how I said it. I asked Ian what was goin' on and told him that was the bracelet I saw in the tub the last time I was wit' him. I questioned him about why dude's bracelet would have been in the tub if all they were doin' was having a business meeting.

"They looked at each other, then at me. I started to get nervous because I didn't know what they were going to do to me. Ian started huggin' all over me and said everything was cool. He reached into his pocket, pulled his hand out and slipped me a hundred-dollar bill. Meanwhile, dude had gone into the living room and was sitting in the chair. Ian kissed me, lifted me up and carried me over to where he was seated. I was scared as shit because this man was so big. When we reached him, he stood me in front of him and dude started rubbin' on my thighs and ass. Then Ian lifted me up again and dude took my shorts off. I was so scared that I couldn't even scream, and fighting them was out of the question. Ian put me down and started kissing on my stomach. I heard dude unzipping his pants and could tell he was taking them off behind me. Then he clutched my hips and eased me back onto his lap, so I would be straddling his legs. I could feel his thing all behind me. Ian got down on his knees and proceeded to have lunch. I knew then that it was true; Ian and this dude were bisexual. While Ian was feasting on me, dude's dick was also there at my entrance. Ian sucked and licked both of us until we came."

My blood pressure has gone into overdrive and I'm feeling like I might explode. I'm about to jump across this table and beat this bitch's ass. Why is she telling me all of this? Honestly, I must be crazy because I keep asking myself why I'm listening, but I'm still sitting here!

She goes on, "I didn't say a word. I was a little confused because as nervous as I was, I was diggin' that freak shit! The next time I came over, Ian had another woman there and we also had a threesome. I never wanted to be with a woman, but I was down for whatever. It wasn't that bad; we didn't really have that much interaction, although I think he wanted to see more. Afterwards I asked him why he didn't have you there, and he told me he didn't know but he'd talk to you."

"What the fuck did you just say?" I demand.

"I thought maybe you all were into that because of his answer. So, the next week, Ian called and told me not to come over because he wouldn't be there. I saw him later at the club, he told me you had stayed home from work, and he slipped me a couple of dollars and said he'd make it up to me. We couldn't hook up all week and when I got there the following Tuesday, dude was there again. I was kind of mad because I figured Ian and him had been together and I didn't really like the thought of him being with me after that. I was wrong; he didn't leave when I came in. He was the one who took me to the room and sexed me better than Ian ever has. Ian watched. Afterwards, Ian joined us. He didn't have sex with me; instead I took it in my mouth and before I knew it, dude was up on Ian and the next thing . . .you were at the door.

"Your reaction didn't sound like it was from somebody who was into what we were doing. I realized then that Ian wasn't honest with me and I was scared of what you might do – that you might put it in the streets. I was crying and screaming when Ian came back in. He got mad and kicked me out and hasn't talked to me since. I don't know what he's said about me. I've seen him a few times with Mike . . ."

"Who?" I ask.

"Mike, that's the dude."

I yell, "That bastard! I knew I recognized him!" He had that man right in my face and Mike had the nerve to try to come on to me. That's the one he said Davon was helping and Davon didn't know who I was talking about.

"Ashlei, are you okay?"

What type of question is that for this bitch to ask me? "Okay? Now you want to know if I'm okay? You fuck my man, in my bed and now you spill your guts about everything and you ask if I'm okay? For real, why the hell did you want me to come here? Why did you send me the flowers and stuffed animals?"

"First, I didn't send you no animals but the flowers were because I'm real sorry things went down like they did. To

136

answer your other question . . .when I was cleaning I picked up one of your business cards; that's how I know so much about you. I saw pictures of you and Ian all around, so that's how I knew it was you when I saw you at the clubs. Anyway, I think you're really pretty, actually very sexy. After that shit went down with Ian, that woman, and me I *really* wanted to meet you. I know he probably wants you back and you and I could perform for him." Reaching for my hand she says, "I really want you, Ashlei."

"Bitch! What the fuck are you thinking? My man . . .in my house . . .then I catch you sucking his dick in my bed and now you think I'm gonna rub coochies with you? What I'm gonna do is kick your nasty ass!" I couldn't get up out of that chair fast enough. Pushing the table over and her backwards in her chair, I jumped on her, commencing to kick her ass. "What the fuck do you think I am, some kind of freak?"

"Ashlei!" I hear someone calling me. I'm being grabbed from behind. It's Kevin. He manages to stand me up and the waitress rushes over to Maria on the floor. She's crying and holding her lip.

Helping her up, the waitress questions, "Do you want me to call the cops?"

"No. Just let me go." The waitress lets her go and then leaves. Maria cuts her eyes over at me but doesn't say a word and she'd better not have. I'll jump on her again.

"What the hell just happened here?" Kevin asks.

"I'll tell you in a minute. Get the waitress back in here and let me take care of this mess."

Kevin goes to get the waitress while I try to fix my clothes. I don't know where Maria went, but I'm glad she's gone. I can't believe that woman thought that . . .eww! . . .I don't even want to think about it. She took me so far out of character. I should've left once I saw her, but something inside of me had to have the truth. I am so glad this saga is over.

Rushing back in the room, Kevin pleads with me, looking very confused. "Ash, please tell me what happened in here."

After I explain everything to him, he agrees she should've gotten beat down. "If I had known she said that to you, I would've slid a punch in before I pulled you up!"

We continue drinking and talking right up to closing time. Assuring my safety, Kevin walks me to my car, gives me a peck on the cheek and demands, "Call me when you get home."

"I will."

"And Ash, I hope your day is better tomorrow."

Driving home I smile at the thought of having a friend as nice as Kevin. He restores my belief in men.

Pulling up in front of my building, I'm taken by surprise. Damn, that can't be that black Maxima parked out front! Feeling a little shaken, I call Kevin as soon as I get inside. It takes him longer than normal to answer the phone. "Hello."

"I'm in."

"Are you okay? You sound funny."

"I'm fine. I just saw something." I stop because I don't want to sound crazy. "Never mind. Thanks for being there for me tonight. I really appreciate that."

"No problem. You know I'm always here for you. You've become a very special part of my life."

"Well let me call Desz and tell her I'm okay. She was worried about me going. She wanted me to take Davon, but I felt more comfortable asking you. Thanks again."

There's only silence. Then, "Davon?"

"Yeah, Davon. I thought I mentioned him to you a while ago. I didn't?" I knew I hadn't but I somehow needed to let him know about Davon.

"No, you didn't."

"I'm sorry."

"Yeah, so if he's your new friend, what am I?"

"Kevin, my friendship with you has nothing to do with him. We will always be friends."

"I have to go, Ashlei. I'll talk to you later." Dial tone.

I have to talk and be up front with him about my feelings. I'm calling him back.

He answers abruptly, "Yes."

"Kevin, can you come over?"

"For what, Ashlei? I'm getting ready to go to bed."

"Please."

After a long pause, he answers, "I'll be there in a few."

"Come through the garage. I'll call the guard."

Watching TV, I doze off while waiting for him. I'm awakened by sounds of someone touching the doorknob. I sit up just as the doorbell rings. Snoopy runs to the door barking. "I'm coming," I yell, knowing who it is.

I open the door, then turn and walk in the opposite direction.

"Woman, you better stop opening your door without checking to see who's on the other side."

"I knew it was you. And anyway, if you didn't think it was open, why'd you try the knob?"

"Forget it; you still need to double check."

"Okay, okay," I giggle, speeding up a little and feeling happy that we're sharing a laugh.

He rapidly comes up behind me.

When he reaches me he starts tickling me. I'm laughing so hard that I don't notice I've reached the couch. Before I realize it, Kevin's on top of me. He stops laughing long enough to lock his lips onto mine.

Pulling away I say, "No, Kevin." I sit up, not knowing what to do next.

"What did you call me back over here for if you were going to be all cranky?" Again, he comes up behind me and slides his arms under mine, gently brushing over my nipples. He gets real close, pressing his body against mine. "What's on your mind? Let Dr. Kevin help you with it."

Normally I think the little shit he says is funny, but not today. "Stop, Kevin. Why are you acting like this? And what's this doctor shit? I thought you were studying to be a manager."

I stand up, grab the remote, shut off the TV and turn on some jazz. We don't need lyrics adding to this fire and the mellow music may help with what I'm about to say. "Look, we need to talk."

"What is it, Ashlei? What's up?"

"Kevin, you know I appreciate the time we spent together when we first met. You were there for me and you helped me keep it together. It was so comforting having you around. I love you as a friend and please know I'll be here for you if you ever need anything…"

"But? Go ahead, Ashlei. Say it! But what?"

I've never seen this side of him. He's always so calm. "Kevin, please listen. I'm trying to tell you how I feel. Why are you getting like that?"

"Go on, talk."

"We never said that our relationship was anything more than a friendship. Don't get me wrong, the few times we slept together were special, but neither of us ever said it was going any further than that. You are truly a good friend, in fact I consider you to be one of my best friends, but I don't think it can ever be more than that. I could have sworn I mentioned to you that I'd met someone…"

"I don't want to hear about that."

"But I have to be honest, especially after having recently gone through a dishonest relationship."

140

"So, what are you saying, Ashlei?"

"All I'm saying is that I want you to know that I'm seeing Davon, I love you as a friend and I hope that we can continue to be friends. I'm sorry if you took our relationship differently. Kevin, please know I don't ever want to lose you as a friend."

"Whatever, Ashlei. You know since that day in the hotel, you've been the only women I've been with? I haven't wanted to see anyone and now you're just kicking this seeing someone shit. I don't know, Ashlei. I don't know if I can just be your friend. I know we never actually said we were a couple or working on being one, but as far as I was concerned it was understood."

At this point I don't know how to respond. This attractive man is standing in front of me, pleading his case, but I'm not feeling him on more than a friendship level. I know I shouldn't have had sex with him and assumed he understood and accepted that we're only friends. I thought it would be cool and just figured that he could handle it. I guess I was wrong. I don't know what else to say to him.

I move closer and reach for his hands. I look in his eyes and he looks back at me, but the warmth I'm used to is no longer there. Touching his face I say softly, "Kevin, I'm sorry. I really didn't know you thought of us as a couple. Even though sex entered our relationship, that's not all a relationship is about. I truly wasn't concerned about you having another female because there was no commitment between us. I'm sorry I didn't talk to you about this sooner."

I reach my other hand around to the back of his neck so I can pull us closer together. As our bodies touch, I kiss him on his cheek. I guess my thoughts are if I make him feel good, he'll lighten up a bit, but instead he grabs me by my forearms and pushes me back. "Oh, you think that's going to make it all right? You think that if you give me a few kisses, get me all hard, that I'll just want to sex you and everything will be fine? Then you can go off and be with your new friend and I'm just left here with a hard dick and no place to put it?"

What's he talking about? Sex . . .a hard dick? Where'd all that come from? "I . . ."

"Shut up, Ms. Thompson. I don't feel like hearing your mouth."

"Wait, Kevin! Don't walk out like this. Please."

When he reaches the door I'm right behind him, so close that as he turns to face me, he almost knocks me down. "What am I staying for? You made it very clear that I have no reason to be here."

"I didn't say that, Kevin. I really care about you."

"So, this is how you treat someone you care about? No wonder you don't have any luck with men. You have somebody standing in front of you who cares about you, and you're pushing me away. I'm sorry I can't be up on a stage singing for you or behind the stage running the show. Just because I'm not interested in that, does that make me any less of a person? Was I less of a person the times when you were depressed and used my chest as a place to lay your head? How about the times when you couldn't stand to be in this place alone because of what you saw your man doing and I sat here with you? Don't even try to rationalize all of this with me. I don't want to hear it...you'll only make it worse. Just leave me alone."

He walks out and I'm speechless. I know I'm wrong. I should've thought of his feelings in the beginning and not just of my own. Amber warned me to be careful. She was afraid someone would get hurt.

I'll give him a few; then I'll call him.

142

17

"Shit!" I scream as I snatch the shower curtain back. No one's there. "What the hell is going on?" I ask aloud as I close the curtain and finish showering. This is happening way too often now. I have to stop at the guard station on my way out the garage, to see if they have record of anyone coming here – just to make sure I'm not nuts.

"Hey, Mr. Carroll. How are things going?" Mr. Carroll is the guard who works the booth overnight.

"Good, Ms. Ashlei. You sure are looking good today, as usual."

"Thanks. Mr. Carroll, has anyone come here for me?"

"Not through here. Why do you ask? That old boyfriend of yours bothering you?"

"No. I thought someone else may have come by and I knew they would've had to come by you to park."

"I haven't seen anyone for you since you and your friend came in a week or so ago. Sorry I can't help. Ms. Ashlei, do you think they may have come to your front door?"

"I'm not aware of anyone coming to that door either. Oh well, no problem, Mr. Carroll. I was just checking. I'll see you later."

"Okay. You take care, Ms. Ashlei."

It makes me feel a little better but it still doesn't explain that shadow I thought I saw. Maybe I'm just losing my mind. The other night I thought I saw that man's car outside; today I think, yet again, I see a shadow while showering. Tomorrow I'll start closing and locking the bathroom door when I take my shower. That should ease my mind. Let me stop thinking about it and collect my thoughts for work.

I get myself all psyched up with a little pep talk on my way down the hall. "Today's a new day and I'm going in here with a new head. My secret admirer is gone."

"Ashlei, are you talking to yourself?"

"Oh, hi Kara! Caught me!" I laugh at the thought of someone hearing me talk to myself. "Wait until I tell you about the other night. Then you'll understand why."

"Everything okay? I got your message yesterday."

"Yeah, actually better now. That's what I was just telling myself. . .today's a brand new day."

"What the hell?" Kara and I both stand still, staring at a stuffed bear in front of the door. "I don't believe she's still at it."

"She who?"

"I'll always be here for you," it reads.

"This is ridiculous. Let's go in. I want to call Desz. I hope she's still home."

"Hello."

"Hey, Desz."

"Girl, didn't I tell you to call me as soon as you got home? You had me worried to death. I even called Amber and told her what's going on. You're lucky Kara told me that you left a message saying you were okay or I would've been at your place with the cops. What happened?"

"If you would stop babbling, I'll tell you. I'm gonna put you on the speakerphone so Kara can hear too."

After filling them in on the events of the evening, Desz screams in the phone, "I can't believe *you* kicked her ass! It's not like you to let something upset you to the point of brawling. You should've called me, I would've done it for you!"

Astonished, Kara says, "Wait a minute, Ashlei, didn't you say that she said she never sent anything except flowers? And now you're receiving a stuffed animal AGAIN?"

"Yeah, she did say that! I didn't even think about that. Then who could've sent this? Now that I know it was Maria and not Ian wanting to meet me, I can only assume that he got the message when we saw him at the club."

"Sent what? What are you two talking about? Did you forget that I can't see through this damn speakerphone?

I answer, "Sorry, girl. When we got here this morning there was a stuffed bear at the door." I read the card to her.

Desz asked, "Could it have been your new man, you know, Mr. Unknown?"

"It must be. It has to be him."

"Hope so – or do you have another looney-bird out there that we should know about?

"Shut up, girl. Go to work. I'll talk to you later."

"Yo, I was serious about not meeting your friend yet. When are we gonna hang out with you and this fine, sexing my girlfriend up, secret man of yours?" Desz asks.

"You know what? When I talk to him later, I'll see if we can hook up next weekend."

After I hang up, I think about what Kara said and she's right; it wouldn't make sense for it to have been Maria. It was probably Davon. Oh well, I have to get some work done.

Things are going really well. Events are picking up because of the holiday and the contacts I've been making.

"Kara, call Starr Temps and get us somebody for the holiday season. We could use an extra pair of hands. My business is jumpin' and the next few months with the holiday coming are going to be hectic. There's just too much for the two of us to handle alone with the same quality of service we've made a habit of providing."

"Sure thing."

Kara is extremely efficient. I guess I could call her my right hand. I can attribute a portion of my business's growth to having her by my side, helping with whatever's necessary. I don't know what I'd do without her.

This week is full of meetings. My networking skills are

much stronger now and I've made a name for myself in this industry. The best thing that could've happened was last month when I finally decided to move forward with operating ShaGru on a full-time level. I don't think either Kara or I could've continued at the pace we were working.

I found a quaint little office on the outskirts of the city. It's in a small town called Essington, near the Philadelphia Airport. The rent is less expensive and parking is much more convenient. Davon's gift of congratulations was an interior decorator, who came in and completely decorated according to my taste. I feel very positive that this move will be a profitable one.

"Ashlei, the agency is sending someone over for us to meet. They're faxing her information."

"Good."

Nearing the close of my consultation with Chanel Patrick, a local model who's mom works at Winer's and I promised I'd help with her wedding, I hear Kara conversing with an unfamiliar female voice.

As I walk Chanel and her fiancé to the door, I glance at Kara and see a fair-skin and very attractive young woman. I recognize her from somewhere but I can't place her.

After saying my goodbyes, I walk towards the two of them. I extend my hand and introduce myself. "Hello, I'm Ashlei Thompson, the founder of ShaGru."

"Ashlei, this is Shelley Richards," Kara says.

"Yes, I remember. Hello, Ashlei," Shelley returns.

"Do I know you from somewhere, Shelley?"

Kara breaks in, "We met her at Club Hot last month. Actually, she was at a couple of our CD release parties."

I reply, "What a coincidence. I'm sorry, what's your name again?"

"Shelley, Shelley Richards. I talked to you last month about a job and you told me you may need help around the

146

holiday. So I followed your advice and registered at Starr Temp."

"I do recall that night. Well, nice to meet you again, Shelley. I have to go out for a little while. Kara will be going over some things with you while I go out to meet a client."

"Okay, and thanks for the job, Ashlei."

When I get back to the office after an hour-long meeting, I notice a message that Davon called is on my desk. It reads: Seven o'clock dinner reservations at The Lounge.

"Kara, did Shelley take this message from Davon?"

"Yes. Why?"

"Where is she? It doesn't say if I'm supposed to meet him or if he's picking me up. Do you know?"

"I think I heard her say you're to meet him there. Sorry, Ashlei. I should have made sure that she got all the information. She'll be right back. She's on her break."

"I'm kind of glad she's gone. I don't really remember talking to her, but I remember her face. Do you really remember her?"

"I remember her trying to be all up on the celebrities the times we saw her. I just hope she doesn't want to work here because she thinks she'll see them coming here to the office."

"I agree with you. Actually, you're going to be her supervisor. Before she leaves today, you should talk to her about your concerns and make sure she's clear on how things are done here and exactly what kind of work we do. Let me know if there's a problem, but I trust that you can take care of it."

"Okay, Ashlei. Thanks."

At that moment Shelley walks in. "Hi, Ashlei. How was your meeting?"

"Good, Shelley. Listen I got the message you left on my desk from Davon, but you didn't tell me if I'm supposed to meet him there or what."

"Oh, I'm so sorry. He did say for you to meet him. Ashlei, I'm really sorry."

"Don't worry about it. I have some calls to make, so I'll be in my office."

He called for me to meet him at a small restaurant near the studio. I arrive at Crystal's a little late because I had to stop home to feed Snoop and take him out first. I also wanted to change into something a little sexier. I want anyone who sees us to know that I'm his woman. When I arrive, Davon's already seated at a table and he is looking FINE!!

Standing as I approach the table, Davon greets me with a kiss on the cheek. "Hi, beautiful."

"Hey, sexy. Damn, you sure look edible tonight."

"Let me know when you're ready to start munchin' and we can leave."

"Champagne? Special occasion?" I ask.

Avoiding my question, he asks, "How was your day?"

"Good. I had a temp start today. Having the extra help is going to take some of the pressure off me and Kara, so now I'll have a little more free time."

"That's good because I have a feeling you're going to need some time."

"Oh really? Who named you the Predictor?"

"I'm saying, I see things moving forward for you and I think the extra hands will be essential in your continued success."

"You sound like Amber. Speaking of Amber, I want to get together with my friends this weekend so you can all get to know each other. Can we squeeze that in?"

"Umph. Friday is better for me. I have to be in Virginia on Saturday with the female I'm working with, Ecstasy. She's opening for Boyz II Men. Did you forget?"

"What? I don't think you ever mentioned that because

Boyz II Men is my favorite group, and I know if I knew that I would've made sure I was with you!"

"Calm down, woman! You can go if you want. Let's do something informal at your place with your friends. We can have food delivered or something. As a matter of fact, I like that caterer you use, M&M Catering. Why don't you call them and they can do dinner. And, what about Snoop? We'll need to leave early Saturday morning and won't be home until Sunday."

"Oh shoot! Maybe I can get Kevin or Kara to take care of him. By the way, I'm inviting Kevin on Friday too." That will be my excuse to call him and hopefully we can all be friends.

"Sounds good. Enough about Friday, I'm trying to enjoy you tonight."

"I don't have a problem with that." After we've engaged in conversation, I proceed to take off my shoe and slide my toes between his legs, in an upward motion the way I've seen women do in the movies. I must have been successful with my intentions because he excused himself to go to the men's room. I wait until I think it's been long enough for him to finish and then I hide in the little coatroom that's next to the men's room. I noticed the girl who was working in there walking to the kitchen. I slip inside and watch in the mirror on the wall opposite the hallway. I wait until I see him getting ready to pass, then I reach out and grab him. At first he balls up his fist, ready to hit me because I'd startled him. Then he relaxes after he hears me whisper, "Shh . . .come here." As soon as he gets close enough to me, I start rubbing on him and lay a big juicy kiss on him. Man, you talking about an instant hard on. I hear him grunt uh-uh-uh! I love when he does this because I know it's my love that's feelin' good to him. It's definitely heating up in this coatroom and then . . .BUSTED!! The girl is back and we're both so embarrassed that we can't do anything but laugh.

While he's trying to fix his clothes, I try to make the situation less uncomfortable by saying, "We're so sorry. We just got engaged and we just can't seem to keep our hands off of each other!"

She says, "I understand and I sure hope I get to have fun like you two one day. Her face is as red as a beet and she looks as if she'll never stop smiling.

We go back to our table, sit down, look at each other and the laughter explodes once again. "I'm glad she didn't ask to see my ring."

The waiter is standing here laughing just because we're laughing. "I'll come back in a few minutes for your orders."

"Well that's what you get for being a little freak," Davon says.

"I didn't see you trying to stop me. That's what she gets for popping in on us!"

We look at the menu as we sip our champagne. For some reason it seems harder than usual to decide on what to eat tonight.

The waiter returns for our orders. As he's refilling our glasses, Davon apologizes for the delay and promises that we'll be ready in a minute.

Davon takes my hand, looks into my eyes and says, "Ashlei, you know you hit a sensitive spot when you said something about the young lady in the coatroom asking to see your ring. I realize that you told her that just to ease a tense moment, but it really made me think. Things have been great between us for the past few months."

My heart begins beating so fast. It's about to jump out of my chest.

"I think we should start thinking about where our relationship is going next. You know some people date for what seems like forever and don't ever discuss moving their relationship forward. I don't want to be like them. I want us to

150

move forward and not get stuck where we are. We have so much fun together, Ashlei."

"I agree with you, Davon. I often think about the two of us walking that golden mile, but I figure when the time is right, it'll happen and we'll be so happy together. To be honest with you, there were a few times that I thought you were going to pop the question, and one time I was even going to ask you but I chickened out."

"There were times when I came close Ashlei, but I didn't have the ring. I want to be able to put the ring on your finger with the question, not afterwards."

Untimely, the waiter shows up again, smiling, and asks, "Are you two love birds ready to order now?"

Davon orders for the two of us. He's always so romantic and I love it when he orders our meals. I'm glad he surprised me like this; tonight feels special. I excuse myself to go freshen up before our meal arrives.

As I near the end of the hallway, I hear the mâitre d' telling someone that at this time, a reservation is required. The man sounds pissed. I glance that way and our eyes meet, but quickly I look away like I don't recognize him. Oh my God! It's that guy again . . .the one with the white pupil! He seems to be popping up more often and I'm starting to feel more and more uncomfortable every time I see him. He was looking right at me. Why does he seem to be everywhere I go? This has to be more than a coincidence.

I clear my throat and get myself together before I reach our table. I don't mention anything to Davon about this mysterious man because I don't want to ruin the mood. A few minutes go by and the waiter shows up with our food. We enjoy our dinner and conversation. I can sense that Davon asking me to marry him may happen in the near future and I'm definitely ready to say yes, but I don't want to rush it; I want it to be right.

18

Early this morning, I left Kevin a message about dinner on Friday but he hasn't returned my call. Everything's arranged for the caterer to have dinner ready by six o'clock on Friday. Kara said she'd stay with Snoop for the weekend. I've confirmed the time with Desz and Amber. I wonder if Davon's going to ask me in front of everyone. No, he wouldn't do that. Well, I guess I'll just have to wait until tomorrow to see what the night holds.

Since everything is taken care of and I don't have anything going on after work, I think I'll go to the gym because I won't be going for the next few days.

***

"Hi."

"How ya' doin'?" I respond.

"I haven't seen you for a few. Have you been coming at a different time?"

I make it a habit not to talk to people at the gym. It's kind of like the same theory I have about making friends in your workplace. Kara and I have always had a very good working relationship and because of our numerous events we've planned and hosted, we've also developed a friendship. Women can be so catty that having friends at work can cause problems. I feel the same way about the gym. I come here for a serious sixty-minute workout and I don't have time for socializing. I've seen this woman several times and we've had very brief, cordial-type conversations. Why is she stopping me like we're old friends?

"No. I've just been busy."

"Oh. By the way, my name is Sabrina. I don't think we've ever introduced ourselves."

"I think you're right. I'm Ashlei."

"The last time I saw you here, you were talking to the girl at the desk when I came in. I was going to come out and suggest something, but by the time I got changed you were gone."

"Suggest something?"

"Yeah. I thought maybe since we're usually here at the same time, we could work out together. I think working out with a partner is a lot more fun, don't you?"

"I never really thought about it. I always work out alone."

"Oh. My closest friend, who I thought was my man, got married and moved down south. Then I was working out with a new friend but he found another partner, if you know what I mean."

"Sorry."

"Don't be. I was really into him and we seemed so happy. The next thing I knew, he told me he was seeing someone else and that things weren't going to work out for us. I was so depressed. I didn't understand what could've happened. After that I spent too much time feeling sorry for myself. I guess in a way I'm glad I had even a brief relationship with him because it made me realize that there was a person in here who deserved more."

What the hell do I look like, a psychiatrist? Why is this woman telling me, a stranger, all her business? I could care less but I don't want to be rude by cutting her off and walking away. "I hear you. It sounds like you've gotten it together. Well, I need to get in there and hit the treadmill."

She stops me. "You never answered me about working out."

"Sure, we can work out together, sometimes." If it'll shut her up, I'll agree.

We talk while we work out. It is actually more fun. Sabrina seems like a nice person. I've really never worked out

153

with anyone, but it does break up the monotony.

When we finish, she gives me her number.

"I don't have any set workout time because of my work schedule, but I'll give you a buzz," I say.

"Okay. It was nice talking to you, Ashlei. I'll talk to you soon."

"Yeah, see you later, Sabrina."

***

Snoopy's more than ready to go out when I get home. Whew! My muscles are aching! Our walk is going to be a little shorter tonight so I can come home, soak for a while and wait for Davon to come and give me a massage.

Drying off and dressing for bed, I feel much more relaxed. I stretch out for what I think is going to be a couple of minutes and fall asleep. I wake at two o'clock in the morning.

What the hell happened to Davon? Did he call and I didn't hear the phone ringing? I know I wasn't that sound asleep. No, there's no message. I call his apartment. No answer. Let me call his cell phone. I get his voicemail.

"Davon, where are you? Why didn't you call and tell me you wouldn't be home?"

I know I said home, but that's the way it seems. He has stayed with me almost every night since we started seeing each other. He still has his place but he's hardly ever there. I've never actually asked him to move in because it seemed too fast. Everything happened so fast between us and I guess I'm a little hesitant to make it a permanent move until we're engaged, which I think will be soon. I talked to Amber about Davon and me and she thinks we're moving too fast and that I didn't allow myself enough time to get over "stupid," but I don't agree with her. This thing between Davon and me has nothing to do with a rebound relationship. Ian did hurt me, but after seeing him with a man, my feelings for him were quickly erased.

154

This is strange. Davon doesn't usually do this. He normally calls when he's going to be tied up or late. I hope everything's okay. Hopefully, he'll call when he gets in. I toss and turn for the rest of the night. I'm not used to sleeping alone and sometimes when Davon's not here with me, I have trouble sleeping. It's only five-thirty but I may as well get up. I can clean up a little so I don't have to do it later, get dressed for work and take Snoop for a longer walk this morning since I cheated him last night.

When we get back inside, I see Davon on the couch. "Oh! Davon, you scared the shit out of me. Where the hell were you last night? You had me all worried. I couldn't even sleep. You could've at least called."

"I'm sorry, Ash. I went past my place to pick up my stuff for this weekend, I sat down to go through my mail and I guess I was so tired that I fell asleep sittin' on the couch. When I woke up, I grabbed my bags and came straight here. When I got here and you and Snoopy weren't here, I checked my messages, hoping you weren't on your way to my place. I'm sorry, babe. I didn't mean to worry you."

"Why didn't you answer either phone?"

"I didn't hear them ringing. I was knocked out. I'm sorry." He grabs me, hugs and kisses me. That easy, I forgot how concerned I was and melt into his arms, but only for a minute.

Feeling much better, I grab my briefcase and go flying out the door saying, "Everything's on for six o'clock tonight. Please be here early."

"I will. By the way, I like the way 'home' sounded in that message."

I smile outside and scream inside. It's hard to believe that we're so close and so much in love in such a short time but like I've always believed, you can't put a time frame on love. It does its own thing!

***

Dinner is going great; everyone loves Davon. At the last minute I decided to invite my mom and her new boyfriend. I'm so glad to see that my mother is finally enjoying life. It took her too many years to truly feel comfortable dating. So I thought I'd get all the introductions done in one night. Kevin doesn't show up and everybody asks for him, surprised he's not here because they all know that we have been very close friends for a while.

Its eleven o'clock and everyone has cleared out. I confirm everything with Kara and give her a key. She has clearance to pass the guards so everything is straight for Snoopy. Speaking of Snoop, I still have to walk him. The three of us head out. The phone rings as I'm closing the door.

"I hope they leave a message because Snoop's not going to wait for me to talk on the phone. It's probably Desz or Amber anyway."

"Go grab it and meet us out front."

I meet up with them out front. "Was it one of your girls?"

"When I picked the phone up, I heard the person hang up."

Hugged up, we walk Snoop for about thirty minutes. I walk straight to the phone when we come in. The person must have called back because there's a message.

"Ashlei, I'm sorry I didn't come to your dinner tonight but I couldn't sit there, with your friends and your parents, and pretend to be happy for you and your new man. I thought I was going to be your man. How long did you think I'd be just a friend? I know you were aware that I was attracted to you and was feelin' you like that. I can't just be a friend. I'll call you when and if I think I can handle it. And you know what, sitting

156

here, watching the two of you walk Snoop let's me know I'm definitely not ready yet."

That bastard! He couldn't come but he could sit outside and watch what the hell we were doing. How long was he sitting there? What the hell was on his mind? Amber was so right...I should've never slept with him. I thought we could kick it as friends. How was I supposed to know he didn't have a life outside of our friendship? I didn't realize it would hurt him so badly. What's he going to do now, stalk me?

Davon sees me standing there looking puzzled. "What's wrong? Who was it?"

I think it's time I tell him all about Kevin, Ian and our breakup, my secret admirer and this dude I keep seeing who makes my skin crawl.

We stay up for hours talking about everything. "I knew the rumors about him diggin' dudes was true. I knew there was something that wasn't cool about him that night we met in the club. Now Kevin, I thought he was cool because you've said nothing but good things about him. Man, that cat is weird. I have a feeling he's bad news. I'm pissed about going to that spot to meet this so-called secret admirer without me. You should've told me and I would've gone with you."

"That would've opened up the whole conversation and I didn't think it was the time to tell you about that mess."

"I'm glad everything turned out okay and you didn't let that bitch turn you out!"

"What?"

"I'm playing. I know you wouldn't trade in Fester for no woman!"

"Yeah, I'm gonna check Fester out before I get some z's!"

"Hold up! This dude that you've been seeing places – you said you've seen him when we've been together. You have to show him to me next time he pops up because, Ashlei, when you're involved in this business you have to be careful. I don't mean run around scared, but you have to be cautious of your surroundings and if something or someone seems strange, you have to speak up. You never know when some psycho may be following you, just like we didn't notice your buddy Kevin sittin' somewhere outside watching us tonight."

"Okay, Davon. I will. Whew, I'm glad I let all that out. Seriously, I'm glad I could talk about it with you."

"Well from now on, don't keep anything from me. We can't do that if we want to make it together. Now . . .back to Fester!"

***

I made Kara promise she would take the weekend off and relax. Her work habits have become obsessive like mine. She'll be here watching Snoopy for me, which will be the perfect time for her to sit back and chill.

I'm so excited about seeing the concert tonight and about being in the same hotel as Boyz II Men! Even though I've been around Dru Hill, Next and other celebrities, Boyz II Men are my favorite. Tonight, I actually feel giddy like I used to when me, Desz and Amber used to run around trying to get backstage or hang out at the back of the arena and catch a glimpse of the groups leaving or trying to get on their bus. It's amazing that I feel like this since I work around performers all the time, but my favorite group is here and I've never had the pleasure of meeting them. I'm doing a good job hiding it. Let me hurry up and finish getting myself together. There's a private lunch being provided for promoters, management, musicians and the groups.

Upon entering the ballroom, its elegance is breathtaking. The chandeliers are dim, the chairs draped with cream-colored covers and the floral centerpieces on each table contain a bird of paradise. Davon and I are early as usual. We like to check

158

everyone out as they're coming in. There are a few people here, so we walk around and socialize. Oh shit! Nate and Sean just walked in! There's that person behind that deep voice, Mike! There he is . . .there's that singing machine, Wanya! They look just as good in person as they do in the videos! I can't believe I haven't met them, since we're all in the Philadelphia area. Look who it is . . .Mariah. We heard she might be here. It's my understanding that she's not on the ticket with them, but when her schedule permits, she makes a special guest appearance to perform "One Sweet Day" with them.

While eating, I can't help but look over at their table every now and then. It seems like each time I look, Wanya catches me and lets go of one of those gorgeous smiles. I better stop before I get in trouble. I'd hate to be some place with him by myself and hear him let out one of those notes he bellows out on stage. It would be on!

I figure it won't be long before they work the room to thank everyone for coming. Here they come! I'm going to sit here, eat my cheesecake and try to stay cool.

Introductions are made and everyone shakes hands. While Ecstasy and I are the only women at the table, we receive hugs from everyone. I hope Davon didn't notice my nipples getting hard. Wanya is last but definitely not least. He gives me a firm hug, a beautiful smile and a little kiss on the cheek. This has to be the best day of my life. I just really love these four men and how they keep it real through their music.

They finish making their rounds and all of us head back to our rooms. I convince Davon that us sneaking in a quickie is essential to the completion of a wonderful afternoon and the success of the concert. Of course he laughs at me, but before he says anything else, he whips Fester out!

Being backstage at a concert is so different than seeing it from the crowd. I've always imagined what it would be like,

159

but my imagination never touched the truth. There is so much going on back here. There's producers, musicians, singers, champagne, food, performers that aren't part of the line up, the stage crew and let's not forget the press snapping pictures and trying to get interviews. You name it, it's going on. It's so hype!

While Davon is making sure everything is straight for Ecstasy, I think I'll take a stroll and shake hands with the rich and famous. I wish my girls were here. I remember years of us trying to be in this type of environment and now here I am all up in the mix. I'll be sure to let them know that I had the opportunity to meet a few more of my favorite performers that were hanging out, including Brandy and Teddy Riley. I met several people who said they'd heard about me and will look me up when they come to Philly.

The music is flowing when I get back to the dressing room. As I open the door, Davon looks surprised to see me. What? Did he forget I was here that quick? Ecstasy is sitting in front of the mirror where she's adding her personal touch to her makeup.

"Where's your makeup artist, girl? You shouldn't be doing that yourself."

"I know. I think she went to the ladies room, so I thought I could sneak in a little something."

"What's up Davon? Surprised to see me?"

"No . . . well yes. I wasn't expecting to see you back so soon. I know how you get when you start networking."

"You're right, but I thought it was almost showtime."

I can't get the look on his face out of my mind. Did I walk in on something? Is there more to Ecstasy than getting her signed to a label?

A knock comes at the door. "Come in," Davon instructs.

"These flowers were delivered for Ecstasy," says this

160

unfamiliar person.

"Thanks," Ecstasy replies.

***

The concert is great. They really pack 'em in down here at the Hampton Coliseum. Ecstasy's performance is sensational. Now I see why Davon has been working so hard with her. She's accepted well by the crowd. Of course, Boyz II Men are their normal . . .FABULOUS! Me, Davon and Ecstasy go to the after-party briefly, and then we head back to our hotel. The evening was a big success and Davon seems extremely pleased with Ecstasy's performance. I'm so happy for him and me too.

Davon and I look at each other as we sit on the side of the bed. We kiss and both of us, simultaneously, lay back, sigh and fall asleep. The next thing I know, the phone is ringing with what I assume is our wake-up call even though I don't remember him requesting one.

"Hello? Hello?" No one's there. I hang up and roll over – but no Davon. Where could he be?

Sitting up, I rub my eyes, trying to focus on my surroundings. I notice fruit and coffee on the table. "Mmm, just what I need...a cup of coffee – but not before I go to the bathroom. After drying my hands, I reach up and feel Davon's washcloth. It's wet. I wonder what time he got up and left out of here. Wondering where he disappeared to, I have a flashback of when I walked in on him and Ecstasy last night. Oh no, please don't tell me he's messing around on me! I take a minute to think back on the past few weeks. He's been late, no-showed and been unusually tired lately. And I know he's been working with Ecstasy a lot in the studio. "Stop, Ashlei," I say to myself. "Stop creating a scenario. You know this man loves you." But where is he?

I walk over to the table and start pouring myself a cup of coffee. I know I'm not quite awake but it looks like something is in this cup. What the heck is in here? I use the spoon because the coffee is too hot for me to stick my finger in it. I hope it's not a bug or something...eww!

I scream! I can't believe it! Where is he? How could he not be here? Oh my, God! I run to the phone and call Amber.

"Hel . . ."

"Amber, call Desz. Hurry up!"

"Ashlei, what's wrong?"

"Call Desz, hurry."

When they're both on the line I scream, "I got a diamond. He gave me a diamond ring!"

"Ash, slow down. What? He asked you to marry him?" Desz asks anxiously.

"No. I don't know where he is. It was in my coffee cup!"

"What do you mean, you don't know where he is?" Amber asks.

At that moment, he comes in the door. "Hey, sleepyhead."

"Oh my God! Here he is! I'll talk to you two when I get home!"

I jump up, run and leap into his arms. "I can't believe you did this to me! I was in here wondering where the hell you were and then...oh, Davon! It's beautiful."

"Ashlei. You still haven't given me an answer. Will you . . .?"

"Yes . . .yes . . .yes!!!"

Then we go at it . . .stronger than ever. Although I always want it to last longer, I really don't want this moment to end. I make him lay down and I climb on top so I can rest my hands on his chest and stare at my ring. This is truly the best weekend of my life.

Back home to my Snoopy with my fiancé.

162

19

The past couple of months with Davon are what I consider to be close to perfect. Davon has moved in with me and we're getting along well. I'm so glad I met him because being with him is exposing me to a different part of the world I've always wanted to know. I've been comfortable with him since day one and it seems like we've known each other for years. I feel so important and glamorous when I step in the room on his arm.

***

The phone rings. "Hello."

"Hey, Ash. I can't believe I'm catching you at home. You're not sick are you?"

"Well hello to you too, Desiree. I actually have a night with no plans, so I'm taking it easy. I've had a few nights like this but I use them to catch up on my rest."

"How are things? How's everything with you and Davon? Did you set a date yet? How's my Snoopster?"

"Wow, you're full of questions. Snoop is fine, frisky as ever. Work is crazy busy. No we don't have a date. Honestly, there's no big hurry."

"What? As excited as you were? What's going on? What did he do?"

"Desz!"

"Well, I know you. You wouldn't be putting off setting a date if there wasn't something going on, not to mention, I can hear 'We Can't Be Friends' in the background. Girl, Deborah Cox and R.L. sing their asses off in that song. I've known you long enough to know that when something is going on in your life, your music reflects your mood. You've probably been standing in front of a mirror out-singing Deborah."

"You make me sick! You're right. We're still getting along good, still making plans, but there's something different. Listen; please don't say anything to Amber this time because I know she'll tell me I'm imagining things. There have been a couple, well a few too many times that Davon has come home really late and a few times not at all. I know his line of work sometimes requires him to be out of town, long hours in the studio or in meetings, but I'm not talking about that. I'm talking about times when there was no excuse or one so weak, he may as well have kept it to himself."

"Aw man, Ash, don't tell me he's messing around."

"I don't know, Desz. I remember that weekend he gave me the ring; I thought I walked in on him and Ecstasy, but when I found the ring, all suspicions were gone. I never questioned him because I'm not sure if I feel this way because of what happened with Ian or if I'm really sensing something. But it's different than it was with Ian. Davon pays a lot of attention to me. His actions haven't changed towards me like Ian's did. I've just been playing it cool around him but it's weighing me down. I really don't want any drama again. That's the main reason I've been staying to myself."

"I hear ya. You don't have to do that, Ash. You know, no matter what, I'm here for you. Girl, we been sisters for too long for you to go through anything alone. Now for Davon, have you seen anybody unusual around him when you're out? Have you found any phone numbers or anything?"

I start crying as I answer, "Negative to all of that. Only what I just told you. What's wrong with me, Desz? Why can't I keep a man? I don't do anything wrong . . .all I do is give them my all. As soon as I think things are going good for me, they always pull the rug out from under me. I must be a horrible person."

"No you're not," Desz answers. Why would you say that?"

164

"Well, can you explain it?"

"For once I don't know what to say, Ash. Maybe it's nothing. You just have to keep your eyes open and if there's something going on, it'll come out sooner or later. Do me a favor, though?"

"What's that?"

"If something goes down, please promise me you'll call me. Don't go running like before and not tell us where you are for days."

"I promise. Thanks for listening, Desz."

"And Ash...keep your head up. I know this is going to sound like something Amber would say, but if it's meant to be, it'll be, and just remember . . .you don't need *him* to be who you are because you were wonderful before he came along."

"Thanks, Desz. Love ya, girl."

"Love ya back."

Desz is right, if it's meant to be it'll be, and there's nothing I can do about it. I haven't given him any reason to go elsewhere, and after all, we are engaged. He didn't have to ask me if he didn't want to be with me.

It's times like these that I miss talking to Kevin. He still hasn't called me since that night I had everyone over for dinner. Now that I think of it, a lot of things have changed since that night. I haven't received any gifts, I haven't seen that guy with the white pupil and I haven't had the feeling that someone's in here. When I think about it, it's a coincidence but a relief, how Davon's presence has changed a lot of uncomfortable feelings.

I'm going to walk Snoopy to take my mind off all this, and when I come back I'll take a nice long bath, then crawl in the bed and wait for my man.

165

20

I think I'll call Sabrina and let her know I'll be at the gym around six o'clock. For the past few weeks, we've been passing each other. When I'm coming in, she's usually leaving, but I could use a little company today to burn off some of the ill feelings I've been having. My relationship with Davon has had me feeling tense, but after the other night, he and I had a long talk and I told him my concerns. He reassured me it was my imagination and that everything is just fine between us. He even suggested that we start making wedding plans soon. I slipped back into my comfort zone and into his arms and the subject was over.

I get her voicemail. *"Hey Sabrina, its Ashlei. Thought I'd call and let you know I'm working out today around sixish. Maybe I'll see you there. Bye."*

***

At the gym and well into my workout, I feel so energized that I could probably work out for hours. Even my warm-up felt good.

"Hi Ashlei. How are you?"

Slightly startled, I answer, "I'm good, Sabrina. I wasn't sure if you'd get my message."

"Yeah, I did. Actually, I'm glad you called."

"Is something wrong? You seem kind of down."

"Well, kind of. Ashlei, do you have a few minutes to spare after we're done working out? I'd like your opinion on something. I know we haven't talked too much about our personal lives, but I'd appreciate an opinion from a woman who seems like she's got her shit together."

"Thanks. Yeah, it's cool. How about we do the sauna afterwards and we can talk in there?"

166

"Do you mind if we get one of those fresh fruit shakes and sit in the lounge instead?" Sabrina asks.

"Sure. Now get your ass on that treadmill and let's get to sweatin'!"

Today's workout is remarkable. I just love how my mood has changed and how positive I feel. I hope my good mood rubs off on Sabrina and not the other way around. She seems to be distracted today. Finishing up I say, "I'm done for today. Let's go get our shakes."

We go to the shake bar, in the outer part of the gym and order two strawberry-mango smoothies. "Umm, this taste so good. What's up, Sabrina? What's so heavy on your mind that you couldn't get into your workout?" I question.

"I need to talk to a neutral party."

Shit. I sense this is about to get personal and I don't want to know any of her personal business. I don't feel comfortable with her like that, but how can I get out of it? "What's up?"

"A few of months ago I met this nice guy. I wasn't going to talk to him but he had a beautiful smile and was so sexy I couldn't help myself. It hadn't been long since I split with my ex, so I didn't think I was ready but I went out with him anyway. Without giving you long details, we ended up in bed and things seemed to be moving forward . . .at least for me."

"What do you mean?" I ask.

"He sometimes seems a little distant and preoccupied, but says he's not. He has a very hectic schedule so I don't get to see him as much as I'd like to, but I deal with it. Lately I've been mentioning he and I living together. He hasn't said no, but he hasn't said yes either. I'm sure he knows I'm not ready to get married, but I am ready for us to take the next step. I don't want to waste my time like I did before. If we're going to be together then that's how we should be."

"Well, it sounds like you know exactly what you want. I don't understand what the problem is. Why don't you just sit him down and tell him?"

"Is that what you would do?"

"If I felt that strongly about it and didn't want to wait. Are you willing to suffer the consequences if he walks away?"

"Well . . .there's something else. I . . .I'm pregnant."

"So, that's why you didn't want to get in the sauna."

"Yeah. I just found out. My doctor said I can keep doing a mild workout since my body is used to it but no sauna or hot tub. Anyway, I can handle it if he walks away. At least I won't be sitting and wondering where things stand."

"Whoa! Well, Sabrina, what I would suggest is that you invite him over, have on something sexy, make him a drink and after some soothing conversation when he's feeling relaxed, let him know how you feel. Lay all your cards on the table and demand that he do the same. If you feel like you don't want to waste your time, then that's how you have to go after it. Please, just remember that all men don't accept that type of conversation easily and it could scare him off if that's not what he's looking for. That means you'd be alone again, alone with a child."

"I'll have to handle that, if that's what happens. I'm ready to settle down and I don't want to be strung along. I'd rather suffer the loss now if that's how it's gonna be. I'll talk to him, but I'm not going to tell him about the baby until we've talked about everything else. I don't want him to stay with me only because I'm pregnant."

"Well, good luck. Look, I'm getting out of here, but here's my pager number, in case you need to talk after your conversation with him. I hope everything goes okay."

"Thanks, Ashlei."

***

I want to get home and shower before my man gets home. I need to fix something real quick for dinner because I don't feel like being in the kitchen tonight. I do feel like cooking with Davon, though. It's funny how I was disappointed after our first sexual encounter because it was quick, but his foreplay is so strong that I want it as much as possible.

A few hours have passed and Sabrina hasn't paged me. She must not have talked to her man yet. Or, maybe everything is going okay and she set things straight. I'm actually glad she didn't call me. After today's workout, all I want to do is spend the rest of the evening snuggling up under my man, except it's eleven o'clock and he isn't home yet. Something must have come up. Nevertheless, he could have called. Let me call him.

His voicemail. *"Hey, Davon. Call me and let me know what time you'll be done."*

By the time he gets home I'm sound asleep. I hear him when he closes the door. "Davon?"

"Yeah."

"Where have you been? Why didn't you call me?"

"I'm sorry, babe. Me and a few guys went to Joe's Sports Bar for a couple of drinks. I'm not even all that late, only a few hours. Damn, you act like I came home two days late or something."

What? Sitting up on the side of the bed, I attempt to yell but can't because of my sleepy voice. "What's up with the new attitude? That's not the point. Whether it's two days or two hours, you still could've called. It wouldn't have killed you. You know what? Forget it. I'm too tired to argue with you. Just know, that was some ignorant shit and you wouldn't like me to do that to you."

I can't believe he came at me like that. He's never acted like that before. Is he tired or drunk?

"All right, Ash. I'm sorry. What else do you want me

to do?"

"Nothing, absolutely nothing. I'm going back to sleep."

When I wake up in the morning, I get up and get ready for work like nothing happened. I leave for work, saying nothing to him. I'm figuring he'll call me later when he realizes he is wrong and then he'll want to make it up to me by taking me out to dinner.

On the way to work, I listen to my music and try to clear my head. I'm too busy to let myself get all worked up over this, especially something as minor as Davon going out for a few drinks with his friends. I don't know why some men seem to have a problem with picking up that damn phone and making a simple call home. It pisses me off, but what can I do?

As soon as I get to work, as early in the morning as it is, my pager goes off. I check the messages and it's Sabrina. Let me call her real quick, before I get started.

She answers, "Ashlei?"

"Yeah, it's me. What's up?"

I feel for the chick. I only gave her my pager number because I gave her advice and I didn't know if things would turn out or backfire on her. I didn't want her to be sitting around crying all night because of my opinion of how she should handle things and then not be willing to at least take a couple of minutes to talk to her. I figured I could at least do that for her.

"Good morning." She sounds refreshed, which to me signifies that our talk must've helped because yesterday she was a borderline basket case. That man of hers really has her brain twisted. I am so glad that I'm past that 'get to know you' stage with Davon. Once you get past that, you usually understand each other better and things can flow a little smoother.

"Good morning. You sure sound better today."

"I feel a lot better too. I wish I had talked to you a while ago. Ashlei, I'm so glad that I took your advice."

170

"So I take it things went well?"

"Yes, they did. He came over for dinner last night, which turned out very nice. At first he got kind of quiet when I told him how I was feeling. At that point, I got a little nervous but I needed to finish. I went on to talk about us living together and that's when he finally opened up and started talking. He told me he wasn't sure he was ready for that and that we might be moving a little too fast. For some reason, I thought he was going to break it off, but thankfully he didn't. He suggested that we take it slow, one day at a time, and see where that leads us. Then I broke the news about the baby. He was shocked, but he said he'd be here for both of us. He held me for a long time in silence, and although I wasn't quite sure what that meant, it somehow was very comforting. Then he said he had some work he needed to finish up before he went to sleep, so he left. This time, I didn't mind him leaving because for once I felt secure."

"Sabrina, I'm so happy for you. I'm glad everything worked out the way you wanted it to. You're not upset that he wasn't interested in marrying you?"

"Not at all. Don't get me wrong, I would have said yes, but at least I know it's not out of the question and that we are going to be a couple."

"You're right. It doesn't sound like you have anything to worry about."

"Ashlei, I'm gonna let you go. I just wanted to tell you what happened and thank you for talking to me. I appreciate it."

"I'll see you around."

"Okay."

I'm glad things worked out for her. I'm still pissed at Davon, but there's no denying that we're good together. I wish everyone could have a strong relationship like ours and it sounds like Sabrina's is headed in that direction.

171

***

This has been one hell of a week. I'm getting out of here early to pick up the makings for a romantic evening with my man. First on my list is a fruit tray and this dip from Acme. The taste of that stuff could make even the shyest person want to cover their man from head to toe and eat him up. Then I'll grab a couple bottles of champagne and I'll even stop at Victoria's Secret to buy something new, sexy and black. I have shrimp at home that I can steam.

When Davon gets home tonight he's in for a big surprise. I page him and leave a voicemail. *"Hey, babe. I have some running around to do, so I'll see you when you get home. You may want to stop at Starbucks for an extra large Café Mocha because it's been a long week and I plan to release all of my tension on you."* I'm sure that made him smile and his pants get tight.

Despite the times he's stayed out and pissed me off, things really have been great between us. We've spent lots of time together, as much as possible, considering our schedules. We do dinner, plays, movies, shopping and basketball games. I'm shocked he goes shopping with me because men don't usually want to go to the mall with their women. They always say that we take too long and have to go in every store we walk by! Sometimes it scares me that things have been so great. I think that's why I think the worst when he's out and I don't know where he is. I guess in a way, when it comes to insecurity, I could be labeled "excessive." I'm always expecting something to go wrong but it looks like this time I'm being proven wrong. I really do think he's the one. I think it's time for us to set a date and take that walk.

Okay, I've finished setting the scene. It's around seven forty-five; he doesn't have any appointments, so he should get here between eight o'clock and eight-fifteen; the candles are lit; champagne's on ice; shrimp and fruit are on the sterling silver

172

platters on the table, with one small silver plate for us to intimately eat off of together; and the CD player is programmed with just the right music. We'll start with Anita Baker's "Sweet Love," then Toni Braxton's "You Mean the World to Me" and some golden oldies like Marvin Gaye and LTD. I always have to have the perfect songs.

I'll take a quick shower now so I can smell fresh and sensuous when he walks in. This night is going to be wonderful. I deserve it and he deserves me.

Dammit! Somebody's at the door. I hate when I get in the shower and I'm here alone and either the phone rings or someone rings the doorbell. I guess I shouldn't complain . . . at least I don't think someone's standing outside the curtain! I don't know who that could be since I'm not expecting anyone except Davon and I know he has his key. Well, since I'm not expecting anyone and they didn't call first, they can just go back home and call me later. This night is too important to be ruined by someone just popping in.

The doorbell rings again. Dammit. Who's ringing my bell? Let me get out of this shower and see who's at the door. I jump out, grab my towel and hurry to the door, dripping wet.

"Who is it?"

No answer.

"Hello. Is anyone there?"

Still no answer.

Oh well. I start walking away when I notice the corner of an envelope sticking under the door. Oh no! Don't tell me this shit is starting again. I don't feel like being bothered with this tonight. I open the door and there's a small box sitting on top of an envelope. There's nothing on either to indicate who sent it or who it's intended for.

"Who the heck is this from?"

I open the box and smile. A Donnell Jones CD. I met him one weekend when we were away and I really like his style.

Davon must have had it delivered as a surprise for me. There's a letter in here…

Dear Ashlei,

I wish there was an easy way to say this but there isn't. Please don't read any further until you put this CD on and go to track #3.

I do what I was asked to do, even though I don't understand what's going on. I walk over to the stereo, take out Marvin Gaye and put in Donnell, then continue reading.

I know we've come a long way and we've seen a lot of things and places together. I do love you and I love everything you're about, but I'm just not sure that right now I'm the person for you. I'm not sure when all this started happening and I can't even begin to try to explain it. It seems so out of my control. I just need time to think about all of this and put everything in perspective.

Ash, I know you hate me right now but believe me I never planned this. I thought we would spend the rest of our lives together but...but nothing. There's no excuse. I know I've hurt you and I promised you I wouldn't do that but I have to figure out what I'm doing and what's going on with me. Please understand that I truly, truly never wanted to hurt you.

I don't want to say goodbye because I hope that when I get my thoughts together, they lead me back to you. I couldn't face you to tell you this because I'm having trouble dealing with the pain that I'm feeling, but mostly I couldn't stand to see the pain in your eyes. I won't come get my things until I'm sure that this is the way it's going to be. Please try to understand, I'm doing this for both of us. Please just give me this time.

I'm sorry.
Love,
Davon

174

Here I stand, hands shaking, speechless, motionless. What happened? This is my fiancé, not just some dude. What was so bad that he couldn't talk to me, me...his fiancé? How'd we come this far and just like that, it's done? And I'm supposed to sit here and wait for him to get his thoughts together? My towel falls and I barely make it to the couch to sit down. I look around in my own home, yet I feel so lost. I look at the champagne glasses and the food I had set up. All the things I wanted to enjoy with him. I was thinking we were going to set a date. Instead, he threw ...

How could...

Why is...

What is going on? Maybe there's been someone else all this time? Was there something up with Ecstasy? I don't know what to think.

I pick up my towel, wrap it back around me and go over to program the stereo to repeat Donnell's track #3, "Where I Wanna Be"; Toni's "Breathe Again" and " Unbreak My Heart"; Guy's "Goodbye Love"; and "Where Will You Go" by Babyface. I go to my bedroom, lotion down, put on my oversized T-shirt and fluffy slippers. I grab my comforter and pillow and go back to the living room, pour myself a glass of champagne and sit in front of the food that seemed so appetizing only minutes ago. All I can do is sit here, reading his letter over and over again. My eyes are filled with tears and the pain in my heart is overwhelming. This can't be happening. The tears are falling. Now, finishing up the first bottle of champagne – crying, listening to my music and petting my baby. I awake what has to be hours later to empty bottles on the table, my glass on the floor, Snoop curled up on the couch in the curve of my body and the empty shrimp tray. "Snoopy!" The sound of my pager going off is what woke me up. Someone left a voice message.

175

I manage to get up and mosey to the phone, only to find out it was Sabrina again.

"Hi, Ashlei! I know you're busy or I may be waking you but I had to let you know what happened. He came over and said he's moving in! He wants to try and make this work. Can you believe it? I guess he just needed a little time to think things through. I'm glad I gave him the time he needed instead of trying to force the relationship. Thanks again. Call me if you get a chance."

Oh great. She's paging me with good news and I feel like my heart's been ripped out, chewed up, spit out and run over by a Mack truck. I'm not calling her back because I don't want to hear it. I don't want her to hear my sadness and ask me what's wrong. I don't know her well enough nor do I care to share my personal life with her, so I'd end up being rude. As a matter of fact, I'll probably stay away from her for a while. However, one thing she said is sticking with me . . ."giving him time." That's something Davon mentioned in his letter. Maybe I should calm down, give him time and space and then maybe he'll realize that he doesn't want to lose me, especially since he "loves everything about me" and is "hurting so bad." She may have given *me* a little advice this time.

I go to my room, plop down on the bed with my journal and begin to write . . .

Exterior, Interior

when people look at me
they explain what they see as strength, will power,
strong mind, confidence
when I look in the mirror at myself
I see pain
I see eyes overflowing with tears

just months ago, I was so happy
I wonder how, in such a short time, so much happiness
could turn into so much sadness

I've always seemed to be such a strong person
very nonchalant, carefree, easygoing
but there's something
some unknown, unseen force
a force that can break you down at your weakest moment
please believe that a negative force will take advantage of that
moment

restoring strength is very hard
to me, it's like trying to seal a loose brick
if someone moves it before the cement dries, it's loose again

PLEASE, LET MY CEMENT DRY

    I end with tears because I remember that day in the
shower, when I spilled for Davon. He said he was going to
make me a star and now I'm alone...again.

***

I doze off and wake this time to the ringing of the telephone. "Yes?"

"Ashlei."

"Kevin?"

"Yes. Please don't hang up on me."

"Why would I do that?"

"Because I've been acting so stupid. I'm sorry, Ashlei. I couldn't help it. I know I was wrong for thinking . . ."

"Kevin, not now. It's cool. As long as we can get past this and still be friends, that's all that matters."

"What's wrong? You don't sound like yourself."

There's something calming about his voice that makes me start crying.

"I'll be right over, okay?"

"Yeah," I whisper. I hang the phone up, fall over to the side, curl up like a baby and sob continuously.

It feels like it's been less than five minutes since I hung up and security is calling for permission to let Kevin back.

I crack the door for him and go lie on the couch. He rushes in and puts his arms around me. "Are you okay? He didn't hurt you, did he? What's wrong?"

All I can do is lean my head on his chest and cry. It's calming to know that the person who helped to soothe my pain before is here again, someone I've counted on since we met. I pull myself together – or maybe my tear ducts have run dry. Showing Kevin the letter, I proceed to tell him how everything happened. He doesn't say anything at first; he holds me . . .the letter and me. A few minutes pass and he lets it out. "I would've never done this to you. You don't deserve to be treated this way. I don't know what's wrong with these men. They don't know when they have a good thing. They must be intimidated by you."

Thinking about what Kevin just said reminds me of one

of those deliveries I received. What a coincidence. I don't respond to his last statement because I sense he's harboring some hostility.

"Kevin, can you do me a favor?"

"You name it."

"Can you walk Snoopy? I haven't taken him out since yesterday."

"Sure."

While he walks Snoop, I call Kara, only to get her machine. I leave a message, *"Hey, Kara. I'm going to take a few days off. I'll check in with you, but if I receive any personal calls, tell them I'm out of town on business. Everything's fine, but I think I've been pushing myself too hard lately and I need a little R&R. Please don't hesitate to call me if you need me."*

Kevin spends the rest of the day with me and asks if he can stay overnight. I assure him I'll be fine and ask him to call me tomorrow. He holds me until I fall asleep, eases me out of his embrace and leaves.

Kara has been holding things down at the office while I've been puttering around at home trying to get my thoughts together. I expected that my first day back would be challenging, but I figured that the sooner I got back in the swing and busied myself the faster I'd get out of this rut. When something bad happens in life and my confidence has been shaken, I'm forced to reevaluate everything: my job, my friends, my lifestyle . . .everything.

It's after ten o'clock when I finally get out the house. The ride to work seems to take forever this morning. All kinds of thoughts are running through my mind. I call the local radio station, WDAS, and request a song. If I can get through, I know Pat Jackson will play a song for me. Right now I'm feeling really emotional and I'm not sure I can handle this. I wish I knew why this had to happen.

A few weeks ago I purchased a mini-recorder to use during meetings and at events when things come up that I need to remember. Today I need it to record my thoughts.

Yesterday, Today, Always

Sometimes we are so close, physically
Yet so far apart, spiritually, emotionally
I may want to hold you, talk to you, laugh with you
Yet you seem to be somewhere else
Why can't you take me there with you
Why do I have to be here all alone
with no one to hold me, no one to keep me warm
You close the door to your private jet
and zoom away, not wanting any passengers
I'm begging......
Please let ME on board
Let ME fly away with you
Again, let me be your partner
The world ahead of us is so bright
Let's hold hands and enter a new dimension
One filled with even more love and happiness
than we already share

Yesterday, Today, Always

    I barely finish for crying. I haven't talked to Davon yet and I'm trying not to call him because I feel like he owes me an explanation, so he should be the one making the call. Eventually, I think he will, but I just hope its not too late. Right now, I'm still willing to talk to him and try to work this out. I wasn't sure in the beginning if his lack of stamina would eventually cause a problem, but sex never played the most important role in our relationship. We shared so much more and I appreciated his other qualities, so it never became an issue. Just thinking about the strong foreplay makes my insides warm up. I love this man and I want him back, but my pride holds me back from jumping and running to him. I have to be strong.

Oh shit! I almost passed the parking lot. I check my makeup to make sure I didn't mess it up crying. I miss talking to Davon on my cell phone on my way to work. He would always call to say nothing, but I loved hearing his voice.

My request is on the air! I'm shocked I got through so fast and now they're playing my phone conversation.

"Hello."

"Hey, can you play a song for me?"

"You sound down this morning. You okay?"

"Not really, but I will be," I answer.

"I hear ya. What can I play for you? Maybe it'll help with what you're going through."

"'Having Illusions'" by Johnny Gill."

"Damn, it's like that? We'll get that right on for you because it sounds like this is deep. Do you want to dedicate it to someone and do you want to give your name?"

"The brown-eyed man and he'll know who I am."

"Sure. I hope it gets better."

"Thanks."

I sit listening to my song. After it's over, I finish checking myself. My makeup is the best it can be today and my hair is in place. I'm ready to go in and take care of business. Amber and Desz don't even know what's happened yet. I promised them I wouldn't disappear and I didn't, but I was honestly hoping Davon and I would work this out so I wouldn't have to say anything to anybody. We're getting together for dinner Friday night so I'll tell them then.

Shit. My pager's going off. I know it's another message from Sabrina. I wish she'd leave me alone. I didn't say I'd be her damn friend because I gave her advice. I should've kept my mouth shut. Some people don't know where the line is between acquaintance and friend and they immediately want to be all in your business.

182

Now that I think about it . . .I gave Sabrina advice that I obviously should've used in my own relationship. Ain't that some shit? At least she could tell there was something wrong. My man had me thinking everything was roses. Oh, I feel a rage coming on. The more I think about what he did, the angrier I get. I should send him Toni Braxton's CD and tell him to take notes to "Just Be A Man About It" because that's what he should have been, man enough to talk to me face to face. I'm really feelin' her song today. He really shocked me. I thought we were better than that.

When I get in my office, I call to retrieve my message. Sure enough, it's her. I lose my man and she's calling me sounding like Sally Sunshine.

Separating your private life and your home life is difficult at times, but it's something I have to do right now.

Look at all these phone messages. One of them is from Davon! That piece of shit, he called Monday. It took him all weekend to pick up his fuckin' phone and dial my number and now, two days later, he still hasn't made an effort to call me at home after not receiving a return call from me.

Well, maybe since he did call me it'll be okay if I call him back. On second thought, I'll wait for him to call me again.

The day is going smoothly and we've managed to get a lot done despite my occasional mood swings. I'm careful not to reveal them to Kara and to stay focused on what's going on here. By six o'clock, I'm definitely ready to quit for the day.

Riding home, I realize that getting up, getting ready for work and my ride in this morning were difficult, but it was therapeutic to be in the office and be back in touch with my clients. I think my level of confidence has risen a little, so I don't want to sit home tonight for fear that I'll begin to sulk again. When I get home, I think I'll jump in the shower and get out of this house for a few.

***

Now this is outrageous. I spoke to Mr. Carroll and he said that no one has come here. Security took Ian's key back and changed the locks, so without me inviting someone in or giving them a key, nobody can enter my place except security, maintenance and me. I haven't seen Davon to get his key, but I know he wouldn't be creepin' up in here. So, why is it that my bed that I made before I got in the shower is messy like someone sat on it? Where's my bra? I know I laid everything out that I'm putting on. I know I have lots on my mind these days but I'm not crazy.

I may have to get my locks changed again. That just seems so crazy since I know me and Davon are the only ones with a key.

I try to calm myself by saying to myself, "Wait, Ashlei, maybe I didn't put the bra out and maybe Snoopy jumped up on the bed after I got in the shower. I'm not going to panic. I'm carrying out my plan and I'm going to do the opposite and go out for a little while tonight if I can catch up with Kevin.

184

2 2

It's been a long and rough week, but like before, Kevin has been here to help me through this. The difference this time is, I didn't let sex enter our relationship. Even though I've been tempted a few times, I didn't want our relationship strained again. I told Desz and Amber about Davon when we went to dinner last week and they were as surprised as I was. They offered their shoulders, but understood that I didn't want to talk about it. Kara has also been very supportive and extremely helpful in handling whatever she can to give me more time to myself. I never called Sabrina and I haven't been back to the gym.

All of this and I still haven't talked to Davon. My pride remains strong and hasn't allowed me to break down and call. We're probably waiting each other out. In four days, ShaGru is hosting the release party for Ecstasy. I'm not only uneasy seeing Davon, but also the two of them. I know seeing him is inevitable and I'm not sure I'm ready, but in a way . . .I am.

***

This Sunday, I'm relaxing, undergoing my own private therapy. I'm curled up on the couch, drinking a cup of chamomile tea and reading "Not A Day Goes By" by E. Lynn Harris when the phone startles me.

"Hello."

"Ashlei, it's me."

I'm silent.

"Ash, please say something."

I thought I'd be able to handle talking to him, but the sound of his voice gives me chills and tears begin to roll down my face.

"Ashlei, I'm out front. Can I please come in?"

"You have a key, Davon."

"I know, but I didn't want to take it upon myself to walk in without asking you."

"I'm here."

I hang up, but my mind is racing, unsure of how to deal with whatever's about to happen. Within minutes, I hear him coming in the door. He ambles into the living room.

He kneels in front of me and takes my hands. "Please forgive me. I don't know what I was thinking, but I do know I need you by my side." He pauses for a minute, and then continues with tears in his eyes, "My head's been real messed up; I can't concentrate and I think about you around the clock. Being in love with you made me appreciate everything as a total package. I love you, Ashlei, and I realize after having time to think about it that I don't even enjoy what I'm doing as much as I thought I did. I've been in this business for a while, but I never felt the gratification from my work as I did when you were a part of me. We are good together, personally and professionally, in the scene and behind it. I need you."

I can't find the words to say back to him because I'm speechless. I struggle to ask, "Why Davon? Why'd you do it?"

"I'm going to be honest. When I told you about moving here, what I didn't mention is that I left North Carolina not only for business but to start over personally too. I broke up with a female I was dealing with, but she wouldn't leave me alone. I caught her cheating on me with a member of some local rap group. She wouldn't accept me not forgiving her, so she started stalking me and I didn't want it to interfere with my career. One of the advantages in my line of work is that I can pick up and move and still work. So, I came here."

"What's that have to do with me?"

"About a month before I left you the letter and CD, I was at the Black Lily with a couple of people and she walked in. I was shocked. We talked for a few and she asked for a ride

186

to her hotel. Ashlei, I'm sorry. Things went too far that night, but only that night. I had too much to drink and she fully took advantage of that."

"That's no excuse, Davon. You should've been able to control yourself."

"I know . . .that's why I left. I wasn't sure if there might still be feelings there and I needed to be true to myself and especially to you. That's why I asked you for time. After a few days, I knew it was you that I needed, but I wasn't sure how to come to you since you never returned my call. Somehow today, I knew I couldn't wait any longer. Ash, I'm miserable. Can I please come back home?"

We look each other in the eyes and I open my arms for him to come back into my world. My man is back. He messed up, but he's human. We all make mistakes, but it's the bigger person who can sacrifice their own happiness to protect someone else and then own up to their mistake, no matter how humiliating it may be.

"Davon, I love you."

"I love you too."

***

Everything has fallen into place for another successful launch party. I know Ecstasy and Davon will be satisfied with the turnout. He should be arriving soon, with the star of the evening.

"Ashlei, this party is the shit, girl! Thanks for inviting me," Desz exclaims. "I'm glad to see you so happy, since you and Davon worked things out. It's been a while, but you should be on top of the world today, your man's solo artist is off to a good start and you set it off right for her in her home town."

"I'm glad you could come. You know I love the support – and I am happy."

"Ashlei, Davon's looking for you. He and Ecstasy just

187

came in," Kara says.

"Thanks, Kara."

"Okay, girl, tend to your man. I'm gonna grab me a cutie and get my dance on."

"Oh, Desz . . .did you hear from Amber?"

"Damn, Ash, I'm sorry. Yeah, she called me today. She said she didn't call you because she knew you were busy. She wasn't sure if she'd make it but she was going to try."

"Okay. Go get your dance on girl. Have fun."

"Excuse me. Do you wanna dance?"

"No, not now!" I snap without even looking in the direction of the voice. I realize what I'd done and turn to apologize. "I'm . . ." My mouth flies open, my body jerks like a bolt of lightening just hit it. It's him! The person asking me to dance is a man with dark shades and locks in his hair, and he's standing there with his head lowered and his shades slightly down on his nose, exposing what causes him to be embedded in my memory . . . that eye. He walks away.

"Shit!"

"Ashlei, what's wrong?" Kara asks.

"It's that man again!"

"What?"

"I can't explain now. I have to get . . ."

"Hello Ms. Thompson."

I'd know that voice anywhere. It's just as sexy today as it was the first time he came up behind me. I turn to look him in his eyes, those beautiful brown eyes.

"Oh, hey Davon."

"Oh, hey Davon? What's up?" He asks.

"I'm sorry. The guy I told you about before is here."

"Where is he?"

"I don't know where he went."

"Let me know if you see him again. I'll take care of him," he replies. Then, Davon hugs me and makes me feel

188

secure.

"Hey, long time, no see. I see you've met my sweetie," this familiar female voice rings out.

I know the voice, but who... "Excuse me, but . . ." I turn to look at the person and can't believe who's standing in front of me. I knew I recognized the voice.

"Your sweetie?" I ask, not knowing who she could be talking about.

"Yeah, Dee," she responds. "You two know each other?"

"I'd say we do."

Davon shouts, "What the fuck are you doing here Brina? Didn't I tell you to stay the fuck away from me?"

"'Brina'? Davon, what the hell is going on here?"

"Tell her, Dee. Tell her who I am," Brina demands.

"Ash, this is the person I told you about."

I stare in his eyes and ask, "Her?"

I redirect my stare. "Sabrina, you fuckin' liar! You told me your man left you and moved down south. So your little story about wanting to be workout partners was a skit to get closer to me so you could get to my man. You bitch! And you had the nerve to ask me for advice about how to get my own man."

Sabrina's tone suddenly becomes hostile. "He's not your man, Miss Priss Ashlei. He never was and he's not now. He'll always be mine."

Pointing my finger in her face I say through clenched teeth, "So, this is why you put our engagement on hold? This is why you slid a CD under my door? This is why you weren't man enough to talk to me face to face? Because this bitch got pregnant to try and trap you after she rode your dick because she liked your smile?"

Sabrina is speechless and rightly so. I can't believe this is happening in a public place and at my event. At this point,

Kara is completely shocked, along with me. Now I'm remembering all the conversations I had with Sabrina about her and her man. Ain't this a bitch? The day I told her to put her foot down is the day I got Donnell's song dedicated to me.

"I can't believe this. You two know each other?" asks Davon.

"Dee," Sabrina pleads.

"'Dee' shit! You were working out with her and talking to her about me? You knew all the time she was my fiancée, didn't you? What kind of shit are you runnin'? You followed me up here and fucked my shit all up...you psycho bitch! I didn't want you when we were in North Carolina and I still don't.

"Ash." He turns towards me begging, "Ash . . ."

Oh my God. I can't believe what I'm hearing. She set this whole thing up. I knew I shouldn't have been friendly to her ass. I should've stuck to my "no friends at the gym" policy. I'm not standing here listening to this shit. She's crazy and he's definitely not ready for me.

Shaking my head I turn to Kara. "Can you handle this one by yourself?"

"Sure, Ash. Where are you going?"

"I have to get out of here, away from all this drama. I have to get my head together so this doesn't set me back another minute. I'll see you in the morning – oh and let Desz know what happened please. Call me if you need me."

"I'll be fine. Go chill." For the first time, Kara hugs me.

I have to say something to both of them. I can't just walk away like this. Kara tries to stop me. "Ashlei . . ."

"It's cool. I got this."

Meanwhile the two lovers are still going at it. Looking at Davon I interrupt, "Excuse me. Don't argue on my account. What's done is done. Remember brown-eyed man – business is

190

business. Make sure you pay your bill on time and give me a call for your next event." I laugh. "As for you, I hope his loving lasts longer for you than it did for me and I mean that in every sense of the word." I move real close to her. "By the way, make sure our paths never cross again or I will fuck you up." I slowly tilt my glass towards her cleavage and pour my drink on her.

She acts like she's going to do something, but he grabs her.

"But Dee," the little heifer cries.

"Get the hell away from me, girl. You playing games is messing up my life, and I guess you think those tears are gonna make a difference? Whatever. You deserve that and more. And I want a paternity test as soon as that baby's born because you're probably lying about that too."

She runs towards the bathroom in hysterics.

I never saw Davon mad before and as mad as I am at him, I find him so sexy.

"Ashlei, wait."

I glance back at him and keep walking. I stop at the DJ's booth and request a song.

Nearing the door, I hear the DJ announce a dedication. "To the brown-eyed man, from your star." Toni Braxton's, "Just Be A Man About It" starts playing. I see Kara watching me, smiling.

Enraged, I storm out of the club and head straight for the parking lot. After walking up and down a couple of aisles, it's obvious I wasn't thinking straight when I left the club. I didn't drive here tonight – I rode with Desz. Shit! When I turn around I have to back up a little. What the hell did I run into?

Without looking up I let out a little yelp! "Ooh! I'm sorry. I didn't see you there."

I try to move around the man but I'm unable to. I can tell it's a man from his shoes. What the hell is he trying to do?

I'm not in the mood for this shit right now. Well, this man is getting ready to get cussed out because I don't have time for games right now. I want to get away from this place, away from my used-to-be man!

"I said excuse me! What are you doing?"

The next thing I know I'm against a car and a strange man is all up against me. I look in his face and can't believe it...the man with the shades...with the white pupil. He's all over me.

"Stop! What are you doing? Why are you doing this?"

"Oh, now you have words for me," he says calmly, like he's not violating my body.

"What? What are you talking about? I don't even know you."

Things are happening so fast that I can't think clearly. Before I know it, the car door is open and I'm being shoved backwards into the back seat of the car, a black one. Here I am, upset over losing another man that I thought was going to be mine for life and another link to the entertainment world. Now this man who's been popping up all over the place is climbing on top of me, kissing me and trying to rip my panties from under my skirt. Why did I leave the club? Why didn't I just stay in there and deal with Davon and his crazy-ass ex-girlfriend? Why didn't I find Desz instead of coming out here by myself? Why me? What did I do to deserve this?

"Why are you doing this to me? Please stop!" I begin screaming and crying.

"Why? You want to know why? I've seen you in the clubs and when I've asked to buy you a drink or to dance, you always turn me down. But let somebody come up to you that looks like he's got a wad of cash in his pocket . . .you start grinning and then anything goes. Well, anything goes now, doesn't it bitch! Where are your money-makers now?"

To think he's been watching me while I was out places.

The more I struggle the more angry he becomes, but I can't just lie here and give in. I can't just let him rape me!

"Why don't you stop fightin' it? You know you like it rough. I know just like you do, that you're a freak. I've seen all those kinky toys you have and your little thongs. If you had me, you wouldn't have to take your toys in the shower with you. Who the fuck you think you're foolin' bitch? Shut up, lay there and enjoy it, like you enjoy your other men."

Oh my God! What is he saying? How does he know this stuff?

"The shower? What are you talking about?"

"You know what I'm talking about. I know you knew I was there. You almost saw me one time so I know you knew somebody was there, and don't tell me you didn't notice that I swiped your bra."

Damn! This man was in my apartment; he's been following me; watching me. Oh my God! What am I going to do?

"Men? I only have one boyfriend? What are you talking about?"

"Yeah, right. Shut up!"

Just as he raises his hand, I feel his body pounce down on mine, but it begins to slide backwards. Someone's pulling him. Thank God! I frantically struggle to get out. Now I can see two men at the rear of the car and can make out that the stranger is struggling with someone. It's Kevin! Kevin pulled that deranged man off me. Where'd Kevin come from?

"Kevin!"

He turns to look at me and, taking advantage of the open opportunity, the stranger bolts away, weaving through the cars in the lot. I run to Kevin with tears streaming down my face. "I'm so glad you came when you did. How'd you find me? When did you get here? Should we call the cops? Kevin, are you all right?" I cry, hugging him. "I don't know what..."

"It's okay, Ash. He's gone."

"Call the cops. I want to report him."

"You don't need to do that. He's gone. What are they gonna do? He's gone and they probably won't do anything anyway."

"No, Kevin. I have to report this. He's been following me. He's even been in my apartment. He's crazy and I don't feel safe."

"I'll stay with you. You'll be fine."

"Why don't you want me to call the cops? That fool just tried to rape me. What are you thinking?"

"All I'm saying, Ash, is that you were leaving a club, you're in a parking lot alone, you're fine and he's gone. What do you really think they're going to do to help you, honestly?"

"I don't know, Kevin, but I need it to be on record in case something else happens. I've seen him a lot lately and I know it's not a coincidence because he told me he's been in my apartment. He even told me he has my bra! He's been in my place several times while I was showering. How'd he do that? How'd he get in? I need the cops and building security to know all of this. I'll call myself, and if you don't want to wait with me, then don't!"

"I'm sorry, Ash. You're right and you know I'd never leave you here alone."

We call the cops and they arrive twenty minutes later. I tell them everything that happened tonight and prior to tonight, including a description of the stranger. As it turns out, Kevin was right; they can't do a thing. After running the plate, the police find out the car is stolen. They tell me they'll patrol the area but can't make any promises. If I have any more problems, I'm to call them. They also suggest that my building's security obtain a copy of the report and I should get my locks changed immediately, plus consider an alarm. I can't believe that's all they can do. This man is running around out here and I'm supposed to feel safe with them telling me to call them.

"Ash, why don't we go back to my place, I'll grab some clothes, take you home and stay with you tonight? I don't want you to be alone. Tomorrow you can call to have them change your locks and an alarm installed."

Thinking I really should go back inside to let Kara and Desz know what happened, I decide against it because I don't want to cause a big scene. Despite what has happened, I know if I go in upset, Davon will want to know what's going on and I don't want him involved.

"Thanks, Kevin." The ride to Kevin's is silent. I'm fighting to hold back the tears but it seems impossible. I've never been as scared as I was tonight. I knew there was something up with that dude. I knew it wasn't a coincidence that he kept turning up all over the place. Thank God for Kevin. I don't even want to think about what would've happened if he hadn't shown up tonight. How is it that he always seems to be around at the perfect time?

"Ash, are you okay?"

"I guess. Just thinking."

"About?"

"Everything," I answer.

"Like what, Ash?"

"Like, how we met and became good friends and how we almost lost our friendship. You know, in such a short time, we've really become close. Hey Kevin, I was just thinking about how you never talk about or take me around any of your friends. Why is that?"

"Why?" He sounds irritated.

"I don't know. I was just wondering. We've been friends for quite some time and I don't know anyone else in your life and you know everyone of importance in mine."

"Well, with your schedule, I really didn't think it was that important. It's not like we're a couple, remember?"

Okay, he got me. Shut me up with the quickness.

Things are fairly quiet again, from that point on until we reach his place.

When we get inside Kevin offers, "Do you want something to drink?"

"Sure, some wine, if you have it."

Kevin gets me a glass of wine, and then turns on some music. "Relax while I go grab some things," he says.

He's only in his room for what seems like a total of one minute and the doorbell rings.

"I'll get it."

"I got it," he demands.

What's that all about? Why doesn't he want me to answer his door? I've had enough for one night – I don't need more drama from a female friend of his. I'm not in the mood for a catfight. He closes the door and steps out in the hall. I'm curious to know what's going on, but either the music is too loud or they're talking too low. I approach the door and recognize the other voice.

"What are you talking about, man? Why wouldn't I come here? How was I supposed to know you were bringing that bitch back here?"

"Keep your voice down. It wouldn't have ended up like this if you hadn't gotten carried away. Rape was not part of the plan. What the hell were you thinking? Why would you try to rape her when you know I'm in love with her?"

"I don't know, man. She was lookin' real good and smellin' good too. I just thought . . .What difference does it make? She doesn't want either of us like that. She deserved it. She always be playin' you and you keep lettin' her."

"No. You didn't think!"

"What do you care? You're probably gettin' ready to go over her fancy little place and hit it anyway, just like you wanted. I should've been the one hittin' that. I was the one

196

who did all your little dirty work, like plantin' the fuckin' bug in her place. You did the fun shit, like watching her in the shower and making sure you were around after I scared her so she'd run to you like a little bitch. You even have the damn bra! Shit, I deserve a piece of that action too!"

Oh shit. It's been Kevin all this time. He's behind all this. What do I do now? I'll call Amber. Hopefully, she's made it home by now.

I use my cell phone.

"Hello."

"Amber, it's me. I don't have time to explain…call the cops and have them meet you here at Kevin's apartment. Please hurry up. Trust me, he's crazy and this is an emergency. I'm in some serious trouble. Please hurry." I give her the address and hang up. I hear her say okay, but I hang up quickly fearing that he'll come back in and catch me on the phone. I put my cell back in my pocketbook, sit down on the couch, lean my head back and play it cool.

Their voices seem louder than before. "Cops?" I hear him say.

"I tried to stop her but I couldn't. She wouldn't listen."

I can hear someone touching the doorknob. "Come on, man, you know I can't do that," Kevin shouts.

I can't hear the response but I hear Kevin follow with, "Whatever man. Fuck you! I told you I'd take care of you and I will."

There's a brief pause and Kevin walks in. I feel him approaching me. Pretending to be startled, I yelp, "Oh! I didn't know you came back in. I guess I was in my own little world."

"Your world is everything but little," he says with a smile.

"Who was at the door?"

"One of my boyz who lives with his girl. He wanted to bring some other girl here for a few hours."

197

"Oh. Why didn't you let them in since we're leaving?"

"He can take her somewhere else. You're here."

"Do you mind if I have some more wine?" I ask trying to play it cool.

He goes into the kitchen and I slip into his bedroom to see if my bra is in there . . .this can't be true. It couldn't have been Kevin. I only make it to the third drawer and I hear him coming.

"Ashlei, what are you doing in here?"

I don't even know what to say. "I, uh . . .I wanted to see if you have pictures of me in your room." That was stupid because I've never given him pictures of me.

"Oh, so really you wanted to come in here for something else, right? You changed your mind? You miss that good lovin', don't ya? You can be honest with me. I know I was giving it to you like you like it and you turned it down; now you want it back, don't you?" At this point, he has me backed up against the dresser and is trying to get all up in my face. He sets the wineglass down and lands his hands on my ass.

"Kevin, stop. Kevin, stop! Kevin!"

"Why Ashlei? You heard me talking to my boy outside, didn't you? Is this what you want?" He goes over to the bed, reaches under the pillow and pulls out my bra. "I keep it under there since I can't be the one sleeping with you at night. Take your blouse off and let me see you. You're so sexy. I don't know why you couldn't have been my woman. Why'd you have to have that Davon person? Where is Davon now? How come he's not here helping you? Oh, I forgot. He's with his ex-girlfriend."

How'd he know about her? How'd he do all of this? What, does he have my apartment and me bugged?

"Don't look at me like you're confused. Yeah, I know about Sabrina. It's amazing what you can find when doing a little research. It's not like people in the music industry have a lot of privacy. It didn't take much to convince her to come here. That's what he gets. Why'd he have to ruin it for me? We were doing just fine without him." Now he's silent while holding me, kissing on my neck and chest. He's breathing real hard and his eyes look glassy.

"Kevin, you're scaring me. Please stop." His touch is starting to feel rough. "Kevin, you're hurting me. Stop, Kevin!" I hit him on his chest. He pulls me closer to him, squeezing me. I hit him again. He keeps kissing my neck and pulling at my clothes. His erection is pressing against me. I can't overpower him; I'm not strong enough. I have to go along with him so he won't hurt me. I begin kissing him back and pulling at his shirt.

"That's right baby, don't be scared. Just go with it. Give it to me; like you were giving it to Davon that morning I called you for breakfast. Let me take care of you the way your toys take care of you. I promise, you'll like me better. Yeah, baby, I knew you wanted me. I knew you wanted me all this time." With one hand, Kevin unbuttons his pants and they drop to the floor. Then he lifts me up on the dresser by my hips, causing my skirt to rise, and he rips my panties off.

I hear my cell phone ringing. I hope Amber is outside.

I try to push him off of me but he won't budge. "What are you doing? Why are you stopping me?"

"I need to get my phone."

"Fuck your phone! I've been waiting for this for too long. What makes you think you can just treat me like I'm one of your girlfriends and talk to me about your men? Did you really think I'd go for that? I guess I'm supposed to sit and hold your hand while you find your next boyfriend. You're mine now."

My body is shivering. I'm scared to death.

Boom! Boom! Boom!

"Who the fuck? I told him to get away from my apartment." He jumps up and stomps to the door with his thing hanging out of his boxers.

I jump down, grab my pocketbook and run out of the room. I enter the living room as he opens the door. The cops come rushing in with Amber trailing behind them. She runs towards me and, crying, we embrace.

Talking to Amber on the way to the police station, she tells me that not far from Kevin's apartment, someone was arrested while trying to steal a car. Once there, I find out that the person was the white-eyed man . . .Kevin's friend. He told them everything from Kevin bugging my apartment to tonight in the parking lot, hoping to make it better for himself and worse for Kevin.

"This is like one long nightmare," I say to Amber. "I'm vowing to stay away from men, on a personal level, for quite a while."

Amber and I hug and head for her car. "I'm going to stay with you tonight. I already called to let them know I won't be coming to work tomorrow. We'll call Desz when we get in the car and I'm sure she'll come right over."

2
3

It's been a while since I've been up to having fun. If I hadn't come to this show tonight, I would've been mad at myself forever.

Fanning myself, I say to Desz and Amber, "Girl, that concert was the best we've been to in years! No matter how old I get, I still love going to concerts. I don't know who had me more mesmerized . . .Cisco, Joe or Tyrese. I can't believe they had all of them on one ticket."

"I think they were trying to kill us women," Amber adds. "Don't they know at thirty-two, we can't keep up like we used to?"

"Who, you two? Speak for yourself. I know one thing; I'd love to be the one they sing to on a daily basis." Desz says.

"I was thinking to myself how happy I am that we at least matured enough to not follow these men back to their hotel!"

"You got that right, girl! Remember the time we went to see LL?"

"Boy do I. Dag, Desz did you have to bring that up? I remember it like it was yesterday. Damn, I should have taken my hotty-boddy home that night. Then my nightmares would have never begun. I am so through with men. I don't care if I lose all of my clients and have to go back to being an admin, I'm through with the drama."

"Ash, I hate the way you feel. Let's go to the coffee shop on South Street and talk for a few," suggests Amber. "Are they still open?"

"Yeah, they're open until about midnight, or later."

Once we're out of the First Union Center parking lot, it's not long before we're walking into The Coffee Room Café. We sit on the comfortable, living-room style couch instead of at

201

a table and, luckily, it's not crowded.

"Now Ashlei . . . "

"Uh oh, Ash," Desz interrupts Amber. "You're in trouble now. Mother Amber is getting ready to lay a don't-be-down-on-yourself speech on ya."

"Shut up Desiree. Seriously, you've been talking like that for the past, what...six months? I don't care if you don't want to date anyone, but why are you being so hard on yourself? They didn't have anything to do with your success. You started your own business and from what I can see, you're doing well. What makes you think if you didn't date those losers that you wouldn't have been successful? They didn't do the job...you did and still do! Davon and Ian may have introduced you to some folks but it's been months and your clients keep coming back, plus more."

"I hear what you're saying, Amber, but did you forget that my major clients are in the music industry and they came from me being with the men I've dealt with? When they find out I'm not with them, I'm afraid they'll call someone else. I view the industry as a big happy family. Once you break away from it, you're out. You know how they say, 'outta sight-outta mind'?"

"I don't believe that. These people have grown to trust you and they know you're very talented. They'll keep calling you based on your skills and professionalism. You have a great reputation with lots of people and I don't think being on the arm of some man is going to change anything. Ashlei, you're an intelligent, beautiful and talented woman and you don't need any man to define your self-worth. You've got your shit together and I personally don't want to hear you down yourself anymore. Trust me, you'll appreciate everything you have when you know that you're getting it on your own and not because of who you lay with at nighttime. Look, Ash, I'm sorry if I've said anything to hurt you, but I couldn't help it. I don't

202

mind talking to you about things that are going on in your life, that's what best friends are for, but I do mind the constant beating up you're doing on yourself."

"Okay, Amber, but what you don't seem to understand is that if either of these dudes spreads some ill rumors about me, I'm through. The majority of my clients are celebrities, and without them in my corner, I'll be out of business."

"Ash, think about what you're saying. They don't have anything bad to say about you. Remember, you didn't cause the breakups; they did. It's been a while now and I don't think you have anything to worry about. Ashlei, I probably haven't said this to you since we were teenagers, but why don't you think about coming to church with my family and me one Sunday? Who knows? Maybe the sermon will be on something that will help you get past these feelings you're harboring."

"Maybe you're right, Amber, and I know you're right about me being down on myself. I have been..."

Desz finally interrupts. "I got it! Let's schedule an appointment at Layers. We can have a girls' day and get massages, maybe do a little shopping and go to dinner. Despite the men who have come in and out of our lives, we've managed to still have each other and I think we should celebrate that."

"You're right, Desz. That sounds good – just like old times. Let's do it! Call me and let me know when."

***

Sitting in my office, the morning after a great concert and a fun evening with my best friends, I lean back in my black leather chair, thinking about what Amber said to me last night. My business *is* doing fine, despite my years of feeling like the survival of me, as a business entrepreneur, rested in the hands of a man. I've had plenty of time in the past six months to get in touch with myself and now that I think about it...I'm all that! I started my business on a part-time basis, got it off the ground, took it to a full-time level, and now I have two people working for me and have acquired a very reputable name for myself.

So, why am I still sitting around punishing myself? Were all the bad times punishment for something I've done? Did I ask for it somehow? Is this what happens when you don't look inside to discover your blessings, your inner self, your own self-worth? Have I actually done this to myself because I was looking past me to find me? Whoa! I think to myself Ashlei, girl, wake up! You've been playing this game all wrong. Men always want to play but always want to keep all the prizes. They think they're the only ones who can win. Well, they are wrong. Ashlei Marie Thompson will no longer be taken advantage of. I will be in control of my own destiny.

Amber and Desz were right. They always said I could get the things I wanted on my own. Granted, those men introduced me to lots of people, but I proved my business savvy on my own. When I stop and think about the people I know now, the clients I have, the connections . . . why couldn't I see my own potential? I've been so hooked on the glitz that I've managed to place my inner self behind a black curtain so that I couldn't see what was there, when all the while, I've had what it takes to succeed. I've schmoozed most, dined with the best and partied with the hippest. Everything else has fallen into place and I've been so busy thinking about not having one of those men that I failed to see my blessings and how much *they're* worth. I've been my worst enemy and now I must be my best friend.

I refuse to be down any longer. I've wasted enough time and I'm not wasting anymore. As a matter of fact, I'm tired of sitting in this office moping around, feeling sorry for myself. I'm cutting out of here, going to that new gym I joined about two months ago and enjoy a good workout.

"Hey gang! I'm leaving for the day. Why don't you two get out of here too? We can catch up tomorrow. Go enjoy

204

your day!"

"Sure, Ashlei." Kara asks, "What's up?"

"I'm picking Snoop up, dropping him off for a shampoo and I'm going to the gym. I need to go get a good sweat on and get rid of this horrible aura that's been surrounding me. I know I haven't been myself lately, but I'm making my comeback. I want to let the two of you know that I appreciate everything you've been doing over the past few months. Tomorrow, I'm writing out a plan of action and putting it to work. We'll have a fresh start tomorrow. Shelley, call and order us some coffee, danish and whatever else you all want from the bakery and ask them to deliver it by eight-thirty."

"Wow, Ashlei. We haven't seen you this excited in weeks," Shelley says.

"I know and I'm sorry. I'm going to make it up to all of us. I'll see you ladies tomorrow. . .bright, early and energized."

I go past my place to pick up my little guy and my workout clothes. Snoop brings a smile to my face as he jumps in the truck. I still love the way he sits in the passenger seat and looks out the window.

"Hey, Snoop! Mommy's back! There are two good things that came out of that Ian/Davon nightmare – you and my business. Mommy's going to treat you to a bath while I go workout and then, before I pick you up I'll go to the produce stand to get fixings for a salad. I'll stop at the pet store to get you a couple of those all-natural chicken biscuits you love. As a matter of fact, I think I'll get you a new collar and scarf!" He looks at me, tilts his head to the side and goes back to looking out the window. I swear he understands me.

After dropping Snoopy off, I head straight to the gym. I rush in to get changed because I can't wait to get started.

Man, this workout feels good. It's been so long since

I've worked out. I can't do this to myself again. Why do we women take it out on ourselves when the men in our lives turn out to be jerks? Why don't we realize that's the time we should improve our appearance? We would feel so much better about ourselves. Instead we go into this little self-pity thing and make ourselves feel worse. Not me . . . not anymore.

24

Whew! This workout is intense today. I'm feeling really good about myself. Finishing on the adductor, I move to the abductor. After adjusting the weight to suit me, I sit down, put my knees against the cushions, position my back really straight, grab the bars on the side of the seat and start the outward-inward motion. That's my third set of fifteen. I have to take a little break. Look at that chick over there on the floor mat. She looks like she's in good shape, but she has on entirely too much makeup for someone coming here to workout. But then again, she's lying there relaxing like she just finished her Oreos and milk and now it's quiet time. I'll assume she's here to pick up some men.

I hear a couple of very deep male voices coming towards the door of the room I'm in. These voices sound like they could belong to two good-looking men. Isn't it funny how you always try to put a face with a voice? Most of the time you're wrong. What you picture is usually nothing like what the person really looks like.

The chick on the mats hears them coming too. All of a sudden, Ms. Hottie puts her hands on the mat, lifts her hips and starts doing pelvic tilts. I can't believe it. She's moving like this invisible man has jumped on her and is giving her a workout.

Well, well, well. In the door appears a medium height, muscular man, with shiny black hair and beautiful cream-color skin and um, um, umph...the sexiest green eyes. Damn! Those things are sparkling from across the room and his exceptional build can't go without notice. This man is very attractive. The first sight of his structure made my muscles twinge, but he'll never find out. The guy he's talking to is also nice looking. He's a little shorter, same complexion but with a sexy baldhead.

This soap opera is getting better and I have to watch. The two men are having their conversation right in front of Ms. Hottie. She's keeping up her nasty motions but with her knees further apart and now her hands clutching her pelvic bones like it's really hurting. Actually, I guess it is. Her muscles are probably screaming at her, *"You dumb ass, stop killing me to impress these men."*

Let me hurry up and finish on this machine. The last thing I want to do is come off like I'm trying to entice them. I don't want them to think that I'm still on here to just give them a quick look at my goodies. I'm telling you, I have seen and heard so many females that are here for the wrong reasons that I sometimes am so self-conscious that I will change what I'm doing when certain men walk in the room. I know I shouldn't feel this way, but I've put the male species on a No-Ashlei-Diet and I try not to do anything to make them approach me. I should have gone to an exclusively female gym, but they tend to not have the same kind, nor do they have as much equipment as you find at a co-ed facility. It's cool, though. It's not like I don't like men or don't enjoy looking at them, I just am not ready to have one of my own.

Ms. Hottie is in her glory. Just what she wanted: two good-looking men, standing in front of her while she puts on her act. Now she's exhaling hard with every tilt upward. They're probably ready to book their own private show.

I'm so engrossed with this...this, whatever I'm watching, that I've lost my count. I figure I've done at least twenty-five, if not more, so I'm stopping to rest for a minute.

Now I guess I'll go to the lat pull down. When I get up I feel my muscles beginning to ache. I've only used this machine a couple of times and it always hurts. But the pain is feeling good today. I adjust the weights and get myself positioned on the seat. I'm so glad I can still see Ms. Hottie and what I'm sure she's hoping will be her two sex leeches. I can't believe she's still going at it. I guess she's trying to show stamina!

I knew she couldn't hang much longer. She stops but it's getting better. She's on her back lifting one leg straight up and pulling it back as far as she can and holding it, then the other one. She's sitting up, spreading her legs and bending forward and now she bends one leg behind her and lays back. I guess these are her cool-down sexes, I mean stretches.

Neither of them has approached her yet. There are a couple of out-of-shape guys in here who look like they're going to have to start masturbating if she doesn't stop.

"All right, man. I'll get wit' you tomorrow. I gotta get home to the wifee," says the shorter of the two and they shake hands.

"All right, Kurt. Catch you later. Tell Karen I said hello."

I figure this is when tall, built and looking tasty will make his move, but instead he's coming this way. He walks straight over to me and says, "Hello. My name is Breon. And you are?"

"Working out," I say, snappily.

"Ouch!" he responds, sounding shocked. "Why so hostile?"

"Because I come here to work out, not to pick up men or be picked up." I stop working out and stare at him.

I glance over to Ms. Hottie and she's actually staring at me. When she catches me looking at her, she rolls her eyes but continues her stare like she's daring me to say something. Instead, I smile at her.

"What are you smiling for?" he asks as if he thinks he's broken through.

"I think that young lady over there is an admirer of yours because she's sure giving me the evil eye."

"You talking about, 'Let me rub myself Mama' over there?"

I strain to hold in my laugh. I can't believe he said that.

"Yeah, you know who."

"Nah, Working Out, you got me pegged wrong. I'm not that type of man and she's definitely not my type of woman."

I almost laugh because he uses working out for my name. "Oh, really?"

"Yes, really."

"So, I'm curious, what is your type of woman or can't you describe her?"

"First let me show you how to use this equipment correctly before you hurt yourself."

"So, you were watching me, huh?" I ask.

"Why not?" He answers.

I couldn't help but smile.

"Maybe after I show you how to do this you'll tell me your name. And who knows, maybe you'll even be real appreciative and let me take you to dinner."

"Dag. You sure do move fast, don't you? And you're a bit over-confident."

"Confident but not over-confident. I just believe in something called karma."

"Oh boy, here we go."

"What's that supposed to mean?"

"Look, I've had enough lines run on me in the past. I'm not up for that at this point in my life. I'm real focused on me; getting to know me; getting in touch with my spirit, my inner being."

"So what's your problem?"

"The problem is that karma crap that you just tried to run on me."

"I don't think that's crap. I, like you, am also very focused on myself. I had to change my way of thinking, eating, sleeping, working and even my choice of friends. Whether you believe it or not, I am after the same thing…a full life. I am

210

satisfied with my career but not with the rest of my life. I want to one day be married and start a family. Even though that seems like it would be easy to do, especially with all the women in the world, it isn't."

"I don't know why not."

"You don't know?" He asks.

I respond, "That's what I said."

"You wouldn't."

"And what's that supposed to mean?" He's starting to upset me now. What he said was sounding good until I didn't respond the way he expected.

"I'm just saying, there are too many women like that one that just stomped out of here. Their what-are-you-gonna-do-for-me attitudes are sickening. That's what so many women are about these days and that's not what I'm about. It's got to be a fifty-fifty thing. I can't do all the giving, but I also don't want to do all the receiving."

"Uh huh."

"What's that mean?" He asks.

"It all sounds good, but…"

"But what?"

I explain, "How can I believe the things you've told me when you came over here claiming to want to instruct me on using the equipment properly and you have yet to do that, but you've managed to suggest that we go out for dinner?"

We both laugh.

He confesses, "You got me there. I did notice that you were using the equipment wrong, but I have to admit, I saw you here before. I didn't say anything to you because I don't normally approach anyone here at the gym, but there's something about you that really grabs by attention. So, I figured I'd offer my help and at the same time, try to get to know you a little better so I can see if my intuition is correct."

He finally shows me the right way to use the equipment

211

and it feels much better than the way I was using it. After he's done showing me, I complete two sets of fifteen and get ready to leave. I've had enough for one day. Not to mention, I met a gorgeous man with potential, but I can't give in like that. I've been through too much to just jump back in. Even though I may be missing something, I'm willing to take that chance.

"Thanks for the help, Breon," I say, walking away.

"That's it?"

"What did you expect?"

Again, he asks, "What happened to your name? Dinner?"

Feeling playful and like I may be up for the chase, I answer, "What do you mean, what happened to it? I still have a name and you'll go home and have dinner."

"Okay. I see. Maybe I was mistaken. Maybe you were the one running a game."

His response pisses me off. "Oh no babe, wrong one . . . I'm nothing like the women you described. Nothing."

"All right, all right, Working Out. Calm down. I didn't say that to upset you and if I did, I'm sorry."

"Apology accepted, but don't make a habit of it."

"In order for me to make a habit of it I'd have to see more of you and that would be slightly impossible considering I don't even know your name."

"I'm going to get changed now. Maybe I'll see you when I'm done – that is, if you're still here." And still interested, I think to myself.

He smiles, showing off his beautiful teeth. I find it amazing when I meet someone and I can feel that there's something good about that person immediately. Well maybe that hasn't held completely true in the past, so I can't let my guard down. If he's interested in finding out my name, he'll still be here when I come out. I can't believe he's noticed me before but didn't approach me. Maybe today is *his* lucky day.

212

I don't know if I'm really ready to get to know someone. I just don't know. I think I'll pass on the added conversation today. And who do I see on my way out the door but Breon himself?

"I'm still here," he says.

"So I see."

"So can I work on that habit?"

"Maybe," I say with raised eyebrows and blushing. "But right now I have to run. I'm late for an appointment. Maybe you'll be here next time I come in." Okay, I don't have an appointment, but so what.

"Maybe?" he says to me with the exact same look. "I'm here often – this is my gym. But maybe I'll have time to talk the next time you come in."

He caught me off guard with that one. I peek back and say, "Oh Breon? Ashlei . . . and I know you knew my name since 'this is your gym'!"

His smile is like the moonlight on a dark river, on a clear night.

Thinking about it on the way home, I'm pleased with myself for not giving in today. If something comes of this, it won't be because I rushed things or pressed the issue. It'll just happen. For once in my life I'm comfortable being alone.

I stop to get my vegetables; Snoopy's things, Snoopy and then I head home. Snoopy and I enjoy a quiet evening together. We eat dinner, he lies by my feet while I watch TV and we both fall asleep on the couch. Just my dog and me.

***

It has taken a couple of weeks but Desz finally coordinated a good time for the three of us to get our massages. I really need this today. I've been so busy that I haven't done much relaxing.

It's been a few weeks since I met Breon and he seems to

be a genuinely nice person, but I still won't let my guard down. I'm very comfortable when talking to him but I don't make myself readily available. We've talked a few times on the phone, at the gym and informally when we went out for coffee.

Damn. I'm letting my mind wander and missed that spot. Finding a parking space on these Center City streets is virtually impossible, unless you have thirty minutes or more to drive around. I'll valet, which is what I should have done in the first place, so I can hurry and meet Amber and Desz in the lobby.

"Hey, ladies. Sorry I'm late," I say as I enter the lobby of Layers. They're both waiting for me, patiently. As I look around, I comment, "Whew, is this the life or what?"

"You better believe it," Desz replies, sipping her herbal tea.

Amber lowers her shades and is quick to add, "What more could you ask for? So, Lady Ashlei, how are things going? You're looking extremely well today. Any new movie stars we should know about?" Amber asks, pretending to hold a microphone.

"Actually, yes. Not a star, but someone."

Desz sits straight up. "What! Are you keeping secrets young lady?"

"Not really. I met this guy at the gym. You know I've never entertained the thought of meeting someone at the gym, but this guy is really nice. Believe me, I haven't bent over backwards to talk to him but he doesn't seem to mind. He's surprised me by being quite patient with me. I know I wouldn't have been if the tables were turned. Other than our limited conversations at the gym, which I haven't been to in a couple of days, we've only been out once and that was just for coffee. We exchanged numbers, but I told him I'm on the go a lot, so we've only talked on the phone a few times and, like I said, it was pretty brief, very informal, but each time the conversations

214

seem to be getting deeper. I'm finding it harder and harder to resist his invitations. I don't mean to say it like he's trying to take me home, but he has offered to take me to dinner, the movies and to a play!"

"So what's your problem, Ashlei?" Amber asks like she's scolding me.

"I don't know. I don't know if I'm ready."

Amber questions, "Ready for what? You're grown girl. You better act like you know. Suppose he's the man for you and you blow it?"

"Yeah, but…"

Desz exclaims, "'But' nothing. Look, we know you've been hurt but you can't stop living. You have to get past that time in your life and move one. You can't put a battery in your man forever! Eventually, you have to replace your mechanical man with one with a face. Those toys don't have tongues."

We all burst out laughing. "Desz, you are stupid but on point," Amber screams.

"Seriously, Ash," Amber breaks in. "You do need to get past this. It's similar to when you were a child and fell off your bike; your mom made you get up and get back on so you wouldn't be afraid to ride again. You have to use those same tactics now."

"What? Ride a bike?"

"Yeah, that's exactly what you need . . . to take a ride. Seriously, Ash, you need to go out with this man. No one says you have to fall in love, but if it happens, then let it happen. Don't go into it with that on your mind. It sounds like he likes to have fun, so why don't you have some fun? What's the harm? What does he do for a living anyway?"

"He's co-owner of the gym I go to."

Desz laughs. "Excuse me, a co-owner? That's a plus – you two have something in common. You both own your own businesses and are workout nuts."

215

"Shut up! Okay, if it continues to feel right, I'll go with the flow but *let me tell ya somethin'*," I say trying to do my best Jim Carey, "if anything starts to seem peculiar, I'm out."

"Let me ask you one more thing, does he know what you do for a living or anything about you?"

"Yes, Mommy Amber. I told him what I do and he was surprised I'm not wrapped up with someone in the industry. I stressed that's exactly what I'm not looking for…a man in the industry."

"Well, enough said. The next thing I want to hear is a progress report on… what's his name?"

"Oops, forgot that part, huh? Breon, Breon Kennedy."

"Hmm, Ashlei Kennedy. Sounds pretty good." Desz jokes.

The assistant arrives to show us to our massage rooms. "Excuse me ladies, I'm Sarah. Do you want to follow me?"

25

A relaxing Friday at the spa led to an early rise this morning. I'm finished my housework before ten o'clock and able to catch up on reading my Essence and Ebony magazines. I'm not expecting anyone to stop by so the ringing of the doorbell shocks me.

Opening the door and seeing Kara standing there, I ask, "Kara, what are you doing here on a Saturday, girl?"

"Hey, Ashlei. I wanted to bring you some paperwork and update you on a couple of calls that came in before I left the office yesterday. I didn't think you'd want to wait until Monday to handle these."

"Kara, you've got to be the best – well, next to me!"

Three hours later and we're still working. The phone ringing interrupts us.

"Grab that for me please, Kara."

She turns to me and says, "Ashlei, it's Breon."

I can't hold back the grin.

"Whoa, look at that smile," Kara says sarcastically.

"Hello."

"Hey, Working Out."

"Hi, Breon. How have you been?"

"Good. How about you?"

"Everything's fine. I've been so busy I haven't had time to come in."

"I'm glad to hear you're okay. Am I interrupting you?"

"No, I'm cool. Kara and I are working on some plans."

"Ashlei, are you free tomorrow?"

"Yeah, why?"

"I'm hoping you want some company."

"Tomorrow?"

"Actually what I wanted to say is, I miss you and I'd

really like to see you."

"You know what, Breon?"

"I know. You don't feel like it. You can tell me, I'll understand."

Kara's sitting beside me, smiling. "Company doesn't sound all that bad. I was going to order something for Kara and me for dinner. Why don't you join us?"

"Tonight?"

I answer, "Yeah, unless your busy."

"No. That'll work. You can order me anything with chicken."

"Okay." I give him the address and hang up.

"Don't say a word, not one word."

"I didn't say a thing." Kara raises her eyebrows.

I fill Kara in on my friendship with Breon and she's happy I invited him over.

It's not long before security phones to let me know Breon is here. The things that happened in the past prompted the change of policy in the building. They now have the list at both entrances and if you're not on it, security has to call. I reach the door the same time as Breon.

"You look gorgeous."

"What? Yeah, right but thank you anyway. Come on in."

Introductions are barely finished when the food arrives. We end up sharing each other's food. After we finish, Kara announces she's leaving but I insist she stay. I break out UNO and after several games, I can't quit because Breon has won too many times. I'm a sore loser.

"Well, ladies, I have to get out of here. I think I beat you two enough."

"Whatever. Come on, let me walk you," I say.

Kara extends her hand. "Good meeting you, Breon."

"You too, Kara. I owe you a rematch."

218

"You got it," she promises.

I walk him down the corridor. "Breon, it was good seeing you tonight."

"Yeah, you too, Ashlei. Thanks for letting me come over on such short notice."

"No need to thank me. Honestly Breon, I wanted to see you too."

His smile is reassuring. I no longer think it's a mistake to let this man get close to me. I think he's worth the try.

"Hey, how about dinner tomorrow? I'll cook," I offer.

"Sounds good. Call me at the gym and let me know what time."

"Seven?"

"I'll be here," he says and lightly kisses me on the cheek.

I can't wait for tomorrow. I feel like a teenager who's just been asked to the movies by the hottest boy in school.

***

It's seven o'clock; the food is ready and security calls announcing Breon's arrival. The only thing left to do is light the candles. I answer the door wearing a sheer, black, wide-legged lounge set with a black lace bra and panty set underneath. I can tell by Breon's eyes, he's pleased with what he sees.

Walking in he says, "It smells good in here."

"Oh thanks. It's the new Moschino cologne."

He has a funny look on his face, not knowing how to respond to that one.

"I'm just playing. I know you were talking about the food."

He gives me a hug and another one of those tender kisses on the cheek that he gave me last night.

A mix of Mary J, Lauren, Whitney and Mariah, with a

219

little wine on the side, accompanies our salad, rice and chicken stir-fry.

The meal was good and our conversation was even better. I don't know if it's because it's the first time we've been completely alone, if it's the wine, music or the fact that it's been months since I've been with someone, but something's making me yearn for this man. He hasn't touched me or said anything to make me think his mind is where mine is, but damn. I want him but I don't want to be the aggressor. On second thought, why not?

"Let me fill your glass," I offer.

"No, let me do it."

While he's filling our glasses, I turn down the lights and go up to my bedroom and light the candles. When I come back down, he's waiting with the wine. He hands me my glass and I reach for his hand. He gets the picture and follows my lead. We barely get in the bedroom and set our glasses down before our lips are interlocked. His kisses are good enough to stay in that position all night, but we don't.

Breon sits me on the bed and asks me to lay back. Standing, he takes his clothes off. I'm glad because it's giving me a chance to check him out in the candlelight. Damn…I like what I see. Does that equipment at the gym work that out too? I guess it's my turn now. He undresses me slowly, looking at every inch of my body. While I'm lying down, he removes my clothes, one piece at a time. Then he leans over me and kisses me again. I thought things I've done and seen in the past were sensual; this man is taking sensuality to another level tonight. His movements are so rhythmic; his skin is soft and the color is so even and pretty; his green eyes seem to be glistening in the candlelight; his body is so cut I can't stop looking at him – and his moans. Damn! I know it always feels different when you're with someone different but this shit is making my body hairs stand up!

220

He's kissing my neck. "Turn over."

Aw-shit. I should've known. He blew it. "What? I ain't into no shit like that."

"I'm sorry – I said that wrong." He kisses me again, longer and more passionate. "Let me give you a massage."

Oh, I can go for that. His hands are so strong. My shoulders, my back, my ass and back up again. I feel his person touching me. He's teasing me but I love it.

"Breon. I hate to stop you but do you have any condoms?"

Without words, he goes into his wallet, removes a package and puts one on.

I've had all the teasing I can tolerate. I manage to get my legs on the outside of him and push myself up, forcing him to lean back on his feet. I lower myself onto him backwards and I hear him moan, "Umm." I put my hands down in front of me to support myself as I raise and lower myself on him slowly. I can feel the full length of his person entering and almost leaving my canal. Judging by the sounds of his moans, I'd say he's enjoying this as much as I am. Okay, this is the shit! This man has won the prize. I know I've thought this in the past but this is real. For once, I'm not infatuated with a man's career, or worried about what he can do for me, but excited about getting closer to this man for who he is inside. His lovemaking is extraordinary. He's not only thinking of himself but is also making sure I get the most out of this. He has his finger positioned in front of his man and is sliding it back and forth on my man in the boat. This shit is feeling so good I don't want it to stop. I feel myself reaching my peak. My thrusts are getting harder and faster, making it impossible for him to continue with his hand. That's okay though...I'm there. I'm now holding onto his outer thighs, giving it all to him. "Shit!" he hollers. I feel his person swelling, pulsating. He grabs my hips and comes back at me just as hard. It's almost impossible to hold

221

back the scream. Damn! His motion is slowing. Mine has stopped. He holds me, slightly pinching my nipples and kissing my back.

Without speaking, I show him to the bathroom. We shower, re-dress and go back to the living room to finish the bottle of wine. I reload the disc player. There's not much conversation, just holding each other with Luther pouring his heart out. Hours later, I wake up still in his arms. Sometime or another Snoop came and lay at my feet.

Things have been non-stop lately. I haven't had much time to spend with Desz and Amber. I try to spend as much of my free time with Breon as I can. Tonight, he's picking me up here at my apartment. He should be here soon. I'm not sure where we're going but I'm sure we'll have fun.

The phone rings. That's probably him saying he's on his way.

"Hello," I answer.

"What's up, stranger?" Amber says.

"Stop it. Hey, girl! I was just thinking about you."

"Well, I never see you anymore. That Mr. Breon just takes up all your time."

"I know. We have been spending a lot of time together. He's so wonderful."

Amber pretends to be shocked. "What? Did I hear you admit that he's wonderful?"

"Yeah, I admit it."

"I'm so glad. I remember when you were determined not to see him; when you thought that you were getting too close to him and that there had to be something that he was lying about because he seemed too good to be true!"

"Yeah, yeah, yeah. You got me. I knew one day you would throw that up in my face." I get serious for a moment. "There was one time when I truly believed he was lying."

Sounding concerned, Amber asks, "Ah, man. What did he do?"

I explain, "After our first time sleeping together, he would call me every day and then one weekend he had to go away on a business trip and I didn't hear from him at all. I wasn't sure what to think. He'd been really good about calling and keeping in touch when he was away on business. So, of course I started to think negative, even though I had no right to get upset. Remember, I was the one who didn't want a commitment."

"So why didn't he call? What was he doing?"

"He finally called and the first thing he did was apologize for not being in touch all weekend. He said he was real busy with meetings, inspections and tours. When they finished, they'd have a couple drinks and go to their hotel rooms. He claimed it was late and he didn't want to wake me, but he did throw in that he was starting to feel like I didn't want to hear from him as much anyway, so he was trying to refrain from calling so often."

"Why'd he think that? What did you tell him to make him think that?"

"He says he was trying to give me space since I'd said I was afraid of getting too close too fast, but listen to this…he said it was so hard for him to not pick up the phone to call me, so guess what he did?"

"What? Please don't tell me he called somebody else."

"Ooh. No, girl."

"He called and left messages on my voicemail at work. He said he needed to hear my voice. Isn't he sweet?"

"Yes, he is. No wonder I can't ever catch up with you. I see why he occupies so much of your time. So things are going real good now?"

"Things are great. We went to the Sixers game last night. They played Miami. It was the first game we've been to since they traded Theo for Mutumbo."

"Oh yeah? You know I don't know who you're talking about. I can't get into sports, but I did hear about the trade on the news. I may not know too much about the game, but you know I know who Allen Iverson is!"

"But of course. So let me finish. Guess what Breon did?"

224

"Asked you to marry him?"

"No. You're so crazy. I'm going to buy you a ticket to Hollywood. But check this out. When we got to our seats.... I don't know if I told you, but our seats were on the first level right behind the Sixers bench. Anyway..."

Amber interrupts, "Wait. How'd you get those seats?"

"Breon has season tickets. I'm not sure if he has them for every game or just certain ones but I know we've been to several. Valentine's Day's game was the best one I've ever been to."

"Why?" Amber asks. "What was so special about that game?"

"Why? What? You don't know? We played the Lakers! We spanked 'em. The atmosphere in that place was indescribable. I absolutely loved it. I was even eye to eye with Allen!"

"Yeah, right," Amber says.

"I'm just playing. I knew that would get you. I thought I told you about that night. I must have told Desz. Sorry."

"What did he give you for Valentine's Day?"

"I asked him not to give me anything."

Sounding confused, Amber asks. "Why would you do something like that?"

"I really don't like Valentine's Day. I feel like this…if you don't do it all year long, then don't do it on this day just because greeting cards tell you that it's the day for lovers. Every day is the day for love."

"That's true, Ash, but most women don't look at it that way. They want those flowers sent to their job and candy when they get home, along with anything else they can get."

"Most of them better hope their man is there when they get home," I say laughing. "They're so worried about a gift so they can grin in front of their co-workers. What's the purpose of showing off in front of them and in two weeks you're coming in all depressed because the stupid man left you for someone else? They should use all that energy to focus on strengthening their relationship instead of trying to bleed that wallet. Just because he gives the gifts doesn't mean he's giving it from the heart. That's why I want mine all year long. That way I know it's coming correct."

"Dag, Ash, you're in rare form today."

Not really, Amber, "Just telling it like it is. Reality. It can be harsh sometimes."

"So did he listen to you?"

"No."

"I knew it. What did he do?"

"He sent me, not one but three dozen roses – peach, white and lavender. They were beautiful."

"That man is so romantic. I'm glad you found someone who's treating you right. You really deserve it. I don't know, girl, he might be the one."

"Don't say that, you'll jinx me."

Amber's voice takes on a more serious tone. "There's no such thing. If it's meant for the two of you to be together and you relax, it'll just happen. It's always better when it's not forced. When you put this kind of thing in God's hands and let Him lead the way, the outcome is always better. That way when it does happen, you both know the other is sincere because the issue was never forced upon either of you. Have you two ever discussed the future?"

"Briefly. One night we talked about it, but not to the extent of making any plans. He asked me how I felt about marriage and I told him I wasn't sure because of everything that happened in my past. Then I explained to him that I know it's unfair to him, so I try not to compare the past to the present – but sometimes it's hard. He understands this is something I have to overcome, and I have to realize that each relationship is different and letting go of those bad memories is not an easy thing to do."

"And what did he say?"

"He agreed. He said he wants to get married one day and have children and that he understands how I feel because he was hurt before too. He refuses to let that stop him from loving and trusting again, especially with me. Since then, he started going to Bible class whenever possible and Sunday service."

"That is great! What about you?"

"I knew you'd ask that question. I've been attending Sunday service for the past seven weeks. I wasn't going to tell you about me going to church yet. I was going to surprise you with an invitation to join us for service when the congregation offers me The Right Hand of Fellowship."

Excitedly, Amber asks, "Ash, you've joined church?"

"Not yet. I'm trying to decide between the one that I've been attending and Breon's. Once I decide, I plan to join. I've met both ministers and talked to both of them. I told them that I was trying to decide between the two churches and both welcomed me."

"I can't believe you didn't tell me that you've been going to Sunday services!"

"I was going to, but I couldn't find the right time. Plus I wanted to surprise you after I joined."

"Right time? Anytime is the right time. I'm so happy for you. How do you feel?"

"You know, Amber, I feel great. When I come home on Sunday, after service, I feel so refreshed. I change clothes, take Snoop for a walk and we wait for Breon."

"Then what do you two do? Knowing you, it's the nasty!"

"Actually, no. Sometimes we stay in and do nothing, just cook on the grill and talk while we load the CD player with soft music. We've even taken the portable CD player and gone for walks, holding hands and listening to the music."

"Sounds so romantic." Recalling the beginning of their conversation, Amber asks. "But hey, what were you trying to tell me when we first started talking about him? Something about the game you went to?"

"Oh yeah, I forgot I was telling you that. I got so wrapped up in telling you how nice everything has been. When we got to the game, we did the norm...got popcorn, hotdogs and soda. While we were in line, Breon excused himself. I figured he saw someone he knew. When he got back, I was at the counter. We got our food and headed towards the entrance leading to our seats. When we got to the opening of the tunnel, the ushers seemed to be grinning at us. I thought this was unusual, but I blew it off because I wanted to get in before they introduced the team; I love that part. The roar in that place is wonderful when Iverson comes out. Anyway, Breon walked in front of me, but when we got to our row, he stepped to the side and let me go in first. When I looked in to where my seat was I couldn't believe my eyes. There was this huge red bow tied to the top of my chair with red ribbons streaming down over the chair."

"What did you say? Ooh, Ash! What was that for?"

"I didn't know what to do or say. I turned to him with a puzzled look on my face.

"'Go ahead, go to your seat,' he said.

"I said to him, 'But...? What...?' I couldn't get it out.

"He insisted, 'Go ahead so we can sit down.'

"'What's all this? Why is my seat decorated?' I asked.

"'I don't know. You must have a fan here,' he responded.

"That was it. The game started and nothing happened. In the third quarter, during a time out, a girl came over to me with one of those cute little Sixers bags with a hat in it. I gave him the eye as I started emptying the bag. Girl, I got to the bottom of the bag and there was a diamond necklace. I couldn't

228

stop smiling. The people sitting around me were watching like they were in on the whole thing."

"Ashlei!"

"For the first time, I agreed to go to his place, but on one condition…"

Amber breaks in, "And what could that be, girl?"

Laughing, I go on, "That we go pick up Snoopy. Of course, he agreed. His house is in that fairly small, subdued section of Philly called International City and it's so beautiful. It's very similar to the house I used to describe when we were younger and we would make pretend. I couldn't take the time to look around since we couldn't keep our hands off of each other. I do know that he loves candles just as much as I do and he lit them all over the room. The next light I saw was the morning sun. When I woke up, he had already walked Snoop, music was playing and I could smell breakfast cooking."

"He cooked you breakfast?"

"Yeah, girl. Before he let me eat breakfast, he played these two Boyz II Men songs for me, "Makin' Love" and "Luv N U.""

"Boyz II Men? Oh shit – I know he got some then!"

"Shut up! He told me if he didn't know better, he'd say that Boyz II Men sang these songs so he could play them for me. After all that, I had no choice but to stretch him out, on the floor. The sun and especially Mike's verses couldn't have been more on point. Amber, this feels so natural, so right. And just think, I almost passed him up."

"Girl, you make sure you hold on to this one. Your time has come. Enjoy it."

"I'll do that. Well, Amber, I hate to hang up but he should be here any minute. I'll talk to you soon, I promise."

"You better."

Just as I hang up the phone, Breon calls from his car saying he's outside.

2
7

The months seemed to pass faster than ever. Breon and I have spent countless days and nights together. Right now Breon is driving me somewhere and won't tell me where we're going. He only says that he needs to talk to me. I can't help but be a little anxious. Where is he taking me and why won't he tell me? Did I let this man into my life, thinking that he's the one, and now he's going to leave me just like the others? Well, I guess I'll know soon, we're turning into a parking lot.

"On The Rise Studios? Why are we coming here?" I ask having heard of this place before.

"I'll explain in a minute."

We get out of the car and head for the door. That's odd. He uses a key on his ring to unlock the door. The place is dark inside, the only light being the emergency lighting.

Immediately after stepping in, he turns to face me. "Ashlei, I have something I have to tell you."

Sadly I say, "Why'd you have to bring me here to tell me?"

"I wanted to come here because one night in the beginning of our relationship, we were talking and you told me about your teenage dreams."

"And?"

"That same night I was going to tell you something about me because I knew I wanted to be with you, so I wanted to be honest and up front about everything."

"So what are you saying? Look Breon, if there's someone else just say it. Please don't bullshit me."

"What? There's no one else. Ashlei, you told me about how glamorous you thought the music business is and how all your life you wanted to be involved in it but then as you got older, you went about it the wrong way. Granted, you've done very well for yourself and after some bad times you realized that you could have a career in the industry and not have to be involved with a man in the *business* as you put it."

"Okay, you've run my past down for what reason?"

"Since that night, I've wanted to talk to you several times, but every time I try something stops me. I guess I was worried about your reaction. Sorry to keep bringing them up, but after your past relationships, you put up a wall between you and men. For a while, you wouldn't even let me get close to you. I wasn't sure at that time if honesty was the best policy."

"So what is it? What are you saying and why am I at this studio? What are we doing here?" I don't understand what's going on and I'm tired of waiting to hear his story.

"Ashlei, this is my studio. It's my recording studio."

I can't believe it. All this time I'd been telling him how I felt about the way I used to be and all this time I was talking to yet another man in the business. Am I right back where I started?

"So this is your studio?"

"This is it. Years ago when I started working in a studio I was fascinated – probably a lot like you. I enjoyed being around and watching the performers record songs but the production process is what intrigued me the most. I decided years ago that owning a studio was what I wanted. I've written a couple of songs for a few artists. I thought I wanted to get more into the technical aspect of it but I changed my mind. I realized that the hours that I would end up spending in here would've been too much and I didn't want that. So, I started saving the money I was making in the studio and off the songs I wrote to purchase a space and the best equipment. I opened this several years ago."

"Yeah, I've heard of it."

"I have people that work for me so I don't have to spend all my time here, but I do visit, often. People come from other cities to record here. I enjoy being around the people, not only the performers, but also the people behind the scenes. I'll always write and I still mess around in there a little so they all give me my respect. They even ask my opinion from time to time, or to do some work with them. I don't mind occasionally getting involved, but I don't want it on a daily basis. I have love and a natural talent for this type of stuff, so I like keeping my hands in it."

My initial reaction was negative, but I know that his secret keeping was a blessing, for him and for me. I am into this man for who he is and not what he does for a living. This is real and I've never been here before. "Wow!"

"Are you cool with this? I know how you feel about everything. This isn't going to affect our relationship, is it?"

"Well, if you had told me in the beginning it may have, but it's too late now. Hey, what about the gym? Do you really own that?"

"Yeah. I went into business with Kurt to help him out. We've always been into fitness. He heard the owner of the gym was getting ready to put it up for sale and wanted to make him an offer before it went on the market. He knew he wouldn't have enough money to buy it by himself and I was doing well enough to make an investment in something else, especially something I enjoy."

We stand in silence. Finally he says, "What's wrong? Why aren't you saying anything?"

"This is unbelievable, Breon. You had a dream and you made it come true. You're so fortunate. Now, show me around!"

After seeing the place, I say, "I don't know much about the equipment. Everything looks so complicated."

Breon disagrees, "It really isn't. Let me show you how things work." He starts messing around with all the buttons, things are lighting up and he's creating some beats. I walk near

232

the mic. I've seen people recording before and it always looks like so much fun when they're standing there with their headphones on, head tilted back and singing their hearts out.

He's looking real tasty to me right now. I ask, "Is anyone coming here tonight?"

"No. I blocked the book out for tonight because I had to find a way to tell you about this and I decided that bringing you here was the best way to tell you. Why?"

"Come here." When he reaches me, I put my arms around him. "I wanted to know before I did this…" I lift his T-shirt and kiss his chest, working my way up to his neck, then to nibbling his ear. I feel what I like to feel rising between us. I run my hand inside the front of his jeans and massage his microphone. I think I'm gonna have some fun tonight. There are some things that have always been off limits when I'd be with someone, but not this time. Breon is so different. It's not the studio or his career; it's him. As hard as I tried not to let myself get involved with him, I just couldn't help it. Now, I'm ready to explore some new territory with him.

"Breon."

"Yeah."

"Turn the mic on, I have something to tell you."

"Now?"

"Yes."

He turns the mic on and returns to me. I take the mic in my hands, the same way I've seen artist do, and I let it come out. What's on my mind at this very minute, is coming out of my mouth…

ooh, i love the way that warm liquid feels inside my mouth

wait, don't walk away
let me explain
i have to make you realize what's going on

you see when i take it in my hands
and wrap my fingers around it
umm, it feels so good, so warm
i take a deep breath
as if trying to inhale its very essence
its strength seems to escape
from the midst of it's steamy existence
as i stare at it, my mouth begins to water
as i wonder if the taste will be as gratifying
        as what i'm imagining
i lick my lips, with a gesture of anticipation
as i begin my personal journey to pure ecstasy
hello you, meet my lips – I think to myself
knowing that once the two meet there's no turning back

the first touch, that unforgettable moment
then a little dab
must take a break
lick my lips again
the flavor, it's got me
gotta go back for more
can't stop
it's all in my mouth
my tongue, whoa it loves it
swish it around, to savor the moment
can't wait any longer

234

gotta have it all
down my throat
damn, you talkin' bout warm
you just don't know
can't keep on going
gotta stop for a minute

second go round
same motions, same feelings
i gotta finish this off
i take a deep breath
lean my head back
and that's it
it's all done...swallowed
received admission to the depths of my torso

pleasurable things never seem to last for long
but the memory of such pleasure
    will keep you going all day long

    I'm not sure I'm ready to look at him because I never told him that I write poetry, but I figured since he's being completely honest with me, it was time for me to do the same.
    "Damn, that was good! Where'd you get that from?" As he's talking he's up against me, getting a little feel.
    "Like you said about being a natural, that's natural for me. Plus, you've got me feeling some type-a-way tonight! You like it?"
    "Like it, I love it! You need to write that down and let somebody check that out for lyrics. You could be making some serious money, woman."
    Oh boy, I heard that before, but I'm not gonna think about the past because the present is looking too good. "Yeah, right. I don't like to let on that I write poetry. I always thought

that the things I write are a little on the risqué side so I only let someone hear something one time."

"What happened?"

"He said something similar to what you said. It was one of my old boyfriends and I'm glad I never gave him any of my work."

"Well, I'm telling you that you need to let me give that to somebody and I can honestly help you. But if you don't want to, I understand. Just think about it."

"I will," I say as I proceed with undressing him in the studio. Before we know it, we're engaged in the most exciting lovemaking that I've ever had. Who would've thought that somewhere so non-romantic, a cold floor and the most imperfect setting, such feelings could be produced? Maybe it's the total honesty, the sharing of things we've been keeping inside. It's like we opened up to each other and everything else just fell into place.

2
8

Things have been sweet for Breon and me. We balance our careers and keep things flowin' between us. Tonight I have to meet him at the studio and then we're going out to dinner with some clients of his. I don't know who these clients are but Breon told me it's casual and to wear jeans. What kind of business meeting is this?

There are several cars in the parking lot when I arrive. I call Breon from the parking lot so he can open the door. There are a lot of people inside, but not many that I recognize.

"Are you almost ready to go?" I ask.

"Almost. Come in here with me. We're finishing up now."

Everybody is always so nice. They all speak like they've known me for years. They probably feel like they do. Breon has pictures of us all over his office.

"Sit right here, babe. It won't be long." He gives me a chair so I'm able to see the vocalists in the booth.

The music starts and the beat is hot! These must be the two he's been talking so much about. She's R&B and he's a rapper. His rap sounds good; voice crisp and clear; deep but not raspy. He sounds sexy and her voice sounds…

"Breon! I don't believe this! Breon, that's my poem! How did you…?"

He puts his finger up to his lips, smiles and walks over to me.

"When we were in here that night, either I hit the record button or you did, but somehow you were being recorded, but only while you were spillin' your verses. A couple days later I came in and Ranjana was so excited about the lyrics I'd left here for her. I didn't know what she was talking about so she let me hear them. Although I knew it was possible, I was amazed. She took your poem and transformed it into a song, a hot song. I told her what happened – well not everything – but that it was you and to keep working on it. I didn't make her any promises but I told her that once you heard it, you would most likely be willing to let her use it."

"Oh my God! I never thought that something I did could turn into something like that! How can I say no to her? I love the sound."

"It gets better. Ranjana got her second offer today. Because she didn't have your permission, they haven't heard this cut yet, but she wants to add it in hopes they'll let it be the first to release."

"Please tell her to go ahead, I insist."

When Ranjana finishes, she comes out and over to me.

"I love it. That thing's hot!" I shout.

"Yeah it is, but it's you. You laid the foundation. You have some serious talent. Do you have more where that came from?" Ranjana asks.

"I do have some other things you may like." She and I are talking, both excited, and during our conversation, I hear this familiar song. That's the song Breon was playing in the room that morning. That's Boyz II Men! Ranjana had my attention and I didn't even notice what was going on behind my back. Boyz II Men is here in the studio!

"What are they doing here? I thought their CD was out already."

Ranjana answers, "They were here before you came, but Breon wanted me to sing that song for you. This is their session. Their CD isn't out yet. They're doing finishing touches now. They're actually being filmed tonight."

"Oh." I resume our conversation, although my favorite group is singing behind me. Ranjana and I are talking about everything but music now and I notice they've stopped singing. Minutes later I hear them singing again, but now their voices

238

are right behind me, literally! As I turn to look at them, Breon bends down in front of me and Boyz II Men move up behind him, along with videographers. They're singing the prettiest song about "the color of love."

"Breon, what is this?"

Before he can answer me, I notice Desz, Amber and Kara, along with Kurt and his wife Karen easing in the door. What are they... He's getting ready to...

Boyz II Men pause, the music softens. "Ashlei, will you marry me?"

The most extraordinary, emerald-cut diamond he is sliding on my finger astounds me. "Oh my God! Oh my God! Oh my God!" My feet and legs are jumping; tears instantly start pouring out of my eyes. "Yes. Yes, Breon, I'll marry you! Yes!"

The singing resumes as my girls rush over, hugging both of us. Ranjana, Kara, Amber and Desz are all crying. We're all a bunch of teary-eyed babies. Breon is being consumed by handshakes, hugs and pats on the back.

The studio becomes one giant party.

After the celebrations come to an end and we're on our way to our cars, I ask Breon, "How did you pull that off? How did you get Boyz II Men to do that?"

"Well, that morning at my house, you mentioned that Boyz II Men has been your favorite group since "Motown Philly" and Wanya happens to be my cousin. Congratulations, future Mrs. Kennedy."

"Thank you so much, Mr. Kennedy. I love you."

"Anything for you. I love you for life."

We embrace and engage in a long, passionate kiss in the parking lot, ignoring the people walking to their cars. This is our night and nothing else matters.

Happiness...YES!

EPILOGUE

1

There's no other way to describe this day but exquisite, from the delicate tulle and white flowers at our house before we left for the airport to the brilliant exotic flowers on the tables and majestic chandeliers in the Grand Ballroom at the Wyndam Hall Plaza in Montego Bay, Jamaica. I'm glad our closest friends and family were able to accompany us. I don't think anyone wanted to miss this day. I didn't want a traditional wedding gown – I'm wearing a Vera Wang gown that fits like a glove and tastefully leaves little for the imagination. Since it doesn't have a train, I had a headpiece designed with a twelve-foot removable veil. Breon is sexy beyond description. My girls – Amber, Desz and Kara – look astonishing in their low-cut halter gowns. Thanks to the beautiful weather, we're able to have our reception on the beach under the moonlight. We're served Caribbean cuisine and champagne. Afterwards, we get our dance on to hip-hop, R&B and of course Reggae.

It's hard to believe I planned this in only one month.

Our friends and family stay for only three days and we bid them a farewell as they leave for the airport. The next four days are for my husband and me. I'm sure we'll find plenty to keep us busy.

***

One month after our wedding and our lives are busy again. It's weird how when we were on our honeymoon, everything else was so far away. We didn't talk about work for seven days. Now we're both consumed with our careers, but never to the point that we don't have time for each other. I'm here at the Ob-Gyn for my annual checkup. Dr. Tia is in the other room and I'm laying here, staring at the ceiling, thinking about my man.

Dr. Tia reenters the room saying something, but I couldn't have heard her clearly.

"What? What did you say?"

Still talking behind a smile, Dr. Tia reiterates, "You're pregnant, Ashlei."

Only four weeks after my wedding and I'm sitting in the doctor's office, being told that I'm having a baby. I finish with the doctor, schedule my next visit and head straight for the gym to tell Breon.

Pulling in the parking lot, I shake my head to make sure I'm not dreaming. Is this really happening?

Kurt is at the counter when I walk in.

"Hey, Kurt. Where's Breon?"

"Hi, Ashlei. Breon's in the office."

"Thanks."

As usual, Breon's eyes brighten when I open the door. "Hey, babe. I didn't know you were coming by today."

"Neither did I. I just came from the doctor."

"Are you okay? Ashlei, what's wrong?"

"I have to sit down. Breon…"

"Ashlei, what's up? Do you need something? Ashlei?"

"We're pregnant. Breon, we're going to have a baby."

"A what? You're kidding! Ashlei, Ashlei, we're having a baby?"

I think he forgets I'm sitting here because he goes running out of the office. Within seconds he comes back with Kurt by his side. "Tell him . . .tell him, babe!"

"We're having a baby," I say to Kurt.

"Aw-shit man! Go head, daddy!" Kurt hugs Breon.

"Come here girl and give your baby's daddy a hug!"

242

2

From the moment of supreme happiness of telling my husband about our child to now, seems like only overnight. How can things turn around so fast? What happened to cause this? My weekly visits to my therapist, Dr. Kline, have finally started to help. I've gone days without talking to anyone, including Breon. I'm not sure how to accept what has happened. I feel so incomplete and don't know how to get past this time in my life.

"You know, Dr. Kline," I say to my psychiatrist, "the moment was so wonderful and the memories of it are so vivid. I never thought things were any less than perfect. I only wish there was something I could have done. Everyone is supportive but that's not what I want. I want my baby."

"Ashlei, you sound like you're ready to explain how you're feeling. Are you?"

"Can I read you something instead, that I wrote from my baby's voice?"

"Sure. Please do."

Jalen's Story

I remember the day my Mommy and Daddy found out about me. From that moment on the bond between child and parent was there. My Mommy told me she was going to do everything she could to make sure she didn't lose me and that I was healthy. She ate healthy things, took vitamins, rested more and worked less. I knew she was trying real hard.

Then something happened. There was someone beside me and then all of a sudden, I had my Mommy's belly all to myself. The doctor said Mommy was going to have twins but had lost one of us. Mommy was shocked and sad, but she said that maybe God had given her two children just in case one didn't make it. Mommy had to stop working for the next four weeks to make sure I was okay.

One day my Mommy got a phone call from the doctor. She told her that she had something called diabetes and that Mommy would have to take medicine with a needle so that I wouldn't be affected by the sugar in the foods she was eating. Mommy cried. I felt Mommy and Daddy holding me between them. Mommy said she was scared but she would do whatever she had to do so that I would be okay.

I had lots of fun swimming around, flipping and kicking! Then one Sunday after they came from church my pool of water that had been surrounding me went away. I didn't know what was going on, but I knew I could hear my Mommy crying and my Daddy's voice sounded very concerned. My sac had ruptured.

The next day Mommy, Daddy and me went to see the doctor. I heard the doctor talking to them about something called inducing labor. Wow! That meant I would have to leave my Mommy's belly that day. The doctor explained that without the water my lung tissue may not be able to soften and when I was born, I may have trouble breathing or my lungs may not be able to function at all. The doctor said there was a chance my sac could seal or if it didn't, I may still get enough fluid so that my lungs would be fine. My Mommy told my Daddy she couldn't let them take me and he agreed. I heard them say they would just pray and ask God to handle everything. They made Mommy and me spend the night in the hospital so they could watch us closely. The next day we went home.

After that night things seemed different. I never got my swimming pool back. My Mommy and me lay in bed all the time. My Mommy talked to me a lot and we did lots of praying. I would feel her rub me and she would sing me songs:

"Jesus loves me, this I know, for the bible tells me so. I

love you Baby,
oh yes I do, I don't love anyone like I love you. When
you're not with me, I'm
blue, oh Baby, I love you."
I used to smile and go to sleep.

I remember Mommy and me going to the doctor every week and they would take pictures of me. Then on a different day someone would come to our room and listen to my heartbeat. That always made Mommy smile.

I'm not sure what it is but something is going on today. My Mommy is in lots of pain, she's crying. I keep hearing her say to Daddy, "I'm scared." She keeps saying to me, "Don't worry, Baby, you're going to be all right." Then she rubs me.

Now the time is four forty-nine and the doctor has taken me out of my Mommy. Mommy is asleep and can't talk to me yet, but my Daddy is right here, I see him. It's kind of cold and now the doctor is doing things to me like they were to my Mommy. Things really feel different. I can't breathe like I could before. The doctor is trying to help me, but I don't know how long I can keep this up.

I hear my Mommy's voice! She's finally awake! Now I feel safe and can take a nap. Oh no! They're waking me up! Someone is praying over me and putting water on my head. What does "christen" mean? Whatever it is, thank you. I feel more comfortable now.

Yeah! My Mommy is back! I hear her. She's holding me and telling me she knows I'm going to be okay.

It's around one-thirty. I'm getting tired. This machine is not helping me enough. I hope my Mommy and Daddy don't get mad. I really just want to go to sleep. The doctor disconnects the machine and takes me to my Mommy and Daddy. My Mommy is holding me, she's looking at me, she's touching me, and she's kissing me. Now I know my Mommy is not mad, she understands. Mommy doesn't want me to suffer.

Now my Daddy is holding me, looking at me, talking to me. My Daddy is not mad, he understands. Daddy doesn't want me to suffer.

Now I'm back with my Mommy. All three of us know that we love each other, but my lungs just didn't develop enough. We knew it might happen but we tried anyway. We fought a nine-week battle of no water, lots of rest, constant medical care, lots of praying and lots of LOVE, but it's over.

Turning my head towards my Mommy's heart, I'm taking my last breath. I know I will always be with my Mommy and Daddy, but I must go home with God.

As I look down on my Mommy, I think about how we spent a lot of time together. She had so many dreams and plans for us. I know she is hurting and she will miss me, but she has my Daddy to help her through this.

Daddy couldn't wait for me to be able to play with him. I know he is hurting and will miss me, but he has my Mommy to help him through this.

Please understand, "Everything Happens for a Reason." The three of us knew how things could turn out, but we were willing to do what it took to give me a chance. Things didn't turn out all that good, but my Mommy and Daddy wanted me to have a full life, one equal to or better than theirs. I couldn't have that because of the problem with my lungs. I am in a better place. I am feeling no pain. I am not suffering. I am at peace.

I love my Mommy for being the best Mommy she could be, for giving me her all. Thank you Mommy for trying and Daddy, thank you for being by her side.

I will always be a part of the two of you.
Your Miracle,
Jalen Breon

"Ashlei, that's beautiful."

246

"Thank you. I gave that to everyone I know. I needed to tell his story the way I thought he would tell it. It has helped me somewhat to deal with the situation and answered questions that I didn't want to hear from everyone."

"I think you did right by finding a way to express yourself that helped to relieve some of the pain. You're a strong woman."

"Yeah, so they say."

"I'm sorry, Ashlei, your time is up for today. Will I see you next week?"

"I'm not sure, Doc K. I really can't say. I'll let you know."

3

Breon has been such a pillar of support for me. Today I'm kind of antsy. "Babe, I can't seem to relax today. I think I need to get out of this house. I've been in here for months. I'm so tired of sitting in here being afraid to go out because I'm scared I'll see a baby or that I'll run into someone who doesn't know what happened and they'll ask how the baby's doing. I've been avoiding certain things on TV because I don't want to see family shows."

"Maybe it's time for you to get back out there, around people. Do you think you're ready to go back to the office?"

"Maybe so, but right now I want to get out for a few."

"Do you want to go see Desz and Amber?"

"No. I just want us to put some music on and take a ride, anywhere."

It's such a relief being out of the house. As we pass through the city, it feels like forever since I've been here yet it seems like only yesterday that I lost my little boy. It's a beautiful Wednesday night, midweek. The streets are fairly empty and traffic is close to none. As we approach Penn's Landing I have to smile, remembering the many nights Breon and I would come here and have sex by the water. Sometimes people would still be walking around, but we didn't care, and by that time of night, no one pays attention to anyone else. That was back when we first fell in love and nothing else mattered.

I'm so deep in thought I don't know when we parked.

"Let's walk," Breon says.

"Okay."

Walking in silence and holding hands feels so good. I feel my insides smiling as we approach one of our old spots. I feel Breon leading me in that direction. As we near the edge closest to the water, he slips up behind me and wraps his arms around my waist. We stand in silence.

Turning me towards him, holding me, he says, "Ashlei, everything will be fine. We'll try again. Don't worry, baby, we'll have another child. We have our whole lives ahead of us. We can't change what happened, but we have to keep living. He'll always be a part of us, no matter what."

My face wet with tears, I part my lips and whisper, "I love you, Breon."

"I love you too, Ash."

We stand near the railing overlooking the water, holding each other and talking about the future for what feels like hours. The chill of the night air coming off the water makes us decide to head back to the car. I suddenly feel so much better. Time away from the house must have been the medicine I needed.

"I think I will go to the office tomorrow. I do miss being in touch with everyone. Kara's been doing a great job, but I'm sure she's ready for a vacation. I know I'll probably have my moments, but I think I can handle it."

"I'm glad. Hey, I want you to listen to something."

He slides in a CD. It's a female singer with a great sound, but I don't recognize the male voices in her duets.

"Who is this?"

"This is Ranjana's debut CD. She recently signed a phat deal. Most of her recordings were done at my studio. She finished it about a month ago and she wanted me to make sure you listened to it. I didn't think you were in that type of mood so I didn't mention it to you, but since you seem to be in better spirits and ready to jump back on track, I thought this would be a good time."

"She sounds good. I know she'll be creating a buzz soon. As soon as the world feels her energy and catches a glimpse of her natural beauty, she'll be at the top."

"Yeah, I think so too."

***

Getting up for work is a little strange for me but I'm glad I decided to go today. When I walk in the office door a look of surprise covers the faces of Kara and Shelley as I walk into the office.

"Welcome back, Ashlei, we really missed you," Kara says rushing to greet me.

"Boss Lady!" Shelley screams, running towards me.

"I missed you gals too and I'm happy to be back. So, enough mushy stuff…whatcha got for me?"

We sit down and go over everything that's on the books. Getting back in the swing is easier than I thought it would be. Kara is absolutely against taking a vacation. She said she's fine and having me back to work is all the vacation she needs right now.

It isn't long before I'm attending events again. Kara and Shelley did a great job handling the events and our clients were very understanding. I spoke to each of them via telephone but didn't go to any functions.

Only one week back and tonight, Breon and I are partying. This is a Welcome to Philly/Congratulations party for Jonesy; the newest and hottest radio personality in the city. She's on our newest radio station, 1039 The Beat and her rating hit #4! She and her crew – J-Black, Bent Roc and S-Class and let's not forget the boss man, Colby Colb are doing the damn thing!

They made sure this party is hot tonight. I feel like I used to back in the day, when me, Desz and Amber used to party until we couldn't stand it anymore, but now I'm partying with *my* man instead of looking for one. Breon and I haven't danced in so long. This feels good – a welcome change. Word travels, so lots of people come over to us, offering their condolences and giving us hugs. After Jay-Z's "Excuse Me Miss" has us on the dance floor, we're ready to leave and return home for whatever may await us.

"Ooh, wait, Breon."

"What's up?"

"We can't leave yet!"

"Why, what's the matter?"

"Do you hear what's playing? You better get back on that floor and let me get my dance on!"

"Woman, they should have asked you to be in the 'In Da Club' video as his leading lady, as much as you like dancing to this. Come on, let *me* get up on that booty!"

4

The past nine months have been extremely hectic. Ranjana's CD dropped and due to all the collaborations with top artists and producers she had done, the pre-marketing and media hype, it soared straight to PLATINUM. The song she adapted from my poem ended up being her debut single. I can't believe it – I'm a songwriter! I never thought people would be asking to see the things I've written. That song was her debut single. When people in the business read the credits, they recognize my name and ask if it's the same Ashlei Thompson who's been coordinating their events. I've retained my maiden name for business reasons only. The phone has been ringing off the hook with calls for events and people wanting to see other stuff I've written. Something I kept private is now a sellable commodity. I received a call yesterday from someone with the NBA who wants to do a huge party here in Philly, with a local author, because of all the publicity that her book "Threesome" is getting and her next one, "Fourplay" is due to release soon.

Amber opened a boutique on South Street that she named Da'Girlz. She specializes in trendy clothing. She says she hates seeing everyone walk in somewhere in the same thing. She's getting married this summer to a man she met at her church. She really seems happy.

Desiree is still hanging in the clubs but only because she's a manager there! I introduced her to the owner of Club Escape, one of the largest clubs in the city and they really hit it off. The next thing I knew, Desz was wearing a ring and carrying the title of manager. His wedding gift to her is a second club called Z's! It'll open after their honeymoon.

Breon and Kurt opened another gym. Kurt runs both of them and Breon is more of a silent partner. We both still workout on a regular basis. I lost the weight I gained when I was pregnant and my sugar levels are down to normal range. I hope they don't elevate with our next pregnancy.

Speaking of this, I stopped at the drug store earlier today to pick up one of those home pregnancy tests. My period is only one day late, but we've been a little careless lately. This is the first time since Jalen that I've had to do this. I'm afraid to take the test. If it's positive, I think I may be afraid to be pregnant, but on the other hand, if it's negative I'm afraid it'll really upset me. I'll never be over Jalen and he can never be replaced.

***

The aroma of dinner meets me at the door. Good. Breon's not home yet. I have Mike from M&M Caterers preparing a romantic dinner for us. I've been looking forward to some scrumptious stuffed flounder, roasted garlic red potatoes and stir-fried string beans and a relaxing evening with my sexy husband. I thank God daily that he brought the two of us together. I can't imagine what it would be like without him.

Realizing I could succeed without relying on a man was a long, hard lesson; I wish I had listened to Amber years ago when she told me, in her own special way, that *I had my own hit movie inside of me and didn't need a man to direct it.* I can't change the things I went through, but I can thank God for all of my blessings, my husband and my friends.

Stepping out of the shower singing "Love" by Musiq, my favorite sight meets my eyes...Breon, sitting on the bed.

"Hey, baby! Why didn't you let me know you were here?"

"I just walked in. Dinner smells good. What, did you come home early today and cook?"

"No. Mike took care of that."

"Oh. What's the special occasion? Did I forget something?"

"You are so crazy! No you didn't forget anything! I was going to wait until later, but I guess I can tell you now."

I walk over to the dresser, take the pregnancy test out of the top drawer and toss it on the bed.

Eyes widening, he says, "Ashlei…"

"I'm only one day late but we did slip up a few weeks ago and this is the first time I've been late since we found out we were pregnant with Jalen."

"How do you feel?"

"Kind of scared."

"Do you want me to go in there with you?"

"No. I'll do it by myself."

I finish drying, put on my oversized T-shirt, and go in the bathroom.

"Ashlei. Ash, are you okay in there? You've been in there for ten minutes and I know it only takes two to get a reading. Ash? Please don't be upset if it's negative. We can start trying if you want. We can start trying tonight after we eat that dinner that smells so good. Ashlei, please don't do this to me; don't shut me out. We'll have a baby, soon."

The door unlocks but it's hard for Breon to push it open. I had slid down the door and I'm sitting with my knees up to my chest, crying…not saying a word.

"Ashlei, are you okay. What happened, baby?" Breon asks kneeling down to hold me.

Another five minutes passes and Breon asks, "Ashlei, where's the test? Let me see it."

I look up at him with tears streaming down my face. I point to the side of the tub.

I grab Breon's arm as he's attempting to reach the test. I ease him gently into a sitting position, climb on his lap, straddling him and looking him straight in his eyes. "I love you so much."

"I love you too."

We engage in a long, passionate kiss. I manage to loosen Breon's belt and remove his gender from his boxers. Laying him on the fluffy white rug, I lower myself on top of him. My kisses are endless and never more passionate. The tears are still flowing and dropping on his face. I know Breon doesn't know what to think. He loves what's going on, but he wants to know. He won't stop me because he doesn't know what I'm thinking right now. I feel empowered surrounding his manhood and he feels helpless inside of me.

"Ash."

I kiss him more.

"Ash."

I won't let him talk. He reaches his arm up to grab the test off the side of the tub. Just as his fingers touch it, I begin to climax. My rhythm changes. I rise up, only working the tip but with tight muscles.

"Oh shit, you feel so good. Ashlei, Ashlei!"

I dig my face into his neck and begin to bite the muscle in his shoulder. He feels my tears wetting him. He's with me now; we're together. We've reached our climax at the same time. The heat...the intensity...

I scream, "Ahh!"

He grips me with one hand, the test in the other.

Our movements stop.

Our breathing is still heavy.

I look at him.

He looks at the test . . .

GOTTa HaVE It!

ABOUT THE AUTHOR

Shawna A. Grundy, born in West Chester, PA, resided in Ahoskie, NC for several years and has spent the majority of her life in Delaware County, PA. After studying Business Administration at Penn State University, she later made the decision to change her career path. She embarked on her natural talents, thus received her license in Cosmetology. As a professional makeup artist she assisted with Boyz II Men's video, "Sympin' Ain't Easy". This break led to assignments with a local advertising agency, displaying her makeup artistry skills on people such as Jill Scott.

While completing a book of poems and short stories, along with her first novel, Shawna is still an avid reader and displays her support by attending many author appearances in the area and actively promoting authors at private events. With the same passion she has shown through her public relations ventures, she will now promote *her* literary works. On the many days when she didn't think it was possible, her love for what she does kept her moving.

Even with the numerous things on her plate, Shawna believes that a strong family unit and spiritual bond aids in the success of her career, and for this reason, insists on devoting lots of time to her husband, Barry; son, Sean; and dog, Snoopy.